For an instant Gus thought the jolt had turned up his hearing aid. Then through the sun roof he saw what it was. A helicopter was matching speed to hover just above, dangling a piece of jagged concrete from a cable like some yachtsman's homemade mooring. The chopper was hovering over them, lowering the chunk of concrete, struggling to correct its aim.

"Wouldn't do for them to use explosives," Albert said. "On the other hand, what's one more dent in a wrecked car?"

Gus pushed buttons frantically until the sun roof opened. Blinking and squinting, he snatched the 12-gauge from its clips. As the chopper passed over them, Gus saw the pilot's dark, Latin-looking face behind mirrored shades. He pulled the trigger.

A fist-sized hole appeared in the plastic bubble directly in front of what had been a face; in the instant before cracks began radiating, the chopper moved enough for him to see a mortal gusher spouting upward through the formless mass atop the erstwhile pilot's shoulders. The opposite side of the plastic bubble was abruptly obscured with a grisly spatter.

Gus concentrated on reloading. "Funny," he muttered. "I'd swear he didn't know we were armed."

Albert glanced up to be sure the gun was set firmly in its clips. "Just stupid I guess," he said.

THE MAN WHO CORRUPTED EARTH

G.C. EDMONDSON

SF
ace books
A Division of Charter Communications Inc.
A GROSSET & DUNLAP COMPANY
51 Madison Avenue
New York, New York 10010

THE MAN WHO CORRUPTED EARTH

An ACE Book

First Ace printing: July 1980

2 4 6 8 0 9 7 5 3 1
Manufactured in the United States of America

The Heavy Lift Launch Vehicle rumbled like a well-orchestrated groundswell of public outrage. Gus held his breath; even inside the solexed Mark V he could smell the acrid stench of booster fuel. He reached for the air conditioner and found it was already on, the limo's idling engine drowned in the roar of rockets. As the flame stopped mushrooming and the hundred-ton payload managed to make its first tentative thrust into space without toppling, Gus tried to relax.

The car was shaking so much from the lift-off that the 12-gauge threatened to spring from its feltlined clips above the windshield. Albert pushed it back with a gloved hand. Slowly the limo stopped trembling.

By now the Heavy Lift Launch Vehicle was an eyeblinking dot in the Mojave sky. Gus wondered why he tortured himself watching. He nodded and Albert began driving. "Ought to get rid of this dinosaur," he growled. "Wastes nearly as much fuel as that goddamned thing!" He gestured toward the smoky, already dissipating trail in the sky.

"We could get a Honda." Albert said, perfectly straight-faced.

"Gasoline goes up any more and you'll get a ricksha."

"Where to, sir?"

"Where indeed?" Gus paused a moment, then half turned to look at his driver. "Anybody gives you a choice in the matter, Albert, don't ever grow old."

"Little late for that, sir," Albert said. "Some mornings I feel almost as old as you're actin'."

Gus glanced at him but Albert's graying head was intent on the road. It was only 0930 and the whole day stretched ahead as bleak as their high desert surroundings. He fished through his pockets and found an appointment book. After a moment he stuffed it back into his pocket. "Hypocritical, parasitical son of a bitch!" he muttered.

"Yassuh! He sho' is dat."

"Please, Albert, not today."

"Sorry, sir. Is there nothing you can do?"

"There's always something. The question is, what *should* I do?"

"Hamlet was a good deal younger than you are," the driver said.

"Got to get rid of this damned car."

"Sho' do suh. Man down to his las' ten million got to eeconomize."

"God damn it, Albert!"

"Yes, sir, things are truly tough. Course, you've been talking about playing golf for damn near thirty years."

Gus sighed. "Don't know why I don't pension you off."

"I don't either. But I know you won't—no more'n you'll take up golf. Now what do you really want to do?"

"I don't know."

"You could paper the corporate walls with injunctions," Albert said. "And you could woo a proxy out of all those widows. But Mr. Dampier, you gotta get off the stick and decide."

The limo moved sedately westward past the dry lake bed, onto the freeway, and then off it a quarter mile later. Gus gave his driver an incurious glance. The Oak Creek and Willow Springs roads were narrow and about as interesting as their names but this route was no longer than the freeway and at least they wouldn't have to breathe diesel fumes.

The limo climbed to fifteen hundred feet. Gus tentatively turned off the air conditioner and opened a window, then decided it was still too hot for fresh air. He closed the window and turned the air conditioner back on. "Albert, are we running on a soft tire? What's that racket?"

Intent on his driving, Albert pointed skyward with one gloved finger.

As Gus was pressing the button that would let him see out the sun roof, the limo's rear window exploded inward, peppering the back of his neck with gravel-sized grains of tempered glass. The limo lurched and one wheel hung precariously over the canyon. Then Albert managed to force the car back onto the road.

For an instant Gus thought the jolt had turned up his hearing aid. After the glass had exploded, the roaring, thrumming noise had continued. He shook his head, felt glass shards slide off his hair and down his collar. Then through the sun roof he saw what it was.

A helicopter was matching speed to hover just above. It was a tricky job of piloting in this canyon but the pilot stuck with them. Albert struggled as the chopper's downdraft buffeted the car. "What do the sons of bitches want now?" Gus growled.

"Couldn't say," Albert said through clenched teeth.

The helicopter was dangling something from a cable. It was a piece of jagged concrete with an eye bolt cast into it like some yachtsman's homemade mooring. The chopper was hovering over them, lowering the chunk of concrete, struggling to correct its aim.

"Wouldn't do for them to use explosives," Albert said. "On the other hand, what's one more dent on a wrecked car?"

Gus considered this. Some people could undoubtedly manufacture their own, but even totally untraceable explosives leave a bad smell in the public record. "On still another hand," he said, "there's no rule says you can't drive good enough to avoid a fatal accident."

"I hope you're right." Albert drove with both hands on the wheel, eyes darting occasionally to the extra mirror that looked upward for traffic-control choppers. This one was not traffic-control—unless the California Highway Patrol had adopted a novel method of enforcing speed laws. The half-meter chunk of concrete swung ponderously past the tinted windshield. Albert braked and practically stood the limo on its nose. The concrete continued forward a hundred feet, then began moving back.

Gus pressed buttons frantically until the sun roof opened. The full force of the desert sun reminded him that his blue eyes had not been evolved for this pitiless open country. Blinking and squinting, he snatched the 12-gauge from its clips. The canyon road was too narrow to turn around in, but Albert was backing up at forty miles an hour. Gus stood on the seat and braced his hips against the edge of the sun roof opening.

The chopper didn't turn either; the pilot obviously knew that the instant he spun his tail Albert would be half a mile back up the hill. The chopper rose fifteen meters and continued backing down the road. As it passed over them, Gus saw the pilot's dark, Latin-looking face behind mirrored shades. If he'd ever seen him before Gus couldn't remember where.

Behind those sunglasses, the pilot's eyes saw Gus aiming the shotgun and his mouth opened wide, distorting his pencil-thin mustache. Gus pulled the trigger, knowing with a mystic certainty that this time his aim was going to be perfect.

A fist-sized hole appeared in the plastic bubble directly in front of what had been a face; in the instant before cracks began radiating, the chopper moved enough for him to see a mortal gusher spouting upward through the formless mass atop the erstwhile pilot's shoulders. The opposite side of the plastic bubble was abruptly obscured with a grisly spatter.

Albert braked, dropped the limo into Drive, and raced out from under the disabled chopper. As he scooted down in the seat and closed the sun roof, Gus saw a billowing mushroom of flame. "There's a law against startin' fires like that," Albert said.

Gus concentrated on reloading the shotgun before putting it back in the clips. "Funny," he muttered. "I'd swear he didn't know we were armed. You suppose nobody bothered to tell him?"

Albert glanced up to make sure the gun was

firmly in its clips. "Maybe he was just stupid."

"You haven't touched it since it was fired," Gus reminded him. "Put rubber gloves on before you clean it."

Albert said drily, "Best tend to washin' your own hands."

Gus surveyed the ruined back window of the limo as he picked broken glass out of his collar. Moments later they topped the pass and turned into the private airport just outside of Tehachapi. "What are you goin' to do?" Albert asked.

"Damned if I know," Dampier replied. "Except to try to act natural. I was going down to the boat for the day. Want to come along?"

Albert studied him doubtfully, suspecting Gus wanted to be alone. "You'll take care?"

"Would I be this old if I hadn't?"

"Guess not. I gotta see to the car and there're some other things here need lookin' into. You'll be back tomorrow?"

"I'll call you."

Albert nodded and drove as close to the idling Vertical Takeoff Or Landjet as he could without hitting a wing. Gus took a deep breath, opened the limo door, and scurried into the waiting plane. When he glanced back, Albert and the limo were already gone.

To give the plane a complete checkout would take time and mechanics—neither of which he had at the moment. Anyhow, Gus told himself, he was too old to waste his little remaining time trying to prevent something that was, sooner or later, inevitable. He performed the rituals necessary to propitiate Traffic Control and a moment later took off running, not inclined to fiddle with

vertical liftoff as long as he had half a mile of
runway.

Should have checked the plane out first. He
shrugged and tried to concentrate on his flying. If
he didn't watch it he was going to see assassina-
tion in everything. And there had been no exag-
gerated reactions—no surprise at seeing him still
alive when he came to the airport.

He locked onto the Balboa beam a hundred
miles south of Los Angeles, scissored over a pair
of dry, concrete-lined riverbeds, and twenty minutes later took the controls again to get onto the
San Diego beam. Ten minutes over the cloudless
ocean with islands to his right and mountains to
the left, then he was once more over land. He
squeezed into the traffic circle and landed as con-
ventionally as he had taken off. Vertical maneuvering made him nervous. He called the tower
and there was a boy standing by with tiedowns as
he taxied into his space.

"No car waiting, Mr. Dampier?"

Gus shook his head. It was cooler down here
near the beach. He stood in the shadow of the
stubby wing while the boy finished securing the
VTOL, then rode back to the tower aboard the
boy's golf cart. As can happen even when a man is
down to his last ten million, there was a taxi
waiting. Gus left a bill jammed into the golf cart
cushion and let himself be carried across the tide-
lands to the marina.

The gate swung open in response to his key. He
paid the driver off and went into the club house.
Should have called ahead and had somebody rig
the boat, he guessed. But there were times when
he suspected that, in sailing as it had once been in

lovemaking, the greater pleasure was in the preparation. But first, a shower and change of clothes to get rid of all that damned broken glass.

Gus was in faded denims and canvas deck shoes, heading toward the sail lockers, when he heard somebody calling his name.

He felt a tiny twinge of fear, knowing a skilled assassin could bring him down anywhere—in view of dozens of witnesses—without fear of reprisals. But a skilled assassin would not call attention by using his name.

The stranger wore a conservative business suit with a vaguely old-fashioned, British-cut tie. He was very dark and pronounced Dampier with the accent on the wrong syllable. *"Yo soy,"* Gus said. *"¿Qué se le ofrece?"*

There was a moment of confused silence, then the stranger said something in another language. The only words Gus caught sounded like *"mokh arabi."*

"Sorry," Gus said. "This close to the border, one just assumes—"

"Not the first time," the Arab said. "America rapidly becomes a bilingual country. But neither tongue is mine. Mr. Dampier, could we talk?"

"What about?"

"I'm not selling and you're not buying. That much, at least, we have in common. I ask one hour's converse, for which I offer whatever your consultant's fee."

Gus studied the man for a moment. "Want to go sailing?" he asked.

"May I bring along a radio?"

Gus sighed. Whatever happened to the old days

when even strangers could converse in civilized fashion? "Is somebody aiming parabolic mikes across the harbor?" he asked.

"We live in troubled times," the stranger said.

"You may," Gus said. "If you'll stand within range while I open it."

The dark man grinned and pulled the back off the radio. Gus decided it contained no explosives. "Got to make a call first," he said. He went to the desk and asked for a phone. He was dialing Albert when he changed his mind and dialed another number.

"Hello?"

"Your husband there?"

"Daddy, is that you?" Tina's voice was shrill with worry. "Where are you? What's happening?"

"Happening?" Gus asked. "Why, nothing much. Any reason for asking?"

"Daddy, I haven't heard from you in three weeks. Don't you think we worry?"

"I'm sure you do. But I'd still like to speak with your husband for a moment."

"He's not here. Can I give him any message?"

Gus glanced across the lounge where the Arab waited, his radio emitting squawks of rock and roll. The stranger had not even looked his way while Gus was phoning.

"Daddy, where are you? I can have him call back."

"No need."

"But what shall I tell him?"

"Just tell him I called." He hung up and added, "That'll make the son of a bitch's day."

He nodded to the Arab. Together they went

down to the second locked gate. Gus waved his key and they walked out onto the dock. "Ever sail?" he asked.

"Many times, Mr. Dampier. Would you like me to set the jib?"

Falling. Half awake. Memories—dreams, who could tell. Still she was falling. Have to pee, too, but ignore it, for now. That would mean full awareness. Just drift and fall and remember.

Should've played safe, played dumb like all the rest of them. But you were different: you could beat the rules. Take all the wrong courses: Math, Strength of Materials, Math, Thermodynamics, Math, Physics, Math, Molecular Biology, Math, Phys. Ed.—how did that get in there? Nothing wrong with your physique.

Sure they're going to let women into space. Just as soon as ships get big enough to need stews. You got the body. With a shape like that you need an IQ?

"Hmmmmm. Head of the class. Brilliant thesis. So how fast can you type? What's a nice girl like you doing in a place like NASA?"

Hiding, I suppose. Surely not going anywhere. Window dressing of course. Out of the typing pool . . . into handling showcase PR—someplace where that body could get NASA some extra footage on the evening news. See how liberal we are at NASA—blacks, chicanos, gay libbers, handicapped—even women!

"Oh, you've got a pilot's license. Got a driver's

*license too? A library card? Ever been checked out
on a Selectric II?"*

*Still falling, still drifting. Still have to pee, but
still too much trouble. How did she get into this?
Remember? She'd thought he was just another
dirty old man. Sure. And Simone de Beauvior was
just another bra-burner.*

"Oh, for Christ's sake! A trip around the world?
Are you thinking of all the interesting things that
could happen in zero grav? Just the two of us,
alone in your little spaceship? Well, did anyone
ever tell you about bathing, or flushing toilets in
zero grav? Do you know how romantic a module
smells after the first day or two?"

How had he put it? Something like, "My dear, I
assure you I have no designs upon your admit-
tedly attractive body. I do have designs on your
even more attractive IQ, however. I have no intention of accompanying you on this trip. And even
though I'm sorry to say I can't pay for your services, I'm sure you'll find the project well worth
your while."

She remembered wondering just how in the
hell he expected her to leave a safe, dependable
job with the only people in the world that could
get her into orbit. NASA was the only outfit this
side of Russia that even owned a ship that could
break loose from Earth. And she was already in
NASA. But when that "dirty old man" had told
her who he was, and when he'd given her a *self-
erasing* tape to view, fergodsake, well, she
thought she'd look a bit further into his most
unusual proposition.

*And here she was. Falling, drifting, having to
pee, and knowing how impossible it was to do it
neatly in zero grav.*

She came fully awake with a sigh.

Still falling. She'd been falling for months and
there was nothing Freudian about it—even if she
did happen to sleep in foetal position. It was the
only way anyone could sleep in zero grav and
even then the uneasy doze, punctuated by nightmares of falling, came only when she had stuffed
everything loose into the net hammock to create
an artificial womb. But she had to pee.

And no matter how careful, there was always
the drop that got away. To hell with it. She was
good for another hour. She backed up, then scrolled forward through hours of graph on the CRT
display. One flattened bell curve and one nearer
miss that looked like a spike. Neither had been
close enough to trigger the alarm.

She checked the battery condition indicator.
Down to half-charge again. Grudgingly, she had
to admit that the old bastard had been right about
not fitting extra solar panels. Instead, every spare
centimeter of the tiny pressurized compartment
was loaded with bicycle pedals, bar lifts, and
hand cranks, with every piece of body building
equipment geared to the small generator that kept
those batteries pumped up.

NASA had worried about decalcification but
despite months in zero grav and recurrent nausea,
Sin's bones were still there. Had to be if she were
to spend that many hours each day pedaling,
cranking, and weight lifting just to keep those
batteries up. The old bastard had a sure cure for

laziness. If she wanted to lounge about and decalcify until she could never set foot in normal gravity again, all she had to do was relax and let the batteries go dead and in return she'd go dead. Why couldn't NASA have thought up something as simple as that?

Maybe because even with an economy-minded congress NASA was never broke. But she doubted it. The real reason was that NASA wasn't violating half a hundred laws. NASA had never dreamed that the first exploration of the asteroids would be in a stolen ship!

So far nobody even knew it was gone. Maybe from now on they'd put locks on them—or put guard dogs in their parking orbits.

"There's a half-dozen clunkers parked up there," he had explained. "They're all near the end of useful life for Earth landings but a shuttle's still a shuttle. If you don't mind a little claustrophobia—say, midway between lighthouse keeping and one of the more rigorous monastic orders—it'll serve our purposes."

"Our?"

"Are you in or out? Has somebody offered you a better deal?"

"Well—"

"Well, hell! So far they've put men on the moon, put men in Skylab, and started wrong-end-to with some rathole satellite program that'll probably get cut off at the Nader or the congressional level long before it shows any hope of success. Even if it does work, when are you going up?"

"Just as soon as they run out of men, boys, and hermaphrodites."

"Obviously, you'll never be the first man on the

moon. So does anybody remember the first European woman in America? Will anybody give a damn when a woman finally gets up to the Colony?" He paused and struggled for breath. "But nobody's been to Mars yet, man or woman. Nobody's been beyond the moon. If you want to get your name in the papers why not try for the asteroids?

"Sure, I know a shuttle's only for getting into low Earth orbit. But with all those degrees and all that IQ you ought to be able to guess what even an old and nearly wornout shuttle could do if it were to start out freshly fueled from a holding orbit—with that cargo bay full of food, water, and oxygen, every bit of extra space taken up with solid fuel boosters, and with a few hundred tons of boosters strapped around."

"Not enough."

He had given her a shrewd look. "I know about the IQ, which means you're clever. Could you possibly be smart too?"

"It's not enough thrust," she said. "I'd like to get out there and back at least as quick as Magellan."

"You will. You'll also spend at least six months prospecting. In addition to what's strapped around, you'll be pushing a hundred tonnes."

"Like a towboat heading for Cincinnati?"

"Except the cables don't have to be nearly as strong when you'll never land, and maximum thrust will never be more than 1/10 of a G."

She had stared at him, trying to remember some grade school bit of geographical inaccuracy about standing in wild surmise. "But how would we keep in touch?"

"You want to be stopped before you start? The only thing working for us is that constitutional bit about *ex post facto* legislation." He was silent for a moment. "Wonder what they'll call it once they get around to making it against the law?"

"But with a stolen shuttle?" she protested. "Surely they'll find something about profiting from a crime."

Gus muttered something about Watergate, then added, "Not if some fuzzyminded old philanthropist buys one of those relics to turn it into a park-museum-Disneyland for all the generations to come."

Sin had grinned, remembering whose whimsical 18th-century wills leaving the moon to lovers. If they'd only known the legal tangles they were setting up. . . . "All right," she had stalled. "Assume I come back alive and sane from this fun trip. What's in it for me?"

"What do you want?"

"You *are* an old man. Do you plan on being alive when I get back?"

"If I'm not you'll inherit fifty percent of my debts." He shrugged. "Any agreement is worthless. Look what they did to me. But if you'll be happier, draw up anything you want. If it's not too outrageous . . ."

She stared, wondering if he were wholly sane.

"It's risky," he'd agreed. "It's crude and the equipment's obsolete. There are better ways to do it but nobody's using them. They're going to futz around mining the moon, setting up that crazy catcher's mitt thing, playing with slingshots and hoping for a return before the whole world bands together to put a stop to all this bluesky colonialism. But do you know what's really nice about our scheme? It's cheap. It's state-of-the-art. It's your only chance and it isn't five, ten, or fifty years away. It's *right now!*"

He was on his feet and screwing his hat down over white hair. "Tomorrow," he'd said. "By then I'll expect either yes or total amnesia." He touched her hand, gave the faintest hint of a bow, and was gone, leaving Sin to wonder what that damned verse had been. It wasn't until she was stepping into a sunken tub that she remembered it was Keats who'd gotten his geography all screwed up and put Mexico where Panama belonged.

> He stared at the Pacific—and all his men
> Looked at each other with a wild surmise—
> Silent, upon a peak in Darien.

So in the end of course she had gone, after carefully erasing her tracks with a resignation from NASA, ostensibly to "find herself."

And being a woman, albeit an intelligent and well-constructed example of the species, she had had secret misgivings right up to the last minute—had half-expected to wake up one fine morning in a luxuriously appointed dungeon where she would the spend the rest of her life for the secret delectation of some dirty old man. It had seemed terribly final, the way she had ordered her social and financial affairs to disappear without even exciting a trace of curiosity.

Physically, she'd thought she was ready. She had scuba dived. Hadn't everybody? But wet-suiting had not prepared her for twenty immobile hours in a spacesuit, in a crate, in an unpressurized cargo compartment, in an HLLV where she had fainted momentarily from the acceleration in spite of all the **HANDLE WITH CARE** and **THIS END UP** stencils on the crate.

She had awakened to her first real appreciation for Poe when the crate had drifted silent, lifeless, weightless, her ears filled with the sound of her breathing and the telltale flutter of her shallow, zero-g heartbeat.

Then two men in spacesuits—at least she supposed they were men; in spacesuits it was hard to tell—had broken the crate open and helped her get her equally spacesuited arms and legs working again. Conversation over the suit radio had been limited to grunts but she had known when they had finally realized she was a woman. They had done her the ultimate honor of treating her like a man as the trio worked harder, longer than she had believed it possible for human beings to work.

She suspected they were afraid of their suit radios being overheard, for most communication was by sign language. The one called Jeff seldom reacted to his name, which she supposed was not his. The other man was simply called Army. It was hard to see into a spacesuit but she thought Army was black. They worked until ready to drop but in zero g one does not drop. They slept fitfully and ate from squeeze tubes and Sin suffered from constipation and worse things and she hadn't even left low-level orbit and there were years ahead before she would see a tubful of water again and ooooh damn, she had known it would be sticky and greasy and creepy and she had known it was going to stink but only a week already?

Then they had gotten a compartment pressurized and she had assured the men she could handle it from then on and they'd better get back where they belonged before somebody got suspicious. And then they were gone and at least she could get out of that damned suit and it was luxury to scrub her whole body with those tacky, glycerine-soaked tissues and were there really enough for two years?

She had known hair—no matter how short— was going to be a nuisance but there were always wigs and she could grow it again. Meanwhile, as long as she kept the batteries pedaled to full charge, the electric shaver would work and as long as she ran it over her entire body a couple of times a week it was possible to feel almost clean with an occasional wipedown—as if she were a hairless, poreless statue instead of a living, breathing, sweating human.

But if NASA could put a man on the moon and a machine on Mars, why in the name of Capitalism couldn't they invent a toilet? Every time she looked at this thing she was reminded of one reporter's observation: "Near as I can figure it, the shit is *supposed* to hit the fan."

If only it would. If only she didn't have to spend hours with butterfly net and sponge.

Damn it! She had to pee. And once she had peed and tidied up she would have to have some coffee. God, wouldn't it be nice to drink out of a cup again instead of sucking those silly nipples! She was slipping the container into her tiny radar stove when the alarm began chirring.

Sin checked the screen and realized immediately that this was going to be the biggest she had come across in the three–plus weeks she had been officially inside the asteroid belt. The read-out matched velocities and it was a definite possible—not too fast nor too much of an angle.

She punched information into the keyboard and corrected course with a few grams of thrust, utilizing the minutelong hint of gravity to sponge a few elusive spills off the aft bulkhead. Then the burn was over and everything was adrift again. She went back to heating her coffee. Twenty-four hours later the asteroid was in sight and close enough to affect the freefloating needle of her magnetic compass. She had come out here for iron and/or nickel. It looked like she had a hundred-meter diameter, roughly-spherical chunk.

She suited up, hooked lifelines, and took all the precautions one woman with neither backup nor moral support can take. Three days later she had verified just how many solid fuel boosters it would take to make this eccentric-orbited asteroid go just enough more lopsided to intersect with Earth.

The answer was: too many. She could push that nickel-iron chunk close to Earth in 18 months for just about every booster she could spare. Or she could have it cross Earth's path in 10 years for 1/3 the fuel.

She spent the next six hours dithering. The asteroids were unexplored and no matter how fiction had them grinding like ice floes, this was the first usable chunk of metal she had found. She might make the entire run without sighting an-other. She ran the numbers again to make sure she would be keeping enough boosters to get home in one piece. Bird-in-hand, she finally decided. And if Gus didn't see any return for ten years she might as well not bother. She opted for the 18-month orbit.

It took another week to rig booster rockets and send the iron sphere toward Earth. She was exhausted. But when she went into the cabin the lights were dim and the fans turned at half speed. Sighing, Sin unsuited and climbed naked astraddle the exerciser. She began pedaling. An hour later she guessed the batteries were pumped up enough to survive while she slept. She cooled out, wiped down, and climbed naked as usual into her sleeping net. And as usual, sleep refused to come.

A hundred-meter sphere of pure iron would weight four and a half million tons. In 1975, the last year the US had really gone all out dumping iron into Vietnam, total raw steel production had been a little under 117 million tons. What would a single chunk equivalent to 1/25th of the last boom year's production do to the world market? She smiled and finally went to sleep.

F. X. M'Meath was a responsible man, one who did what had to be done no matter how unpopular. He had striven mightily, had been blessed with a couple of small breaks as is practically everyone; but, the main difference between F. X. M'Meath and the losers was that he had known when and how to exploit those tiny strokes of fate.

Even his name . . . such obvious ethnicity locked him into a cultural box from whence he could never emerge into the WASP power structure. But the Kennedys had done it. And since then times had changed. A little. He recalled the first time Tina had introduced him to an aunt.

M'Meath had known he was entering unknown territory but how alien it was had not dawned on him until that aunt had asked what the X. stood for. Then, studying him with myopic benevolence, she brightened. "Francis X. Bushman! Your mother had a crush on the actor." Pause for one beat then, "Your grandmother?" Pause two beats and then in a plaintive voice, "But I never did know what the X. stood for."

M'Meath had goggled at the old lady, wondering if he was being put-on. Finally he had explained that he, the silent film star, and countless batallions of Francis X's were named in honor of a peripatetic Basque who had spread the word of the one true God among Moslem, Buddhist, Hindu, and Jew with a fine and impartial disregard for pagan learning.

"Xavier?" the old lady had mused. "Some kind of a foreign name?"

Francis Xavier M'Meath had managed a mute nod. From the edge of his vision he had caught a hint of amusement from the delectable Tina. But only a hint. M'Meath had spent the rest of the weekend in that condition of befuddlement that his namesake would have called a spiritual crisis. Tina called it mindblown.

When he had linked his destiny with hers in a rite as blandly nonsectarian as everything else among these uncaring worshippers of the one true God, M'Meath had still been moderately mindblown. But he was beginning to suspect. It was sad in a way. As long as he could suffer or die for it, a man's faith was a living thing. But how could a man make his valiant stand among those who would not even afford him the honor of ridicule? The Church Militant had combatted pagan, heretic, and Protestant. It was powerless against a yawn.

"Pray for their conversion," the voice behind the screen had said. But something in the tired voice told him there was little hope. "More important," his confessor had added, "is to realize that you are now moving into spheres of unbelievable power. Money can be used for good or evil."

M'Meath said his Hail Marys and received absolution. And for the next nine years he never returned to confession. If he was sinning it must be in some diabolically clever way that he could not see. The delectable Tina had produced two children equally divided among the customary sexes. Nine years and two parturitions had left that lovely blonde as delectable as the day he had glimpsed his main chance on the newly coeducational campus. M'Meath had liked her even before he learned how much money went with this only child of Gus Dampier: the Augustus Dampier of exotic metals and aerospace, spiritual heir to Schwab and Carnegie, wunderkind of the '60s who had taken on a corrupt government and singlehandedly made the media realize there could be coexistence between morality and big business, that not every manufacturer of jet planes and chain saws would let himself sink into a moral morass, lockheedless of the public good.

M'Meath saw plenty to admire in his father-in-law, even if he did have to admit that in these enlightened days old Gus looked like the last of the dinosaurs—a robber baron straight from the era of Rockefellers, Goulds, and Vanderbilts. Gus Dampier was larger than life.

"Fruit of an unnatural union between Barry Goldwater and Daddy Warbucks," an enemy had once called Gus. Which only made M'Meath love him all the more; but then, M'Meath was still in no man's land, having shed one set of principles and not yet settled comfortably into the loose fit of his new skin.

He really felt bad about it but it had to be done. Platitudes about living by the sword and dying by the proxy aside, it was really admirable the way M'Meath had pulled the fragments together and managed to salvage something. He kept telling himself that someday old Gus would thank him. But life as a Christian had already taught M'Meath that gratitude is scarcer than a guaranteed 40% return.

It was time for the old boy to be put out to pasture anyhow. In his seventies and still wheeling and dealing like some crazy Texan! It had to be done. And F. X. M'Meath didn't see anybody else with the family interest at heart who could protect the senile old fool from the wolves—from himself.

"Mr. M'Meath?"

"Yes."

"A few minutes if you can spare them."

M'Meath studied the stranger—a man about his own age, but with that undefinable something possessed only by those secure in their positions—or in show business. Definitely, this man was not peddling insurance. "Well, I—"

The stranger handed him a card. While M'Meath was trying to read it without his glasses, the other added, "Philps Averill," and held out his hand.

M'Meath was puzzled. Obviously the other man expected to be recognized. M'Meath made a series of, for him, rapid calculations concerning the merits of an apologetic *vs.* a screw-you attitude. Never knew when you might need somebody. He landed on the side of prudence. "I'm sorry," he began. "I've heard the name many times but I seem to've lost track of just what you're into at the moment."

"I'm with the government."

Oh shit—why didn't I pay off those antitrust sons of bitches? Then as his eyes came into momentary focus he saw an acronym that looked like ECPAD superimposed diagonally across the card. He riffled through his memory. Damn it. He'd heard something about them. Plenty of clout. Who in hell were they?

"Environmental and Consumer Protection Administration," Philps added. Or was his last name Averill?

Light burst in M'Meath's benighted belfry. This was Ralph Nader's agency. He switched his mind to automatic and emitted an Ivy League version of "Pleased t'meecha," while wondering what possible mileage he could get out of that collection of oddballs and freaks. Surely they didn't—were they out to get him? But that wasn't their style. ECPAD's victims seldom knew they were even targets before the fine morning some 'friend' ruined breakfast with a sympathy call about the hatchet job that usually started with a blast in one of the more influential news magazines.

"I've been following your career with some interest," Philps—or was it Averill—said. "You're a young man on the make." Before M'Meath could bridle the conspiratorial chuckle came. "So am I. Perhaps we can do each other some good."

M'Meath was not fool enough to voice his doubts. He glanced around quickly at the familiar, slightly dingy surroundings of the transit lounge where he was waiting for a chopper from Burbank to LA. What the hell? Hadn't all the world's truly great men been offered temptation in the midst of one desert or another?

"Welcome to the club."

"I beg your pardon?" M'Meath struggled to concentrate.

"You know. Ivy League and all that."

"I do?"

"You're in it. Doesn't take much doing to be born into it. But when an Irish Catholic makes it he's got to have about twice as much on the ball as will be required of the first black Jewish president."

"Are you after that job?"

Philps Averill flashed a grin and looked squarely at M'Meath. "Jesus, no!" he said. "Why do you think we keep bringing in new blood?"

"Clay," M'Meath muttered.

"Yes," Averill agreed. "We gods all have clay feet."

"I was thinking of pigeons."

Averill turned on his Ivy League smile again. "There's that too."

Somehow this conversation wasn't coming together. "You're with ECPAD?"

"Nader's Raiders, otherwise known as the Environmental and Consumer Protection Administration. Your father-in-law probably has a different name for us."

M'Meath could see that he was supposed to ask a question at this point. He had no idea what it should be. He waited.

"Economic Chaos, Panic, and Despair," Averill said with a triumphant Ivy League smile.

For one wild moment M'Meath thought the power structure decided to run him as the next Clay Pigeon candidate for president. Then he realized if they planned on that they wouldn't have made jokes about it. What did Averill Philps want?

Philps Averill, damn it! He was going to have to say it out loud a hundred times.

"Shameful the way they worked over the old man."

"He knew what he was doing," M'Meath said.

"Like hell he did! The name of the game was nonpolluting. Old Gus just about had it licked when they changed the rules. Now the game is fuel economy."

M'Meath almost said, "That's what he gets for trusting government." Now that Nader's Raiders were in civil service, drawing annual leave and piling up retirement benefits he wondered how they felt about government. Even more he wondered when this snakeoil salesman would get around to sinking the harpoon. What in hell did he *want*? He glanced at his watch.

Averill took the hint. "Can you turn him?"

My God, right out of James Bond! "Turn whom?"

"Who're we talking about?"

"Ralph Nader?"

Averill shrugged an apology. "Let's put it this way," he began. "You have access to information we could use. Do us a favor and we'll do you two."

"I'm afraid we move in different circles," M'Meath said. "I don't know any spies. If I did I wouldn't know how one goes about selling out a friend."

"The same way one sells a father-in-law."

M'Meath wondered why he hadn't been better prepared for an attack on his single vulnerable point.

Albert pulled the limo into a **24-Hour Emergency Glass** place just off San Fernando Road. The shop manager glanced up, went back to his figuring, and sauntered over a minute later. "Looks like you'll need some metal work too," he began.

"Can you?"

The Mark V had survived extensive and expensive revisions not apparent on its surface. But none of these were obvious to the shop man who saw only an elderly black with a years-old Continental. "Any insurance?"

Albert shook his head. "My employer prefers to make book on his own risks."

"Bookmaker, eh?"

Albert ignored the question. He extracted a rubber-banded packet from his pocket and began silently counting green documents. There were several C notes in the stack. One brilliantly executed engraving of Grover Cleveland graced a $500 bill.

"Yes, sir, we can do it."

"In one hour?"

"Well, I don't know about—"

"How much?"

The shop man studied the jagged remnants of the rear window and the minor dents around it. "Could easy run over four hundred," he said.

"I could drive another twenty-five miles down into Watts and get it for half that."

The shop man laughed. "You'd take that car into Watts?"

"Only as a last resort. I'm sure there are other places closer."

"Live around here?"

"Just passin' through."

"Three hundred eighty."

"Double that if I'm out of here within one hour." Albert set the alarm on his watch.

"I run an honest business."

"So does my boss. Now could you recommend a place where I could get some lunch?"

The shop man pointed across the street. "We all eat there."

Albert surveyed the place doubtfully and began walking toward it. Halfway through the overhead door he silently turned and walked up behind the shop man who was punching a phone. "You'll find pertinent documents about my employer and myself in the glove compartment," he said. "But if I've got to be out of here within an hour you'd best spend your time working instead of telephoning."

"I have to order parts."

"Does the San Fernando Police Station stock auto glass?" When the shop man almost dropped the phone Albert knew his guess had been correct. "Guess I'll shuffle off and git some grits," he added. "Us old folks gits cranky when we misses a meal." He could feel the shop man's eyes on him all the way across the street.

The waitress was young and white. She gave Albert a vacant professional smile and put a glass of water in front of him.

"Uh, 'scuse me, Miss. Is there a rest room?"

There was the faintest flicker of hesitation. "Would you care to order first?"

"Might be a good idea." Albert smiled blandly and prepared for a waiting match.

The girl gave up first. "Through the kitchen in back," she said.

"Thank you, Miss. I'd like a potato knish, some cold borscht, and chitlin's." She was still staring as Albert passed through the opening into the kitchen.

In a corner of the kitchen was a tiny table where the help could sit when things were slack. It had been cleared of its usual clutter of newspapers and half filled ashtrays. There was a clean tablecloth. Albert sat down.

The cook was a brownskinned man in his thirties who would have been handsome without the scar that ran down his forehead, across his nose, and down the opposite cheek—as if his creator had changed his mind and tried to cross him out. "Figured you'd be along pretty soon," he said. "How 'bout a couple of nice chops?"

"Lay 'em on me. But how come you knew? Somebody been spreadin' stories?"

There was a flicker of interest in the cook's eyes but he refrained from asking questions. "Saw the car," he explained. "Like to blew my mind, see you come drivin' in here big as life."

"How's business?"

"Can't complain. Fact is, I could probably make a few extra payments and clear up that loan a little faster."

"No hurry."

"Like hell there isn't! Some other brother out there got to catch up to a four hundred year head start."

"Only if you really think you can spare it," Albert said.

"Randolph, did you see an old man come in here—?" The waitress saw Albert and stopped.

"Tha's all right, honey," the cook said. "Mister Albert is an old friend of mine."

"Very old," Albert added.

"But do you really want that—?"

"I'll take care of Mister Albert's order, honey. You jus' take care of the customers out front."

"She know you own this place?" Albert asked when the girl had departed.

Randolph shook his head.

"Too bad you can't—"

"Some other part of town maybe I could. But if I hired a brownskin gal here I'd be broke in thirty days."

Albert sighed. "Next year in Jerusalem," he quoted, and raised his water glass.

"Yeah," Randolph said drily. "Funny how they could go on sayin' that for a couple of thousan' years and never once think about the Arabs."

"Son of a bitch!" Albert said. "Where's the telephone?"

Rascaluna was rigged for singlehanding, with not just sheets but halyards as well run back to the cockpit where a man could raise and lower sail while keeping a hand, knee, or buttock on the tiller. But the old man would not handicap himself with a shortened sail area or jib club, so the forestays'l was overlapping. And, as any sailor knows, the world's best chafing gear and fairleads cannot guarantee the weather sheet won't kink, or whip around a stay, or go any of the thousand wrong ways it can go when coming about in preference to the single right way. This knowledge made Gus motor out of the crowded anchorage.

The Arab was totally out of place in business suit, conservative tie, and street shoes. But he set the jib without droops or Irish pennants, stepping nimbly back to the cockpit to stretch the halyard with a coffee grinder winch. "They told me you were a wild man," he said. "But I see you're not reckless enough to risk other people's property trying to sail out of here."

They cleared the basin and Gus shut off the motor. He pointed high for an instant to let the Arab sheet in on main and jib without having to struggle with the winch. An instant before the sloop would have gone in irons he let it fall off. Sails filled, the deck canted over to a proper angle, and they were under way.

"Beautiful," the Arab said. He looked around. Land was only a hundred meters away but the nearest building was several times that distance. With a shrug of regret the man in the business suit turned on his pocket radio. "My name is Mansour ibn Jezail," he murmured.

Gus puzzled for a moment, knowing he had heard the name before.

"Your factory is about to sell some jet fighters to my brother."

Abruptly Gus saw he was in the middle of a family feud, which is not the best place for an outsider. He remembered the Latin-looking chopper pilot, the way he had mistakenly spoken Spanish to this Arab. There seemed no real urgency but his mind began inventorying the sloop's resources.

The stranger gazed at Gus from mournful, Semitic eyes. "My hand is not out," he said.

While Gus wrestled with the semantics of bribeseeking versus offers of friendship the Arab added, "The sad truth is, I have very little influence on my brother."

A sorehead. That jet sale interferes with his plans for a palace coup. Now which of these cushions uncovers the sawed-off? Gus kept his eye on the head of the mains'l and pointed higher, working mental equations involving leeway, true wind and apparent wind, the tip of the jetty a kilometer ahead, and the slight flutter that was just beginning in the head of the tightsheeted mains'l. "I hope I'm not getting involved in family politics," he offered.

"You became involved when you sold war planes to my brother, the sheikh."

So the chopper pilot was not Latin American. "Should've known," Gus muttered. "But they made the same mistake when that dingbat shot Bobby Kennedy."

"I beg your pardon?"

Gus studied the man in the business suit. They were surely beyond range of any parabolic microphoned listening devices by now. Also beyond the range of any intervention if this darkskinned man in the conservative suit were to finish what his chopper pilot had started with the swinging weight. Gus sat on the windward side of the cockpit, feet braced on the leeside bench. He glanced at the fluttery mains'l and knew that whether he lived or not they would have to come about if they were to clear the jetty. He explored with his free hand and found the steel winch handle.

Too primitive. There could always be somebody with binoculars or a telephoto lens. Even with 10 million dollars at his disposal it would be difficult to defend against pictures of himself bashing a conservatively dressed stranger's brains out with a winch handle.

Gus sighed. Electrical gadgets were notoriously unreliable around salt water. Try giving this Arab a 'heart attack' and Gus might find himself sharing the hot seat. "It would've been simpler if you'd registered your objections before the sale," he groused, and abruptly wondered why a competent sailor would let himself be caught where the boom could sweep him overboard if Gus were to free the sheet. His hand began creeping toward the jam cleat.

"But I have no objection to the sale," Mansour protested. "We live in an imperfect world, surrounded by less than perfect neighbors. Between the Jews, the insane Iraqi, Iran's army and Ayatollah, the ubiquitous Russians—it should be obvious that my brother needs modern weaponry. And your jets are very good."

"Then you didn't do it?"

"Do what, Mr. Dampier?"

"Somebody tried to kill me this morning."

"Oh!"

To Gus's way of thinking there was entirely too much surprise in the other man's reaction. They studied one another for a moment.

"I am truly sorry, Mr. Dampier."

"For what?"

"It was an Arab, I suppose."

"I suppose," Gus echoed. "But he could've been a Mexican or any number of things."

"I fear he was not."

The flutter at the head of the mains'l became more pronounced as the wind veered slightly. Gus glanced at the wake which was slanting off more than it should, then ahead at the tip of the jetty. "Better come about," he growled.

The Arab surrendered whatever advantage of position he might have had and trotted forward to nurse the jib clew around the mast. The sloop settled on the opposite tack and they angled a hundred meters across the channel before coming about again to take another lunge at the jetty tip, but this time with plenty of room.

"You know who did it?"

"I'm afraid I do," Mansour replied. "Did they hit you?"

It took Gus a moment to realize Mansour thought he'd been shot at. He was shaken as he realized how close he had come to blowing away an innocent man. "It wasn't that way," he explained, and told the Arab about the helicopter incident.

"The fine Italian hand of Omar the Beloved," Mansour said regretfully.

"Italian?"

"In a way of speaking. Actually, I believe his mother was a Piedmontese hairdresser. Odd things happen in harems, you know."

"Do I detect a hint of irony in that title?"

"Omar the Beloved? But he is truly beloved. My

brother is a good man and a river unto his people."

"So where do you fit in?"

"I am the playboy—what you would call the black sheep of the family. Surely you've heard of me?"

Now that he put it that way, Gus had. Hadn't everyone heard at one time or another about the man who never went home, who spent his wastrel days on the Riviera, an Arab remittance man whose allowance was reputed to be over a million a month?

"Somehow you don't look the part," Gus said.

"Thank you, Mr. Dampier. But God knows I've tried."

Gus considered this for an instant and felt a sudden sympathy for the studious middle-aged man with the mournful eyes. "Protective coloration?" he asked.

Mansour nodded and shrugged. "Part of Ishmael's curse is to see deeper into the soul than other, newer peoples."

"So you played the clown, knowing your beloved brother would lop you off at the first sign of intelligence or responsibility."

"You see things clearly, Mr. Dampier. Perhaps in your background—?"

Gus laughed. "Captain William Dampier was English. He wrote the first treatise on the global weather system. It was my ancestor who named the Trade Winds."

"And financed the leisure to write his book with a few ventures into piracy," Mansour added.

"I see you've researched my family."

"You are the last of the pirates," Mansour said.

"Therefore I sought you out."

"I'm afraid my ship is a little small for that sort of thing." Gus let the sloop off the wind until the jib stopped fluttering.

"But not defenseless," Mansour said, and glanced at the cushion that concealed the sawed-off. "In any event, we know we're not talking about that kind of pirate." There was a pause, then the Arab continued, "Mr. Dampier, with a family like mine perhaps I'm in no position to give advice but, please do not judge your son-in-law too harshly. He was subjected to great pressure."

"From me?"

"From your enemies, who are not necessarily his friends."

"Goddam meanminded pennypinching Jesuit!"

"We are what we are," Mansour said mournfully. "And the older we become, the more so."

"I know I sound like a mean old man," Gus snapped. "I *am*."

"An angry old man," Mansour said. "And with every right."

Gus pointed high to take advantage of a gust. The wind dropped and he let the sloop droop back on course. Some fifty kilometers dead ahead he could see the vague outline of an hallucination that, on a clear day, sometimes turns into Catalina.

"I hope you don't blame the Arabs?"

"For trying to kill me?"

Mansour shrugged. "Of that we are most assuredly guilty. But I meant the bus project."

Gus paid attention to his sailing. Just as he was about to let it out Mansour sheeted in and the *Rascaluna* settled down to her lines again. "If only you wouldn't print so much," the Arab said.

It was Gus's turn to shrug. "In my lifetime the Mexican peso has dropped from par with the dollar to something like 23 to 1. In the meantime the dollar's purchasing power now buys less than that paper peso we used to make crude jokes about. Were I to do the same thing I'd end my days in prison. When a government does it, it's called 'adjusting to economic realities'."

"But our oil will not last forever. Is it fair to pay us in ten-cent dollars?"

"Wss it fair to change the rules for me in the middle of the game?"

"Equally unjust. Will we be going all the way to the island?"

"Not enough time if I'm to be at work tomorrow."

"You still work?"

"I'm not planning on dying just yet."

"I'm happy to hear that, Mr. Dampier. You realize that my brother, Omar the Beloved, is one of the more moderate voices in OPEC. None of it was planned deliberately to injure you."

"I have no illusions about my relative size. After all, I wasn't big enough to get bailed out like Lockheed."

"Nor were you guilty of gross mismanagement. You were asked to develop a nonpolluting steam bus for mass transit. No one told you that as the project neared success, just when you were in the worst possible financial position, pollution would suddenly be unimportant, that from now on the name of the game would be fuel economy."

"To hell with it. You wanted to talk to me about something else, didn't you?"

"An opportunity to recoup."

"Me personally, or the company?"

"You, Mr. Dampier. With petrodollars it's no problem to buy the companies one needs."

"Your brother send you?"

"No, Mr. Dampier. Nor do I hope to buy you even if my modest resources do overpower yours. I seek alliance for our mutual benefit."

"Who do you want to stick it into? Sheikh Omar the Beloved?"

"My brother lives a simple, religious life and funnels the greater part of his royalties to his people. Do not deceive yourself. Omar commands and deserves his people's loyalty."

"Sounds like reason enough to want to kill him."

Mansour smiled his sad Semitic smile. "You're sure your ancestor did not poach in Arab waters?"

"I'm sure of nothing. What is it you really want?"

"To do something with my life. Omar the Beloved takes the gifts of God and distributes them equably, holding back the bare minimum for himself. But my brother is a simple man. He cannot—or will not see beyond the end of the oil." Mansour paused to let the jenny out a fraction of an inch. "Surely you, Mr. Dampier, must see how vulnerable we are.

"We control the world's wealth. We own the world—on paper. We buy frantically, put our money in the most outlandish things because anything is better than green paper that becomes worthless any time you decide to print more of it. We own real estate. We own banks. We own everything.

"But what can we do? Can we grow food? Can money create water? Can we manufacture weapons to protect ourselves? If your lawmakers bow to their yahoos, can we not be nationalized out of everything we have bought? It happened to the Germans and the Japanese. It happens repeatedly to the Jews."

"Welcome to the club," Gus grunted.

"Yes, it happened to you too, didn't it?"

There was a shrill, batlike shriek in Gus's hearing aid, riding the supersonic edge of audibility. He tried not to wince. "Take over?" he asked. "Just hold her steady as she goes."

Mansour grasped the tiller as Gus scooted through the open slide and began fiddling with what looked like an ordinary ship-to-shore radio.

But this radio was several orders of magnitude beyond ordinary. It was single sideband FM and possessed the usual scrambler. The audio signal was broken into binary bits, which was not all that unusual. What made it impossible to trace or intercept was a silicon real-time device that switched carrier frequencies several times each second in a random pattern and put a reverse dolby on the signal—all in a sequence known only to the single telephone-patched master and the half dozen slave units among Gus's possessions.

Since interference on any band was limited to the faintest of ticks as carrier frequency raced up and down, it had never occurred to the FCC or other interested parties even to look for an unlicensed communications network. Nor did the insulators in *Rascaluna*'s steel cable backstay look any different from the usual ship-to-shore antenna.

But despite the near impermeability of his network, Gus insisted it be used only for matters of dire importance. He fiddled with the receiver and a short-range loop fed the signal directly into his hearing aid. "Yes?" he snapped.

"That you?"

"Who the hell else would it be?"

"That wasn't no Meskin boy who brung us the gift. He was just some ole' peckerneck."

Before Gus could ask what in hell he was talking about he heard the click of a telephone and an instant later the carrier wave went dead.

There were times when Albert was entirely too goddam cute. Then Gus knew what ol' peckerneck meant. Albert was warning him about some OPECkerneck. He was switching the transmitter off when abruptly he went headfirst into the chart table. For some reason Mansour was throwing the sloop about on the opposite tack. He heard the sudden snarl of a racing engine.

M'Meath looked down his nose at the government man who had accosted him. What business was it of this son of a bitch how he had worked things out with his father-in-law? "I did what had to be done," M'Meath finally said, making no effort to conceal his distaste.

"Getting childish, was he?"

M'Meath could not bring himself to lie. "No," he admitted. "But he was getting so slow in his reactions it made me nervous to ride with him. And the Olduvai Gorge fossil of a chauffeur is nearly as bad."

"Wonder how he managed to hang onto a pilot's license."

"If only he could hang onto money!" M'Meath

controlled himself. "It was funny. Just when we'd
be about convinced the old boy was ready to be
committed he'd have a good day and do something brilliant."

Averill was sympathetic. "But when the Senate
committee started closing in, the good days jus
didn't come often enough?"

"I felt sorry for him. I always admired him. And
the way those vultures moved in . . ."

"Some things have to be done," Averill said
comfortingly, "No matter how distasteful."

"Another week and we'd have been out selling
apples."

"So who controls the company now?"

"I do."

"Did you know Sheikh Omar has just about
decided to buy his jets from the French?"

M'Meath smiled. "We've a technical term for
that sort of information. I don't like to talk shop
but sometimes there just isn't any other word will
do."

"What's the word?"

"Bullshit."

Averill smiled. "When you've touched bases
with your own information network, please try to
remember I'm on your side. You have my card?"

M'Meath nodded. Averill tipped his hat and
began moving away, leaving M'Meath to dither.
He was still dithering when he reached the door of
the building—his building. He tried to put some
purposeful thrust into his shoulders as he charged
through the door toward the executive elevator. It
behooved the chairman of the board to look like a
man of decision. But by the time he reached his
office M'Meath was still trying to decide between

Tums and Valium. He sat at his desk and reached for the phone. Before he could pick it up the phone gave a discreet executive buzz. He answered it as if it might contain an explosive device. In a manner of speaking, it did.

M'Meath sat staring at the dead phone. At least he'd had presence of mind to say, "Yes, I already know." But oneupmanship with Company Intelligence was not going to bail him out of this mess. If the company was to survive there had to be some kind of short-term cash flow. He had to sell those goddamn jets. What was wrong with Sales? Had they greased the wrong man?

Trouble was, with those funny clothes and those funny noses they all looked alike to M'Meath. He found himself wondering if Irish faces were that confusingly uniform to Arabs. But damn it! Sales ought to be able to tell one Arab from another. It was their business to make sure the proper wheel got the grease. It was their business to keep this business from going under. He pulled his desk drawer open and studied the Valium wistfully. Better not. The organic matter was going to hit the fan any moment. He chewed thoughtfully on a Tums.

The phone buzzed again. "Yes?"

"Mr. M'Meath, there's a Mr. Averill on the line. Shall I put him through?"

I should have known he'd call to gloat, he thought. "Yes, put him through."

"Philps Averill here. Can I buy you a drink?"

"Where?"

"Wherever the music isn't too loud to drown out intelligent conversation. Are you ready for intelligent conversation?"

As he was leaving the office his secretary, a primly efficient vestal inherited from his father-in-law, said, "Mr. M'Meath, Dr. Johnson is on the line."

"Screw him!" As he said it M'Meath was horrified. He never talked this way in public—and most especially not to Miss Jepworth. "Uh, tell him I'm in conference—I'll call him later."

Miss Jepworth was still exuding silent disapproval as he ducked into the elevator. Jesus! Outside of family, Johnson was the major stockholder. Did everybody know already?

He made his way into the bar and squinted into dim light. "Over here," Averill—or was it Philps?—said, and waved from a corner booth. "Now as I was saying," he began.

M'Meath listened with half his mind and cursed the maddening slowness that was his private cross. He wasn't stupid. But it seemed to M'Meath that he was always half a beat behind anybody else in a given conversation. That his analyses might, in the long haul, prove more accurate was scant comfort when everybody else had moved on to the next topic.

What, for example, was Philps Averill up to? The name positively reeked of Ivy League and old money. Which meant only that it could have been changed from something unpronounceably Slavic. But how many generations did it take to acquire that air of inborn assurance? Or how much experience in summer stock?

Most likely he'd been born with a silver spoon in his mouth. And with a guilty conscience. Whole damned family of them trying to live down the robber baron grandfather who had made it possible for them to afford the luxury of a conscience. They would go in for social change—help the common man, pass legislation for his benefit. They would be willing to do just about anything for the common man except live next door to him.

If Averill went out to do good in a world where his grandfather had done well, would he cut himself totally loose from that greatest of all insulators? Grandfather might have insured against that. M'Meath suspected that Philps Averill would have a comfortable trust fund. But he was guessing. What in hell was the man saying? "So you're with Nader's Raiders?" M'Meath asked.

"We prefer to call it ECPAD but of course you're right." Averill's smile turned into a smirk as he continued, "Amazing how many old classmates who never could give me the time of day when I was waiting tables are now all willing to hang on 'hold' until I'm ready to talk to them."

M'Meath had missed something but he guessed he had gotten the important part: The Environmental and Consumers' whatever-it-was had plenty of clout. Must have. How had they managed to queer M'Meath's deal?

"We have something in common," Averill was saying.

M'Meath raised his eyebrows.

"We're both outsiders."

M'Meath guessed he should have been listening. To hell with it. He could look up Averill's background.

"So you admired your father-in-law?"

M'Meath gave a mute nod.

"Shameful the way they treated him."

M'Meath clapped a hand over the Tums roiling around in his midsection and saw that Averill recognized an ulcer candidate. Was he one too?

"I didn't mean you," Averill said. "If those vultures hadn't backed the old man into a corner you wouldn't have had to proxy him out of his company just to protect the family."

M'Meath gave him a doubtful look.

"I think," Averill continued, "it's time some of their noses were rubbed in it."

A girl in abbreviated costume hovered over the table. Averill ordered a Shirley Temple. M'Meath suppressed a racial memory of blasphemy and asked for a Virgin Mary. "What're we doing in a bar if neither of us drinks?" he growled.

"We're considering ways to redress a great wrong. For once in the history of this corrupt system we're going to do something for the good of the people."

M'Meath sipped tomato juice. "Gus Dampier is not exactly one of the people," he protested.

"There're little rich and there're big rich. Teddy Roosevelt called them Malefactors of Great Wealth."

M'Meath sighed. "I'm damned if I can see where consumerism has anything to do with jet fighters."

"You will."

"Who threw the monkey wrench in that sale?"

Averill shrugged. "I mentioned the French earlier. They do stand to gain."

It was such a supremely logical reply that M'Meath knew instinctively it could not be true.

"Can you turn him?"

M'Meath sighed. That was twice Averill had used that James Bond turn of phrase today. Damn it! This slick SOB was a whiz at slipping them in unexpectedly. What was he learning from M'Meath's reactions? M'Meath didn't know but he suspected he was being interrogated in some subtle fashion. "Are you with ECPAD or CIA?" he asked.

Averill produced an easy laugh. "Sometimes it does seem the same. Let me put it this way: I know you don't have the information we need. The old man does."

"What makes you think he'd give me the offal from his brothel?"

"You're still his son-in-law."

As M'Meath's hand went to his midsection he realized he was telling Averill there was trouble on that quarter too. But he must be able to guess that Gus Dampier's daughter was being torn in two by a father and a husband. He had to order his thoughts. Averill would be bracing for another round of justification. It was time to throw him off balance.

M'Meath spoke not in lofty platitudes. The phrasing was dredged from some ancestral Irish past. "Bedamned if I know what I can do to help yez but I'd trade my cool corner in hell for the chance to make thim dastards go peck shit with a wooden bill like the rest of us chickens."

Averill laughed. "Surely you're mispronouncing 'dastard,' aren't you?"

"Anybody can be born a bastard," M'Meath explained. "But if you want to be a dastard, you have to work at it."

They exchanged private phone numbers, shook hands, and M'Meath hurried from the bar. On his way back to his office he wondered whatever had gotten into him. He'd never been brought up to talk that way. Could he have picked it up from Uncle Seamus who drank too much, who never married, who finally disappeared, and was entirely too Irish to suit the lace-curtain pretensions of the remaining M'Meaths?

He ran the gauntlet of Miss Jepworth's disapproval and closed the door to his office. Then he sat at his desk and waited. The phone buzzed. "Yes?" He strove for amused tolerance. "Yes, I already know the sale is going through as planned. No problems."

But there were problems. Something was still rubbing at the underside of his consciousness. Suddenly he knew what it was. How had Dostoevski put it? *Whenever someone says, "For the good of the people," brace yourself. A great crime is about to be committed.*

TV programs would have the asteroid belt so full of solid matter that planetoids are grinding against one another. Actually, the belt is a wasteland nearly as vast as television and with even less content. Sin had been orbiting through it for some time now and she was still a month short of apogee. A week ago she had been awakened by the clang as a grain of sand furrowed one of the boosters strapped around the shuttle. Since then she had been without interruption.

She was strapped into the exerciser, cranking away with both hands, pedaling with the long straight legs that had never failed to turn heads as she clickheeled down the marble halls of NASA. The machine was ingenious—even stretched her back and abdominal muscles as she continually bent and straightened over oscillating hand and foot cranks. She wondered if it was just boredom that made the job seem harder and longer with each day.

Had she really been four months out here prospecting, cleaning up all the spills and messes during those fleeting moments of fractional gravity when she initiated a course change and everything drifted toward the aft bulkhead?

The batteries were at ¾ charge. She was tempted to leave them but she knew better. Let one thing go and soon she would let another and inevitably some bit of slovenliness would end up costing her life. If she were to make a really big strike and have to work outside for a day or two it was important to have those batteries at full charge.

But damn, was she ever sweating! She remembered her finishing school days. "Horses sweat," Miss Gilpin had proclaimed. "Or occasionally wrestlers. Men perspire. But ladies *glow*."

Miss Gilpin should see her now strapped into this goddam battery charger, globules of *glow* forming on her body—not pouring, since nothing pours in zero g. She felt the prickle of fresh jets erupted amid the eight-inch–long hair on her scalp. Ought to stop this cranking and pedaling long enough to run the shaver over her head and body again. But that would mean two wipedowns, two glycerin towels out the chute instead of one. And anyway, the vacuum cleaner bag that kept bristles from clogging her lungs, her electronics, and everything else in this crowded compartment, was full. To empty it was a delicate and time consuming process in zero g. She would shave tomorrow. She gritted her teeth and continued cranking, pedaling, bobbing, and bending at the whim of a machine. She glanced down at full firm breasts, totally without sag in this gravity, and grinned as she remembered how she had accused old Gus of wanting to make skin flicks. God, she was tired!

It had been weeks since her elliptical meander through the asteroids had turned up anything big enough to entice her outside to examine it. She hadn't been working all that hard. Actually, an hour a day was enough to keep the batteries topped up. Why not knock it off for a while and put in another half hour this afternoon?

Because she didn't want to form bad habits. It must be in her mind. She hadn't done anything to exhaust her like this. A couple of months ago she had whizzed through this battery charging routine without even working up a good . . . glow. She tried to put it out of her mind. If the fates saw fit to afflict her with some degenerative disease at her tender age, that was tough. Tough on Earth. Just a little more so out here. Out here at least she was not being exposed to any new contagions. She continued pedaling and cranking, struggling to ignore the growing nausea.

There was a faint whisper of sound, barely audible over the blowers and pumps that kept this place livable. Sin paid no attention. As long as the alarm didn't start chirring there was nothing on the display that couldn't be handled just as easily an hour or a week from now. She breathed deeply and tried to fight off fatigue.

She wondered if it was within her ability to remove the tiny sprocket-driven fan and install a larger one that would give the illusion of a cool breeze while she pedaled and cranked her bumps and grinds. The charge indicators were almost full up now. Time to cool out: get her vital signs back somewhere near normal before she abandoned the machine.

If only she didn't sweat so much. She was working hard. A certain amount of glow was normal. But she was positively spraying it! She gave herself a hasty wipedown before too much effluent could end up in the filter or on the bulkheads. The damned computer was still—

Well, not exactly printing out. It was storing information on a floppy so Sin could call it back on a CRT and thus not use up several miles of paper. But the screen didn't make sense. It was words instead of numbers. She scrolled it back to the beginning.

ARMY CAN SPRAY SIGNAL BUT PEOPLE BEHIND OVERHEAR YOU IF RECEIVING PLEASE BURST RANDOM NOISE ASTERN 1/3 YR ELLIPSE 20.111133 METERS

Now how was the Army getting into the act? Sin had been able for a while to catch news beamed up to the construction site, but several weeks ago her ellipse had taken her too far away from the beam. She wondered if somebody had blown the whistle on old Gus. Army . . .

Army . . . then abruptly she remembered the two spacesuited figures who had gotten her out of the crate and helped her set up this ship. She was perfectly sure one of them was not named Jeff— unless life in space had left him unable to respond to his own name. But the other one had been called Army. There had been something odd about him.

If she was reading him right he was in her transmitter antenna's blind spot. She fired a few gramsecs from an RCS vernier and began fine tuning the transmitter while her ship began a ponderous, slower-than-an-hour-hand rotation about its center of gravity. Army must really be fine-tuning the way he had insisted on six decimal places. How much bandspread would he have? Then she remembered he could blanket her for half a meter each way. But since her reply was limited to a burst of static the only way he could know he was talking to Sin and not some eddy in the solar wind was to specify an exact carrier wave. She consulted her inertial system and aimed the dish toward what had been dead astern but was now drifting at 3'/min. Now how, she asked herself, does one make a random noise?

She'd had a comb when she lit out on this insane odyssey. But she'd had long blond hair then. Both had gone out the chute. Sin studied the claustrophobic compartment, saw her toothbrush, grabbed it and rasped the bristles over the edge of her mike.

Nothing happened. She was about to try again when she realized how many millions of miles and how many light minutes separated them. She tore the edge from a glycerin wipe and mopperd her face, trying to ignore how lousy she felt. Several minutes passed and then the CRT display said **REPEAT TWICE.**

Sin did.

More minutes and then, **ONE YES TWO NO ARE YOU OK**

She brushed the mike once.

NEED ANYTHING

A bath, a week at Aspen. But what amazed Sin most was that she just needed to talk to someone. Funny. Back on Earth she had always been self contained. She sighed. To hell with it. She had known this was not going to be any fun trip.

ANY RESORPTION

A bit of a scare shot through Sin and for a moment she was *glowing* as profusely as if she had been still recharging batteries. She forced herself to consider the problem. Was that why she was feeling so lousy, so tired all the time? She ran a hand over the bones in her forearm. For an instant she could have sworn one bone had actually *bent.*

The CRT was suddenly full. It took Sin an instant to realize that Army was quoting from some scientific journal: **NEW DATA SHOW RESORPTION IS NOT THE ENTIRE PROBLEM/ THERE IS ACTUAL REDUCTION AND PERHAPS COMPLETE CESSATION OF BONE FORMATION/ THE ANIMALS RECOVERED THEIR ABILITY TO FORM BONE AFTER RETURNING TO EARTHS SURFACE AND THE NORMAL PULL OF GRAVITY/**

Sin felt a sudden wave of panic. How far was she from Earth? How long to get back? Would she have any bones at all? Would she ever be able to function again in normal gravity?

Normal gravity hell! Without some kind of bone structure her muscles would pull her into a quivering, moribund lump of totally nonfunctional . . .

Panic gave way to outrage. Had all the hours she spent tormenting herself on that battery charger been for nothing? Another couple of solar collector panels would have kept her comfortable. Damn Dampier! Then she remembered that he had a stake in this project too. It would be tough on an old man like Gus to take still another defeat. And this one wouldn't just leave him in reduced circumstances. The old man had every dime he owned in this project.

But Mr. Dampier would die on Earth at his appointed time. Sin was still young. She was going to die right out here in the asteroid belt—in zero gravity. She would grow weaker, sicker, unable to clean up after herself. She would drown in her own—

Army didn't like mirrors. Didn't need them either. His black beard was silky fine as his hair. He ran the shaver over his face and scalp. No use doing his body for another week. But it was time to mow his pubic patch. He wondered if he would ever stop fantasizing about hot tubs. Not saunas. He was still fairly close to the sun and the whole ship was a sauna every time he overslept and it rotated until sunlight came through cabin windows. And lately, no matter how much he slept, Army could never seem to get himself quite as wide-awake as he remembered from crisp fall mornings in the city.

Not that he missed the city. Two sisters into analysis, his parents into constant squabbling. And they all acted as if it were Army's fault. As if he had volunteered to join that chickenshit family!

They believed in Causes, the Perfectibility of Man. Back in the '60s when Army was into Pablum they were into marches and protests. They were, he supposed, decent people. Did their best in an imperfect world. How could good intentions spread so much misery in their wake?

Lorie only fifteen and already a roundheels. Cute little blonde like that should have turned out better. And Deedie, at eighteen trying to support a two-hundred-dollar-a-day habit in a world where there was too much giveaway competition from other leggy blondes with straight waistlength surfer hair.

He had to get out before he went round the bend like the others. But where? His siblings had somewhere to go once they escaped the family.

Well, there was always work for an able computerman. Army was able. When he was twelve his IQ had checked out at 160. The examiners had seemed so embarrassed that for a long time Army kept his test score secret. He thought he was subnormal. Later he discovered how exactly right his childish instinct had been. He went out for basketball.

Not a bad choice when you're six five and weight one fifty. Of course, he had filled out since then. But no matter how many points scored, he had always known in his soul that when the World's Worthwhile Pursuits were someday compiled, slamdunking was bound to rank close to the bottom.

But so was computer fraud.

Why bother? So easy. Didn't really need the money. But what was a 23-year-old man to do? He couldn't spend twenty-four hours a day working. There had to be someplace to go, someplace to be somebody. In a dim way he saw the money he was stealing as compensation. Money was never an inconvenience. It had bought him an education, insulated him from the slings and arrows of his condition. Perhaps with unlimited amounts of it he could insulate himself even more—buy an island or a yacht.

He had really grooved on computers. Enough to endure the brotherhood of oddballs and misfits who served the faceless machines. They came from everywhere—all sizes and shapes, united in a freemasonry of bytes and bits, caring more for baud rates than the cast of a colleague's eye. So why had he done it?

A century earlier he might have gone in for mail fraud. Or even something legitimate, so long as it was sufficiently anonymous. There was a limit to how many times a day a young man could endure that moment of disbelief whenever someone got a first look at Armand Fortin's skin. Army was sick of it. Sick of people, sick of the whole miserable mess. Why had they tried to make him into something he was not? Why hadn't they warned him?

He had tried to be charitable. His family had been liberal minded, well-meaning. They'd thought it would work, a black child in a white family. And people have a habit, not just of creating gods in their own image, but of projecting that image onto their neighbors. They had thought Army was just another bright little boy. He would have no trouble making his way—not with all the advantages and education they could give him.

It had never occurred to these well-meaning people that someday the boy would be a man, that others would look on that face and never ask his IQ.

"My own part of town?" he had blazed. "I grew

up in Beverly Hills. My brothers and sisters, whole damn family's white. How am I supposed to know anything about niggers?''

When he went to find out, the only things Army learned were that he didn't care for their music, that he was constantly on his guard, that no matter how he struggled to communicate, his profoundest observation might be interrupted by a ''shit, man, you jivin'.''

A black man, no matter how protective the cocoon he's raised in, expects at some time in his life to get thumped a little for being an ''uppity nigger.'' But to have it happen at the hands of other blacks? And naturally the other business all had to hit the fan the same morning he was doing his best to conceal a black eye and multiple contusions about the head and shoulders.

If he hadn't been so enwrapped in his own misery, Army would have sensed something wrong the instant he'd walked in to work that morning. He had thought they were all being diplomatic, pretending not to notice the eye which, though not noticeably blacker than the rest of his face, was scabbed and swollen. And even then they wouldn't deal with him personally. Detail another black man to do the dirty work.

That old Uncle Tom chauffeur who puttered about on little errands for the old man had been stepping out of Mr. Dampier's private elevator at the same instant Army stepped out of the other one into the main bank of the terminal. Their eyes met for a second and Army saw that the old black man had noticed his shiner.

There was a sudden charged silence as everyone concentrated on being busy. Albert's

grizzled head had nodded in the faintest of ges-
tures as he turned back into the executive
elevator. A moment later Army found himself in
the sacred precincts of old Gus's office. Gus Dampier had given Army a curt nod as he charged out,
his mind midway between Chase and Manhattan.
Army and old Albert were alone. Albert took
Gus's chair behind the desk and motioned Army
into the other.

So much for equal rights, Army thought. Big
man can't even be bothered to fire me. Now I'll get
chewed out by some old uncle who never had the
guts to go for the big score.

Albert studied him mournfully for a moment
and Army was disconcerted to see that the old
black man was not even faintly self-conscious
about sitting in the seat of power. "Looks like they
gittin' onto your ways all 'round town," the old
man said.

Army's swollen eye began throbbing. How had
he ever thought he could get away with it? Hotshot computerman! Should have known robber
barons can afford whole armies to stop a single
Army. His head was aching and his eye seemed to
be trying to close all the way. He sat hunched in
silent misery.

"You into us for damn near a million dollars,
boy," old Albert said. "You got any idea how long
they gonna keep your ass locked up for a punch-
board?"

Army didn't.

"Even if you still got all the money and git it
back to the company within the next ten minutes,
you're in bad trouble."

Army didn't answer.

"What in hell's wrong with you, boy? I know you don't need the money. Maybe you just hate niggers?"

"I'm not a boy."

"You're no man. You jus' some young asshole got to do somethin' stupid an' never think 'bout how the rest of us gotta live here."

"You gotta live!" Army had blazed. "Everybody gotta live. Just where the hell am I supposed to live?" He drew a breath and prepared to expound on this theme and then to his total confusion Army discovered he was weeping. From across the desk old Albert handed him a box of Kleenex.

Finally Army controlled himself. "I must've been a real cute little pickaninny," he said bitterly. "I wonder if they'd've taken me if they'd foreseen all their little blonde daughters going off their rockers from the joy of having a black brother in a white neighborhood."

Albert sighed and muttered something about imprinting.

Army blew his nose. He had not expected such knowledge from an old darkie. "Yeah," he agreed. "I suppose the anthropologists would call me just another marginal man—between two cultures and no place of my own."

"They're good at making up new words," Albert agreed. "Imprinting, all that jive. Now when I was a boy we used to raise mules. You know how to make a mule?"

Army wasn't sure. "Some kind of a hybrid, isn't it? At least I think they're sterile."

" 'Fore you get any kind of baby, couple of people got to do somethin'," Albert explained. "Now you take a mare in heat—she jus' like lots of people in heat. Don' make no difference who 'tis as long as they gets it. But you take a jackass, now he got some feelin's."

"You're not ignorant," Army had protested. "Why the Uncle bit?"

"Protective coloration."

"But we don't have to put up with that crap anymore—"

"World's full of those who'll do me the favor of inflicting their cloddish company on me. Ol' Uncle knows his place—and how to keep them in theirs. Now, you take a handsome young jackass—he don' want nothin' to do with some shorteared, funny-looking female twice as big as he is. He's got more sense—more pride in being a jackass. You want to raise mules, there's only one sure way to do it without ruinin' your ass.

"First you pick a good stronglookin' young jack with the right bloodlines. Then, 'fore he ever gets his eyes open good, you take him away from his mama and you put him with a brood mare. Mamas are all the same—don't care what a youn'un looks like, long's she got one.

"Then you keep that poor young jackass penned up with horses all his life and by the time he's growed up he thinks he's a horse. He's never seen a jenny. All he ever wants to stick it into is one of those big shorteared mares. 'Mongst us ol' mule breeders, tha's what we calls a mule-jack. Ain't fit to hang out around other jackasses. He only good for makin' mules."

"Nobody ever asked me what I wanted to do," Army said.

"Nobody ever asks the jackass." Albert dropped the honeysuckle accent. "I'm not blaming you.

The problem is, just what are we going to do with you?" He sighed. "If I thought it'd cure anything I'd send you up to the Joint. But they got some jacks up there'll really riddle your young ass. What do you think we ought to do about you?"

Army didn't know. The silence grew.

"You're young, strong, in good health," Albert mused. "Do you mind living alone?"

"When did I live any other way?"

Albert sighed. "We're just people too. But I suppose it's too late." He squirmed about in old Gus's chair and examined his fingernails. "Used to be, a boy got in trouble they gave him a choice—jail or join the navy."

"Fuck the navy."

"Wouldn't have you anyhow."

"My record is clean up till now."

"I'm afraid a time-sharing system isn't half as private as most users think it is."

"Is the FBI tapping your lines too?"

"You said it, not me. Anyhow, you try to join any branch of government and there'll always be just one more signature missing from your papers. You'll be as old as I am before you begin to understand."

"Next time I'll just get a gun and stick up a bank," Army growled.

"Never mind that shit. Are you really serious about getting away? Could you stand a couple of years by yourself and never see another living soul?"

"At the moment I can think of nothing I'd like better."

"Well, I think we got a place for you." Albert sighed. "I know you can't do much about your height but if you knew what it costs to lift a pound you'd sure take some of that weight off."

"I'll give you the codes so you can start getting the money back," Army offered. Abruptly he began to understand what Albert was talking about. Son of a bitch—space! He hadn't even known the company was that deep into it. How many more things were there he didn't know about the company?

"Forget the codes," Albert said. "You do the job we got in mind, and keep your mouth shut and that money you stole can apply toward your first year's salary and commissions."

Army had felt a sudden foreboding. There had been rumors of an undeclared war out there in orbit, with each side knocking off the other's spy satellites. Was he going to end up ice-picking some poor Russian in a spacesuit?

For a while he had worked with Jeff who had been up here a little longer, was due back down soon, and so overjoyed at the prospect of a little help that the man whose name was most assuredly not Jeff couldn't have cared less if Army had been black, purple, or little and green with sprouting antennae. And finally the girl was on her way and Army's ship ready to blast off. He remembered old Albert's farewell the night before he had lifted up into low orbit. "You're on your own out there. Get in trouble and we'll feel real sorry. Know why?"

If Army had expected the usual platitudes about the value of a human life he didn't get them. "That ship and all that fuel you're lightin' out with costs more even down here on Earth than you could steal in ten years. Up there in orbit it costs several times more."

"I won't steal it," Army promised. "Where would I go?"

"I know you won't," Albert said. "But Mr. Dampier's been fucked over by experts. You break radio silence and somebody learns what we're doing, you might as well find yourself another planet out there. What we want is that ship and the stuff you're going out to get. Now your ass may be precious to you but it's worthless without what we want. Just keep your priorities straight."

"I will," Army promised.

They had three ships. It was only logical to hit equally divided sectors of the belt. Astronomers were full of theories but when it came right down to it nobody knew anything, except that the asteroid belt was actually only slightly less empty than the rest of space. Or else the probes were lying. Right up to a couple of days before he blasted off, Army had followed instructions to the letter—then he had hogged more than his share of boosters and set off right after Sin, sweeping an adjacent ellipse some ten days behind her.

After all the consideration they had shown him Army couldn't have told anyone why he disobeyed orders. But he had left an explanation hidden in a tapeful of compressed telemetering: Army's explanation had nothing to do with the fact that he had caught a glimpse of straight blond hair, blue eyes, a face very like his sister's. Nothing at all to do with that. The gist was simple: These things aren't perfected. If something goes wrong, we can help one another. Something will go wrong. I can feel it in my bones.

He was feeling it in his bones right now.

Without a lot of equipment, there was no way of knowing if his weight had gone up or down. But during the months in zero g his body had changed alarmingly. In Beverly Hills he had been six-five. Now he was 206 cm, not having thought to bring a Stone Age tape measure with him. Even so, the first time he noticed how short the legs and how tight the crotch of his spacesuit, Army had been so nonplussed he had run the numbers through just to be sure he wasn't doing something stupid. There was no error. He was four inches taller. His waist was eight inches smaller.

"Should have read that stuff," he muttered. But he had. Army knew that without constant gravity the cartilage between his vertebrae tended to stretch, that every joint in his lanky body became even more loosely connected. He also accepted for the first time as one of Life's Cruel Truths and not just an interesting bit of data that body fluids normally at rest in legs and abdomen were no longer held down.

Fluid was crowding his heart. He wondered if diuretics could reduce the edema before it became impossible for his heart to pump even the reduced workload of zero g. He wondered if his red cell production had merely slowed down or if it had come to a complete stop.

But mostly he wondered what had gone wrong—why the hours pedaling and cranking, bobbing and weaving, had not been enough to make his bones retain their calcium. Jesus! It wasn't enough that he put up with years of discomfort. Now he could never come back down into normal gravity and enjoy his wealth. "Some people have all the luck," he muttered. But he was pretty sure the longlegged, longboned girl who had gone out ten days ahead of him was not one of them.

It took him nearly an hour to adapt his detector into a transmitter with enough poop to reach her unaimed antenna. And then he heard the rasp of Sin's toothbrush over the edge of her mike. "Give me another burst if you can hear me now." He said it vocally this time. They were so far apart it was minutes before he heard the toothbrush again.

After that it was simple, though time consuming to carry on a onesided conversation, phrasing everything so that Sin, whose transmission was aimed back toward Earth, could limit herself to one or two strokes of the toothbrush.

Two weeks passed. Army, burning fuel as if the GSA were paying for it, had moved to within a light minute of Sin. With only two minutes between question and answer they discussed— onesidedly—their symptoms. More time passed and finally their intersecting ellipses had angled off enough so that there was little danger of anyone intercepting Sin's rearward messages. She reduced power, narrowed the beam, and for the first time they could actually talk.

In a way it was better than most conversation because there was still enough time lag to force them to organize and deliver thoughts without buzzword or interruption.

"Not to be chauvinistic," Army began, "and God knows, it's lonely enough out here without grounding all the women—" He hesitated. "But decalcification among older women is even more of a problem than among men. Buffalo hump and all that. How are your neck and shoulders?"

He waited a minute for his transmission to reach Sin, waited another thirty seconds for her to formulate a reply, then another minute for it to reach him. Idly, he multiplied 60 seconds by 300,000km/sec. Eighteen million kilometers. How about that! Sin and Army were only 46-½ times as far apart as Earth and its moon.

"I'm not that old." Sin's voice was loud and clear. "Actually I just feel run down all over; about midway between mononucleosis and malaria. I'm afraid to strain any long bones. But my neck feels all right." Pause, and then, "Have you any brilliant solutions?"

"Not brilliant," Army replied. "In fact, it promises to be quite a pain in the ass, but I've got an idea. Meanwhile, would you please doppler my carrier wave and give me a closing velocity?" He kept holding down the mike button long enough for her to get a reading on how far his carrier had drifted up from nominal.

Two minutes later Sin's clear WASP voice came back. "I hope you're not still holding down that button. You should be retro firing."

Damn! Why hadn't he asked her that a week ago? Where had he screwed up? If only he didn't feel so wrung out and just plain lousy all the time. Must've punched a wrong button. It was so easy to leave out a parenthesis or a goto if you let your mind dwell on aches and pains instead of programming. But damn it! Navigational and velocity-matching programs were stored in the motherless machine. How could he have screwed up on something so simple?

Sin was calling out the numbers and the machine, he hoped, was storing them on an erasable loop. He double checked to make sure he wasn't wiping out all her information, then began firing attitude jets to turn the cumbersome shuttle around for retro firing.

Minutes later the shuttle was performing its slow-as-an-hour-hand rotation while he concentrated on making sure the antenna tracked on Sin's number-chanting voice. The vehicle aproached completion of its turn and the oversized, strictly afterthought antenna's blind spot slowly wiped her out. Army fired verniers again, stabilized more or less, and began the complicated process of cutting in the main propulsion engine.

Halfway through the procedure he slammed a fist to his forehead. He turned the switches back off. This shuttle no longer even had any main propulsion engines, but the Orbital Maneuvering System engines were still too wasteful of liquid fuel for this maneuver. Lately he was screwing up everything.

He fed it all into the machine, dumped the result into **RAM**, then tried an alternate method of working the problem. When he flashed the display to compare answers they were not the same. "Brains turning to peanut butter!" he growled. But when he stopped actually to read the numbers instead of just flashing them he saw they were alike until one got down deep into the decimal places. He began donning his space suit.

Probably everything was all right but Army wanted to be sure there were no broken wires or loose connections to put him in a lopsided spin when he lit off all those solid fuel boosters strapped so far outboard.

Then once more he had to stop halfway through the job and redo some circuitry. If he were to fire those boosters as originally planned he would be subjected to almost a full g. Even if his weakened bones could take it he knew the shuttle could not.

Finally he was ready for a burn ten times as long, at one tenth the acceleration. Everything had been rechecked. He addressed a final prayer to Newton's shade and went back inside. Jesus, how that ship could stink after the relatively untainted air of a suit! He took it off and ran doggedly once more through the numbers. And then he flipped a switch. As everything went drifting toward the aft bulkhead he got out the sackful of used bodywipes he'd been saving for just such a chance to catch the ones that got away.

One more interruption as gravity pushed liquids downward in his unaccustomed and overfull bladder, suffusing Army's soul with a need more urgent than housekeeping.

The burn ended. With zero g everything not tied down went adrift again. As he floated up out of his seat he caught a flash of the tiny sun through a port. Now what? There were so many boosters strapped around the shuttle that he had not been able to see anything from the side ports since they had assembled the ship. Had cargo shifted? If his CG had moved, his intersection with Sin's orbit could be off by months and millions of kilometers.

The shuttle was spinning lazily, making a revolution every ten minutes. He began hunting for Sin's carrier, found it, checked his figures against the doppler shift off nominal frequency. "You still on 20.111133 meters?" he asked.

Two minutes later she said, "Yes."

Army sighed. They would intersect sooner or later. Maybe he shouldn't have wasted so much fuel hotrodding out here after her. Would another week have made any difference? If she was feeling as lousy as he was, it just might.

Perhaps it was just nerves. Perhaps it was an intuitive sense of physics and the problems of moving bodies. Either way Mansour ibn Jezail knew what was going to happen from the first instant the jet-ski emerged from the haze. In the minute and a half of its approach he had time to reflect that anyone riding an aquatic motor scooter alone this far from shore had to be either supremely confident of his longdistance swimming ability, or totally heedless of his future. As the jet-ski snarled toward the sloop, skipping and jittering at 40 knots he came to the reluctant conclusion that his latter guess was correct and concommittantly, that some idealist was only seconds short of completing a kamikaze run. Mansour wondered if the target was himself, Gus Dampier, or both of them.

The *Rascaluna* was far enough offshore for crime to be hidden, save from the all-seeing eyes of gods or spy satellites. Mansour took his hand from the tiller. The rig was so well balanced the sloop could sail herself for short intervals. He began rummaging beneath the cushion Gus had been at such pains not to look at.

Mansour was not familiar with United States laws but common sense suggested a weapon capable of scattering this much dismay was, if not illegal, bound at least to be considered *prima facie* evidence of an irregular lifestyle. Fire it and he would have to jettison it. He hoped it would not bruise his shoulder.

As the jet-ski jinked toward him he saw coffee-colored skin in startling contrast to sunbleached blond hair. Were it not for a peeling red nose, the boy who wrestled mightily to control the machine could have been Cherkessi. He glanced up and seemed to see the *Rascaluna* for the first time. He leaned hard right, struggling to force the jet-ski ahead of the sloop's bow. Just as it seemed he might make it the scooter snagged a wave crest and flung its rider in a spectacular windmilling arc. The springloaded throttle slowed to an idle. Steering gear locked in a turn engineered to return the jet-ski within grabbing distance of its rider.

But the boy lay half stunned, floating dead ahead. Mansour called upon the hundredth name of God and flung the tiller over just in time to keep from running down the young fool he had been preparing to blow away. Gus came tearing up on deck and for a nanosecond seemed undecided whether to grab the tiller or the sawed-off.

Mansour pointed astern where the boy was just beginning to stroke uncertainly toward his circling machine. "Perhaps we should make sure he's all right?"

"Steady as she goes," Gus growled. "And please get that weapon out of sight."

Mansour let off the cock and stowed the shotgun under the cushion. "I thought only in the old world," he sighed, and noted that the idling jet-ski had no name. Instead, it had one of those squiggles the western world insists on calling "Arabic" numerals. Probably some enterprising Irishman was renting them out by the hour. Mansour paid attention to his sailing.

Gus sat on the lee side of the cockpit and watched the blond swimmer struggle to board his machine. "You've had several opportunities," he said. "The only conclusions to be drawn are that you have no intention of killing me—or no intention of so doing at just this time."

Mansour smiled a sad Semitic smile and changed the subject. "You do not think then that our interruption was merely some monied moron with a new toy?"

"Morons usually try out new toys under the eyes of bikini-clad females in estrus." The moron in question was piloting No. 13 shoreward at reduced speed and seemed, temporarily at least, to have all the heat knocked out of him.

"I'd not thought of that," Mansour admitted. "Are all Americans as devious in their thinking?"

"No more so than Armenians or Japanese," Gus said. "Our most disconcerting national trait is an occasional lapse into honesty. Unfailingly it comes at the worst possible moment for frankness to rear its ugly farengi head."

Mansour raised his eyebrows. "You speak Arabic?"

"Hardly. But from the way Frank came to signify a lack of politeness in European languages and something midway between foreigner and barbarian in yours . . ." Gus paused. "But then I suppose the Franks were cousins to the Vandals. So what brings you here?"

Mansour laughed. "An Arab could spend days working up to a question like that."

"Do we have days?"

"I pray we do. But perhaps they are better used in your American fashion. I offer you one-half billion dollars."

"For what?"

Mansour had expected at least a blink. He did not get it. "I believe billion is proper American usage."

"A thousand million as they would say in England. And what do I have that's worth that? Is it your money?"

"You have— Well, uh, yes, it is my own."

"Where'd you get it?"

"The first million is hardest. I was born with that."

"I haven't looked into your background," Gus said, "but it seems to me you're given an allowance of something like a million a month."

"Something like that," Mansour agreed. "And I strive mightily to give the impression that I spend a trifle more: a hundred dollar bill to the odd headwaiter or parking lot attendant."

"Takes ten thousand hundred dollar bills to make one million," Gus said.

"And only one to make the headlines," Mansour said wryly. "Every casino will tell you I'm plunging deeply somewhere else." He glanced at his watch.

"Right," Gus agreed. A younger and bolder man might have attempted a flying jibe but Gus went over on the opposite tack and pointed slightly high while Mansour freed the sheets and let her out on a broad reach. Soon they were heading back in, moving at twice the speed but in an illusion of dead calm since the wind was going the same way.

"So you've been investing under other names

and squirreling money away instead of tending to business drinking champagne from starlets' slippers?''

Mansour smiled and nodded.

"What am I to do with your money?" Gus asked. "By the time I could afford champagne my tastes were firmly fixed on beer."

"*Munkar.*"

" 'Fraid I've never drunk that."

"Moral filth," Mansour explained. "That's how my brother and all good Moslem describe it."

"It?"

"Anything alcoholic."

"And you?"

"*Je suis un croyant, mais pas un praticant.*" The phrase came so automatically that Gus was made to understand the countless times the man before him must have explained along the Riviera that, though a believer, his practice of the Moslem faith was less than totally rigid. Gus went below again and returned with a bottle and two glasses. "Say when. I presume you know that Arabs invented the still?"

"It surprises me that you know." They raised their glasses and the *Rascaluna* romped along on a broad reach heading back for Newport. The traffic thickened again. There were half a dozen jetskis up ahead playing some kind of tag. Gus put the bottle away and made certain other preparations.

"We invented the still," Mansour said bitterly. "We introduced modern medicine and modern mathematics into Europe. No matter how often European plunderers assaulted us under the guise of crusaders, we managed quite handily to win every war. Our arms and armor were the envy of the world." He turned to face Gus. "How the mighty have fallen. Do you know what happened to us?"

"Yes."

Mansour managed to hide his confusion. Did Americans do this deliberately, to keep opponents off balance, or was he facing some cultural impasse?

Gus disabused him. "I know why a small band of blue-eyed barbarians bested you," the old man said. "And so do you. But the frankness of my reply must needs hinge on the balance between *croyant* and *praticant*."

"Odd," Mansour mused. "I would never have taken you for an historian."

"Nor I you for a playboy. Do you want a frank answer?"

Mansour shrugged. "Islam?"

"Your crescent and your cross."

"You are Christian?"

"Even less than you're Moslem. I rode the Wheel of Karma full speed through Unitarianism, and misread the sign at the crossroads of the Eightfold Way."

"I'm sorry," Mansour said.

"I'm not. It simplifies life to get all the burning issues out of the way."

"There will be some problem transferring the money inconspicuously," Mansour said. "Perhaps if I merely handed you a power-of-attorney and my portfolio . . ."

"I haven't accepted," Gus said. "And besides, that gives you no protection if I decide to skip."

"To which planet?"

Gus grinned. "There is that. But what do you want?"

"My brother, Omar the Beloved, struggles to better our people. He wishes them to live well, be devout, bring honor and glory to Islam."

"And you?"

"What my brother promises, I wish to deliver. I wish to bring pride and respect to my people. I wish for something that will outlast the oil."

"Why me?"

"You are the one man in aerospace who has not been bought and sold by one Arab or another. If I see you correctly, you care more for your own opinion of yourself than what others may think." Mansour paused and studied the jet-skis frolicking ahead. "They say the world is full of honest men. But perhaps they only confuse honesty with timidity."

"Then you're not interested in a few jet fighters for some *coup d' etat?*"

"Were that all I wanted, Interarm's headquarters are in Monte Carlo. Sam Cunnings offers discretion, and an assortment of arms that would corrode the brass off Francis Bannerman's coffin. Do you know Sam?"

"Not personally," Gus admitted. "But I know many slightly used aircraft pass through that arsenal in Manchester."

"But no spaceships," Mansour mourned. "At least, not yet."

Gus managed not to laugh. "The way Uncle's reaching around trying to save a dime," he growled, "it'd serve him right if somebody like you took over. Might even turn out to be long-range patriotism to let somebody else compete with the Russians. But—'' He faced Mansour. "You know the UN agreed there'd be no private enterprise in space?''

"On May 4th, 1943, Pope Alexander VI divided the world between Spain and Portugal,'' Mansour snapped, "never once considering that we Arabs might live in some parts of it. Nor did the Holy Father make any provision for the British, Dutch French, American, Russian or Japanese empires which followed.''

Gus studied traffic and let out the sheet until *Rascaluna* was perilously close to sailing by the lee. "Well,'' he mused, "all the UN can do about Africa is argue. We'd be a few million miles farther away.''

Up ahead one jet-ski had peeled off from whatever tag game they were playing. It was heading toward the *Rascaluna*. The machine had dumped its rider. Mansour waited for the steering gear to lock in a rider-rescuing turn. It did not. Like a torpedo, the jet-ski bore unwaveringly toward them. He let go the tiller and the sloop rounded up. In the instant before the riderless jet-ski changed course to meet them Mansour saw it was the same No. 13 that had dumped the blond boy a while ago. He was scrabbling for the sawed-off when a burst of rapid fire assaulted his eardrums. Gus was blasting away with a hunting rifle.

There was a shock wave and sudden geyser as the jet-ski blew a momentary hole in the water. From the force of the blast Mansour knew if it had reached the sloop there would have been nothing left. Gus's mouth was moving. He hoped they would not be permanently deaf.

Moments later a blue Harbor Patrol boat was

screaming toward them. Mansour still gripped the sawed-off shotgun. He gave Gus a questioning look. Gus nodded. He let the weapon slide into the water, excused himself and went below for a moment.

Before the police boat was alongside the Arab was back on the deck. "Are they real police?" he asked. He sensed Gus's slight confusion and knew it would be best to enter this confrontation with as few unknowns as possible. He pointed at his tie. The conservative, old school stripe had been replaced by a handpainted and improbably pneumatic nude. Sunglasses covered the top half of Mansour's face.

"What happened?" a policeman called.

Gus shrugged.

The cop was young and blond. He studied the swarthy, middle-aged Mansour in expensive suit and handpainted tie. "Oh," he said knowingly. "You guys only kill each other, don't you?"

"You wanna ask questions, ask." Mansour no longer spoke British. Now he was rumbling in a flat midwestern basso with overtones of garlic.

The other older cop got the boat to stand still for a moment. "Who was shooting?" he asked.

"I was," Gus said.

"What happened?"

Gus told them.

"We ought to take them in," the young cop said.

The older one sighed and muttered, "Someday you'll learn. But why did you shoot at it, Mr. Dampier?" he added to Gus.

"Because it was shooting at me," Gus snapped. "Now, if the owner of that device cares to step forward and make a claim, my guest and I will be delighted to deal with him. If not, then I see little point in wasting a citizen's time with useless reports over the firing of a properly registered weapon in an unpopulated area. You know who I am." Gus turned to the younger cop. "And if you do not, part of your on-the-job training should be to find out."

"I still think we ought to take them in!" the blond cop was saying as Gus and Mansour hauled sheets and got under way. The older officer's reply was lost in the roar of the patrol boat's turbine.

"Why the godfather routine?" Gus asked as the police headed toward scattering jet-skis.

"There is always the possibility that my brother's agents do not know I've contacted you."

"What would you have done if one of those cops hadn't been smart enough to know when to back off?"

"You and your boat are known. If the remains of your fortune are not enough to decelerate the course of justice I could always claim diplomatic immunity."

"That must save you a few thousand a year just tearing up parking tickets."

"I have no car."

"What good's money if you don't want to spend it?"

"I want to spend it. It is just that new cars or new women are not among the things I would rather have than money."

"What will you spend it on?"

"Power, influence, the quality of adjective that will stand by my name in history."

"Hopeless case," Gus muttered.

"You would not rather be known as the man who filled the streets with cheap, nonpolluting buses?"

"I'd be nine million dollars happier never to have heard of the damned things."

"One half billion is 55½ times 9 million."

"Fool sudani." Gus exhausted one third of his vocabulary in Arabic. "What do you really expect to do with that kind of money?"

"Nothing," Mansour said. "I expect you to do it."

"If you hand me the money, what do you suppose I'll do?"

"Pay off a few old scores," Mansour guessed. "And once you've repaid your enemies, perhaps you'll remember your friends. While at it, please consider which ethnic group accepts impossible heat, monotonous food, carries every gram of provision during incessant journeying, and never wastes a drop of water."

"Bedouin in low orbit," Gus mused. "Silently folding their solar collectors and stealing away into the asteroids."

Mansour gave him a sharp look. "You are already there?"

"I'm nowhere," Gus said flatly.

"But you could—?"

"You don't put that stuff together in the basement. I'm afraid half a billion wouldn't even get us desk space in a low-orbit laboratory."

"There is always the possibility of unused equipment." Mansour's eyes narrowed. "Perhaps an informal acquisition—"

"You mean steal it?"

"Did they not steal from you?"

"It's not the morality that slows me down," Gus explained. "I just don't want to be like Caesar's pirate."

"I beg your pardon?"

"Julius Caesar was once taken for ransom. When he asked his captors why they chose piracy for a career their leader explained, 'It's because I have only one ship. With a whole fleet like yours I'd be a conqueror.' "

"Ah? And what happened to the pirates?"

"Caesar's captivity lasted some months. He whiled away the time writing poetry. When the pirates didn't like his verse Caesar promised to crucify them."

"And did he?"

"Just as promptly as every government on earth will cooperate to search out any tiniest law we might violate."

"We must stay within the law," Mansour agreed, "or abandon all hope of keeping any profit."

"It's money you're after then?"

"How else am I to better my people? Do you take me for some sackcloth-and-ashes prophet off crying in the wilderness?"

"I had my doubts," Gus admitted. "But now that we understand one another . . ." They were approaching the inner basin. The harbor police had discouraged jet-ski traffic but there was the usual press of day sailers and dinghys. Gus and Mansour busied themselves with lowering sail and lighting off the auxiliary.

"The cameras will be out in force," Gus warned with a wave at the no man's land beyond the gates of the marina's parking lot. "I could get a VTOL in here if you want to avoid them."

Mansour considered the problem. "Have you urgent business elsewhere?"

"I could get you a room here. Or you can share my suite."

"You'll have calls to make and so will I. I'm sure two suites would be better. And if we don't appear for a day or two perhaps the *paparazzi* will move on to someone more photogenic."

As he left the phone booth, Albert found himself thinking about Armand Fortin. Poor gangling bastard had blown a fuse when he was force fed in a few months those cruel truths most blacks absorb in tiny painful doses all their lives.

Albert had been sure he had the boy in the palm of his hand. But Albert had been wrong before. "Can't change a mule jack," he muttered as he got into the newly rear-windowed limo. "Maybe I didn't explain it right."

But he had. Once Army learned he was not going to be prosecuted he had entered so enthusiastically into the project that Albert knew the boy would have gone willingly even without a million dollar defalcation hanging over him. It had taken him mere days to shift from finance to chemical rocketry. The boy worked delta vee equations in his head.

"But no matter how much thrust you strap onto that old shuttle," Army had protested, "you might as well try farting if you hope to push anything worthwhile within grabbing distance of Earth."

"Even us old Uncle Toms knows how many zeroes sit behind a hundred million tons. If a bonus comes along, like a chunk of iron heading right for just a nudge to get it home, that's frosting on the cake. But mainly, we want to see if there's anything there that'll pay for building a mass driver."

"One of those crazy slingshot things like they keep trying to build on the moon?"

Albert nodded.

"How about ion rockets?"

"You got one that works?"

"Then what'm I supposed to be doing out there anyway?"

"Prospecting. You're going to let us know if it's worthwhile swindling and stealing a bunch of dollars we haven't got." Albert had sighed. "You've been to school. Don't you know anything about history?"

"Like what?"

"Like trade routes. Nowadays we got ore carriers, bulk loaders, ships hauling dirt halfway around the world and making it pay. What do you think the king would have said if one of those old Portuguese explorers had emptied the treasury finding a route to the Indies and then come home with a cargo of low-grade iron ore? Why do you think Columbus died in prison?"

"So if I don't find a gold mine I shouldn't bother to come back?"

"You want to stay out there, that's up to you. But you get that ship back."

"You're only in it for the money. Why don't you go to the moon or build a colony?"

"Why don't we just print money? There's some things the government jus' don't like us poor people to do for ourselves. And since the UN closed off the moon, it's up to us to find some place they haven't thought of yet."

"How about Mars?"

"You got to ship your air and water up, and then lift your product out of a gravity well near as bad's the one down home where all the groceries come from. We're not out there for glory, boy. We're trying to make money."

"Why are you so sure you'll find it in the asteroids?"

"Can you think of some other place to look?"

Albert could practically read the boy's mind as he inventoried the possibilities. Mercury and Venus impossibly hot. The moon was already more ripped apart by lawsuits than by the half dozen hopeful mining ventures there. Mars was out of the question. The Jovian satellites were even years farther away.

"Well," Army had said doubtfully, "the asteroids are already in handy bite sized chunks, but it seems like a lot of money for a maybe."

"It is," Albert agreed. "And just don't you go bein' part of the maybe."

The silence had finally been broken by Army. "I've been wrong about everything else," he mused. "But I think I'm not the only one who doesn't know who you are or where you stand in this company. Why do you keep slipping into that Amos and Andy dialect?"

"I have to keep in practice."

"But why do you use it? People know we don't talk that way."

"The ignorance that exists in this world would positively amaze you. Anyhow, I only use it to keep the bleeding-heart liberals revelling in guilt. To scare a redneck you have to talk better English than he can." Albert stopped. He could see that he was never going to transplant experience into this poor mule jack's head. Only a lifetime could do that. Would this Army ever get his chance at a lifetime?

That night, to keep the paper pushers from wondering why more people went up than came down, Army had gone up, stuffed full of tranquilizers and enclosed in breathing apparatus, crated as freight. Up there he had been greeted by Jeff who had gone up properly, the way God intended people to fly into orbit. This Jeff, who did not always respond to his name, had gritted his teeth, counted the seconds, calculated air tanks against the reduced demands of a tranquilized body, multiplied by six feet five and assured the shuttle crew that yes, he was fine, and no, he didn't need a gram of anything to help him through the night even if it was only $500 and guaranteed pure. Finally they were gone and he could uncrate the newest recruit to Gus's private army.

And then, after all the time and hope Albert had invested in him, that god damned mule jack had lit out in the wrong direction, practically breathing the lovely, longlegged Sin's exhaust fumes. Albert had been close to tears when he had to tell Gus. "That son of a bitch!" he raged. "If ever I get my hands on him!"

But Gus had not been annoyed. "What the hell?" he growled. "They're on adjoining sectors. Not really sweeping the same space. Maybe they'll have to help one another. Remember when you and I needed some help?"

"You means yesterday? Yassuh, I do indeed."

"Why don't you quit that, Albert?"

"Cause you know I'm a full partner and I know it and the fewer others know, the better it is for both of us.

"My life's invested in this business and this isn't any run of the mill government screwup. Somebody's out to shaft us. A poor old black man's got more chance of overhearing things than Mister Augustus Dampier's ever gonna get."

"You may be right. But it's a hell of a way to live."

"Black's bad enough. Don't you go wishin' broke on me too."

"You got any ideas?" Gus had asked.

"Penn Central skims profits, scams stockholders, and Uncle bails them out. Lockheed puts the wings on backwards and the government's right there to keep an American industry from going under. Gus Dampier does an honest job, comes in on time and under the bid—and they change the rules in the middle of the game."

"Maybe they didn't know the Arabs were going to do their number with the oil just then."

"If they can bail everybody else out, you'll excuse me if I don't believe it. This old man's been fucked over before. You ready for that meeting tomorrow?"

"Should've bought the good doctor out years ago." Gus shrugged. Dr. Johnson was the only major stockholder outside the family. He needed periodic pacifying—especially now that every financial page was predicting a dire future for Gus Dampier. But even if Dr. Johnson's senility was surpassed only by his timidity, Gus and Albert both remembered the old days when there would have been no company without Dr. Johnson. In violation of all common sense, neither of them could bring themselves to pronounce a death sentence on a man who was, at most only ten years older than they were. And besides, as Gus always remarked, as long as he had the family in his hip pocket the good doctor's shares would never be a threat. But at ten sharp next morning it had turned out that neither Gus nor Albert were ready.

As usual, Albert presided over the coffee machine, greeting all with the exact mixture of familiarity and reserve that was fitting for an old family retainer.

Dr. Johnson had doddered in, toothbrush mustache distorted into a permanent pantomime of I-smell-excrement. "Good morning, Albert," he said. "Aren't you ever going to retire?"

"Whenevuh you does, suh."

M'Meath took coffee, sipped, made a face and opted for cream and sugar. Ulcer bothering him again, Albert had noted. Gus beamed like a benevolent walrus, doing his best to look like the old lecher on Esquire. No more family appeared. Albert had made too much coffee. Studying M'Meath's smug face, he suddenly knew that too much coffee was to be the least of his problems.

It was brief. It was brutal. Dr. Johnson had given a passable performance as Judas while projecting his own senile failings onto Gus. M'Meath had struggled to play the suave and emotionless croupier, his performance marred by an abrupt dash from the table. From the toilet came clearly the sound of vomiting. "And this is the young blood that's needed to bring us out of the doldrums?" Gus had asked acidly.

While M'Meath continued vomiting Dr. Johnson studied the polished tabletop. Gus had riffled through M'Meath's bundle of proxies, hoping to discover a bluff. Instead he found dates a fortnight newer than those on the proxies in his own briefcase. Now he knew why that bogtrotting son of a bitch had been so busy for the last couple of weeks.

M'Meath emerged pale and shaken. But the quality of his performance in no way vitiated the validity of the proxies he held. Ten minutes later Gus had found himself out on the street, no longer in control of his own company. Albert had restrained the impulse to rush out after him. Instead, he remained in the board room impassively polishing the coffee machine, willing himself invisible.

It didn't work. M'Meath had turned to him and said, "I'm afraid that means you too, Albert. We're under new management now."

The next week had been a critical one for both Albert and Gus. He had driven Gus here and there while the old man brooded and vacillated, one minute resigned and ready to learn golf, the next minute busy with some scheme to recapture the company from a faithless family.

It was enough to make the most unsuspecting of men see a conspiracy. Gus still bore the scars of a year-ago raid that had nearly finished him. And then the government had pulled the rug from under the steam bus project. Gus had weathered that by getting the inside track on the French, and once Omar bought those jets the cash flow problem would be just another memory. And then Omar the Beloved began having second thoughts about American-made jets and what might happen if the United States were to make it difficult to get parts or service or instructors or any of the hundred other indispensables that went with a sale of this magnitude.

Who was out to get Gus? Why?

Albert had pondered. Albert had listened. Albert had made discreet inquiries. Albert had learned nothing. And one morning he had picked up Gus and the Mark V felt odd and he had pulled up just short of an on-ramp to get out and find all the lug nuts on the left front wheel unscrewed within a half turn of eternity.

That afternoon Albert had personally installed a radio controlled starter so he could warm up the car from a block away. He also installed several noisemakers that tended to make him unpopular around parking lots. But these capacitance alarms had stopped the mysterious almost-through slashes on inner sidewalls of the limo's radials.

It solved another problem too. Gus no longer ignored Albert's warnings that somebody was out to get them. But with Gus out of action, out of the company—why?

The old man's stock was worth 10 million—at fair market value. Albert's was tied up in some private ventures to the greater glory of Watts but even with Gus holding the proxies they had been leveraged out, thanks to concerted action by the family and Dr. Johnson. Even if M'Meath seemed somehow to have salvaged the King Omar disaster and sold those jets, it might be years before Gus or Albert could peddle their shares for anything like true value. Twenty million between them and they were—broke.

Sitting there in the limo, he tried to remember if it had been his idea or Gus's to drive up to the high desert and watch the shuttle lift off. Albert was sure neither of them had planned it until moments before they had gotten into the limo. And why the car? Why hadn't they flown up?

Then he remembered the VTOL had been tied down at Palmdale and it was easier to drive a hundred miles than arrange a charter. But had anybody known? Albert knew nobody had. Which had to mean somebody was following him. Albert had learned how to shake a tail before he was old enough to quit smoking. But a years-old, customized Mark V was conspicuous enough in these overregulated and undergasolined days. Dented, with a missing back window . . .

They could take their time, call ahead, pass him from station to station like some ancestor on the underground railroad.

Albert started south on the Golden State Freeway and there it was. He pulled off, bought two dollars worth of gasoline from a glowering attendant, and got back on, puttering along at a sedate 55 and there was the battered VW again.

Albert was tempted to find out how fast a VW van could go but he was more interested in who drove it. A mile ahead somebody blew a tire and the chain reaction began. There was plenty of time to swing a couple of lanes over and avoid the jam. Albert feinted, led the VW into a jam-avoiding swing, then cut back and braked. The van passed, its driver too busy surviving to glace Albert's way. He caught a clear view of a brownskinned, Latin-looking young man with wavy, almost kinky hair. He was too neatly groomed for that battered relic of a— From the angle at which it reared up when the driver braked Albert suddenly knew this was no ordinary VW. Probably there were some four hundred supercharged inches in the middle of the cargo space with a gear belt drive down to the transaxle. Albert began threading his way through the braking cars. Horns blared as he made it to the right and scooted down an off ramp. The funny van was now boxed into the left lane.

Albert wormed his way through the jungle of North Hollywood streets and got onto the Santa Ana Freeway. A half hour later he eased off the Harbor Freeway, scooted over to Central Avenue, and found himself in darkest Watts.

The store was small, dingey, the sign fading. But Albert could still make out *TV Rental and Repair*. He drove around the block into the alley, hoping the shards of wine bottles would not meet his new radials the wrong way. He got out and pounded on the back door.

"Who is it?"

"Albert."

The door opened instantly. "Never know around here," the man who opened it said. "Come on inside and have some coffee."

"I'd like to. But I have a problem. Sort of urgent."

"Name it."

"Could you sweep this car?"

The TV repairman raised his eyebrows but did not ask questions. He was a very dark young man with a thin, nilotic face and almost straight hair. At the end of the block several children were pumping up their courage to approach the limousine. Albert weighed fingerprints against the memory of how long since he had been a child. He shook his head when the young man prepared to run them off.

The thinfaced young man went in to lock the front door, then returned with a handheld sniffer. He swept the Continental and found it immediately: a small beeper no larger than the magnetic extra key box some optimists affix to the undersides of bumpers or fenders. He held it out to Albert. "Smash it?"

Albert shook his head. "Seems like you found it awful easy."

The young man frowned and began sweeping again. This time he spent a good ten minutes. Finally he straightened. "Up there." He pointed at the overhead power lines. "So much rf around here it's damn near impossible to sort anything out from background noise."

"But you still think there's something there?"

"Ain't got no real reason to." Obviously, he did think so.

"You own this car, mister?"

Albert turned to the nappy headed boy child. "No," he explained. "I jus' drive it. But I clean it too so don' you go gettin' no fingerprints on it."

"Can I have a ride?"

"Maybe later on. We busy jus' now."

"Might be something wired into your ignition," the young man said doubtfully. "Only works when you're running."

"I been over that ignition pretty careful." Albert had just installed a remote, radio controlled starter that removed the suspense from each morning's first turnover of an engine that had been sitting overnight. But he fired up the limo and left it idling while the young man swept it again, going over the car's surface as carefully as if he were polishing it. The probe showed nothing. He paced down the alley away from the car, still studying the probe.

There were half a dozen children by now admiring the sleek elegance of the sort of automobile that seldom visited this neighborhood. Albert started to shoo them and the montage of blighted hopes reminded him of so many times in his own youth that he just couldn't do it.

He had been driving all day. The car was bugged but he knew this vehicle too intimately for anyone to have managed to fillet in a bead of plastic explosive without Albert knowing it. He changed the threatening gesture into a wave and a half dozen kids poured into the Mark V. As he started moving down the alley he knew from the sudden change in the young man's shoulders that the probe was picking up something.

"Who own this car, mister?"

"Oh, he jus' some big man from uptown. He pretty good."

"Man, that cat really *live!*"

"He got his troubles jus' like ev'body else." But as he said it Albert knew there was no way anyone in Watts would ever come close to believing troubles could accompany a car like this. He circled the block and headed back down the alley again, sighing at the prospect of finger and noseprints all over the back windows. Finally the children were all out. "You found something?" he asked.

The young man nodded and began crawling underneath. A moment later he was out again,

puzzled. "Got to be around the wheels or fenders," he explained. "I get a whup, whup, in sync
with your speed. Anybody been workin' underneath the car lately?"

"Only me." Albert remembered the new back
window but reminded himself that this bugging
had begun before the broken glass.

The sharp featured young man scooted underneath again and ran his hands over the undercoat-
ing that lined the wheel wells. There were no
unexplainable bulges. He took his probe under
the car. Nothing.

"A transmitter has to have a power supply," he
grunted, and raised the hood. He disconnected
the hot wire from the coil, then removed a battery
cable and checked continuity. Thanks to Albert's
spic-and-span maintenance there was no crud
around the battery to foster tiny leaks. There was
no current draw on the system. He reconnected
the ignition and ticked away at the starter until
the electronic equivalent of breaker points was in
an open position. Still no current.

The young man wiped his forehead. "Being
wired into your ignition system's the only way it
could turn off when the car stops. If it had its own
power supply it'd be whup whupping all the
time."

"In time with wheel rotation?"

"You change tires lately?"

"Several times. Somebody's been slashing
them. But I never went to the same shop twice."

The young man studied the probe which
showed nothing. He crawled under the car again.
"Shocks?" he asked. "When'd you replace
them?"

"Month or so ago. I did it myself."

"I know you got some funny radio in there. You been having static problems?"

Albert shook his head.

"You know about bonding—the way you have to tie every part of a car or plane together so the charge is equal?"

Albert knew.

The young man studied him admiringly. "I know you're thorough," he said. "But I never saw anybody bother to solder bonding wires to the overload springs around shock absorbers before."

"Son of a bitch!" Full speed ahead and damn the dry cleaning, Albert dived under the Mark V. Both ends of the coil spring had tiny wires leading into the closed cylinder of the shock absorber.

"Want me to take it off?"

"No! That's big enough to airmail us to Beverly Hills!" Albert was suddenly sick with fear. "You chillun git out of here now. *Scoot!*"

They scooted.

"Not enough room in it if it's going to work as a transmitter and still keep the back end from bouncing around."

Albert controlled himself and knew the young man was right. But how did the thing work? There were no connections to the limo's electrical system. It only beeped when he was moving. Halfway down the alley the kids sensed the crisis was over. They began infiltrating. "You chillun got nothin' better to do? Why aren't you in school?"

"Hey mister, why your wheel weight growin' whiskers?"

Albert and the young man glanced at one another. "Got a compass?" Albert asked.

"Think I got one somewhere in the shop."

"Never mind. Give me a screwdriver." Albert removed the compass from in front of the steering wheel and crawled back under the rear of the Continental. "Sho'nuff," he grunted. The young man crowded beside him and they watched as the compass card swung back and forth, pointing toward an inside wheel-balancing weight.

"Somebody sure went back to basics," the young man said.

Their bug was simplicity itself. The ceramic magnet had been painted to look like lead and, being on the inside of the tire, the load of iron filing whiskers it had accumulated was not that conspicuous. But this kind of magnet was several orders of magnitude stronger than the horse shoes of fond memory. Whenever it spun past the array of cores and coils inside the shock absorber that coil spring wrapped around it energized the limo's whole body shell into a transmitting antenna. No wires, no power source—it was as self-powered as any magneto and would run forever. "So that's why we found the first one so easy," the young man said. "Want me to pry off the weight?"

Albert shook his head. "Take that other bug and stick it on the first United Parcel you see. Leave this one like we think we got 'em all."

Albert would have liked to give the children some candy but he didn't have any and in any event, children in Watts—those who survive—are hesitant to accept sweets from strange old men who drive magnificent cars. He gave them each a dollar, knowing one candy bar apiece could do little permanent damage to their teeth.

"What if you want to run some little errand?"

"Depends on what we find on the other wheels." Albert began checking them with the compass. Though only one shock was doctored up with cores and coils, each wheel had one magnetic weight. In case Albert were to rotate tires, he supposed. He checked the spare. Ditto. Thoughtfully, he pried the magnet off the spare and tossed it down the alley into—how 'bout that! Somebody was growing happy grass right there between the trash cans. "Get tired of bein' tailed I can have a flat," he explained. "And meanwhile, I'll whup-whup out of here and they can all laugh at how stupid we are."

"I didn't find it."

"The hell you didn't. The man's going to get billed for next month's payment on your loan." They shook hands and Albert went whup-whupping out of Watts, back onto the Harbor Freeway.

It was mid-afternoon. By the time he could reach Newport, Gus ought to have gotten in his afternoon's sail and be ingesting his sundowner—unless the old goat was up to something Albert didn't know about. He wondered how the old man had figured the Arab connection, then realized it was obvious: they had been dealing with Omar the Beloved. To the best of Albert's knowledge there had been no dealings with any Latin American countries for years—not since Gus had finally and reluctantly given up building any more of the old workhorse projects that still held most third-world airlines together.

He was rounding a cloverleaf from the Harbor to the San Diego Freeways at a sedate 45 when the rear tire blew. Albert slowed and got over as fast as he could. The left rear wheel was the one with the magnet-powered whupper. Albert studied it with some dismay. Fifteen minutes ago in Watts that tire had been perfect. He remembered wine bottle shards in the alley and then realized that steel belted radials would never notice a little glass. I'm not that important, he thought as cars whipped past. Still, he wished he'd pulled to the other side of the single lane ramp where he would not be so exposed. A wrecker with an auto club logo pulled up. Albert wondered if such promptness was coincidence. "Need some help?"

The driver was young, blond, with a totally ingenuous face. Albert waved him on. Paranoid, perhaps, but what the hell? He'd already ruined his neat black suit crawling under in Watts. Wouldn't hurt him to change a tire now. He began setting up the bumper jack, trying to ignore the roar and hiss as cars swept past.

Minutes later he swung out on the cloverleaf again, changing his mind to complete the turn and head back toward Watts. This leg of the run would be unmarked by any electronic whup whup. He picked a tire shop he had never visited before. A heavyset man nearly as old as Albert began changing the tire. When he had the carcass off the wheel he looked around the shop carefully. Satisfied nobody else was watching, the heavy man beckoned and pointed. Inside the ruined casing lay the undistorted slug of a steel jacketed 7.62mm bullet. "Looks like you got a friend," the heavy man murmured. Albert dropped the slug in his pocket as the other man pulled a new tire down off the rack. If this kept up it was just a matter of time before . . . He wondered if the

blond boy in the tow tuck had been there by
accident.

The guard waved him into the parking lot. Albert parked, set the alarms, and locked up. He was
striding toward the house phone when he
changed his mind and went back to the doghouse.
He handed the guard a double sawbuck and said,
"Somebody keeps trying to steal that car. Could
you please keep a special eye on it?"

The guard assured Albert that he would. Albert
called Gus's room. No answer. He was about to
have the old goat paged when he saw Gus and a
swarthy middle-aged stranger climbing up the
ramp from the floating finger piers. Albert made
himself invisible and gave them time to get into
the clubhouse, then called for Mr. Dampier.

"Come on up, Albert," Gus said. "We've got a
guest."

"I'll be right in," Albert said. Damn! When
would he get a chance to talk alone with Gus?
Must be getting old. His feet were hurting and he
did not really look forward to an evening of playing old family retainer. But Gus wouldn't have
warned him unless there were something in the
wind. He took a breath and braced himself. By the
time he reached Gus's suite he was almost cheerful.

Gus and the stranger sat sipping watered bour-
bon. Albert slipped noiselessly into the room and
began changing from his scruffed chauffeur's
uniform into a white jacket.

"Albert, will you please stop that. Come sit
down and have a drink."

Albert wondered if he'd gotten his signals

mixed. "Are you sure you ain't had one too many, suh?"

"Very sure, Albert. This is Mansour ibn Jezail."

"Very pleased to know you, suh."

"Brother of Sheikh Omar," Gus explained.

Albert decided it would be wiser to stay in character. Ibn Jezail . . . had to mean something like son of a gun. Son of a flintlock, he guessed. Family name or a descriptive term? His hand touched the steel-jacketed slug that had ruined a tire. "Do you gemmun want somethin' to eat?"

"Our new partner is bringing a half billion into the company," Gus said. "What we'd like is some advice on how to spend it."

"How about armor plating the car?" Albert tossed the bullet onto the coffee table. "Does Jezail mean what I think it does?"

Mansour nodded. "As you Americans say, it goes with the territory."

"His brother the sheikh thinks we're arming a revolution."

"Are we?"

Mansour shook his head and began explaining. By the time he finished Albert sat, drink forgotten. There was a moment of silence. Finally Albert said, "You want Arabs in space. Can you guess who I'd like to see there?"

Mansour nodded again. "It is not small and limited like Earth. Surely there must be room." They looked at Gus.

"I don't give a damn who goes up," the old man growled. "I just want my share of the action."

"*Amil eh del wáqti?*" Albert asked abruptly.

"Tell us how best to spend the money," Mansour began, then stopped. "You have lived in Egypt?"

"Only if Cairo, Illinois counts. Now the first thing to do with that kind of money is remember you have no company. You can build all over—tie up the whole half billion in new plant. Or you can steal back the one they stole from us. The latter is cheaper, quicker, and offers Mr. Jezail a little more protection. He can do it without turning his money over to us or even giving us a limited power of attorney. Of course," Albert added after a pause, "it leaves us wide open to a takeover by Mr. Jezail."

"Takeover of what?" Gus asked.

"That's the point I'm making. If Mr. Mansour wants to grab that company and knows how . . ."

"Companies do not run themselves," Mansour said.

"How much running do you plan on doing?"

"Perhaps I could capture the company alone. Without your willing cooperation, what could I do with it?" He smiled his sad Semitic smile and added, "I will sign any document but surely we all know the exact value of signatures."

Albert decided either he was dealing with the most devious mind west of the Caucasus or else he was in contact with something even more exotic: could this stranger possibly be an honest man? Then he remembered something else. "Uh— about how long ago did this idea first occur to you?"

Mansour thought a moment. "I was in Harvard School of Business when you Americans landed on the moon. But even before then—we are not all camel jockeys, you know. We Arabs are also sea-farers and explorers."

"Sindbad," Gus grunted. "Piri Reis, ibn Batu-ta."

"I don't mean in general terms," Albert explained. "When did you first consider Mr. Dampier?"

"Perhaps six months ago. Even then I had no real hope until the others used you so shabbily. After all, why should anyone whose business was moving along so smoothly even consider becoming involved with a playboy?"

Albert shook his head. "When did you first discuss it with anyone?"

From the Arab's shocked surprise at the thought of such blundering Albert knew he was barking up the wrong tree. "But it's Arabs keep shooting at us," he protested. "You got any ex-planation?"

"Only that my brother sees a plot under every pillow."

"Then it wasn't you that crabbed the sale of those jets?"

"To what end? Even if I had a reason, I cannot imagine how I could influence the sheikh. After all, I am the remittance man—the family clown."

"Yassuh boss, you sho' is."

Mansour grinned. "It may be that we have other things in common," he said thoughtfully.

"I'd sure like to know who's shootin' at us."

"Probably my brother's agents," Mansour said. "We must find a way to stop them. It could spoil everything."

"And cut me off in the first chorus of my September Song," Gus added. "Which reminds me. I'll have to change my will."

Albert's feet were no longer hurting. He freshened drinks all around, then came back armed with a yellow legal pad and several pencils. "Now this is what I'd suggest you do once the London Exchange opens in—" He glanced at his watch. "—about seven more hours. God damn, I'm getting hungry.

"And when the New York exchange opens there ought to be just enough of a shock wave so you could—" From the corner of his eye he noticed that Gus was on the phone calling room service. Mansour was on another line struggling to reach London. Then suddenly Mansour was saying, "Ya Haroun, marhaba!"

Haroun had chosen his lodgings with some care. At times he had enough currency on his person to make Brixton or any other inconspicuous place a bit too dicey. He screwed down his bowler against a raw breeze. There were a few pallid English faces opening up along Uxbridge Road but most shopkeepers were Pakistani. Coreligionists, perhaps, but as alien to Haroun as to their English neighbors. Much darker than Haroun too.

It was a handy place for anonymity and despite its nearness to Heathrow, was blessedly out of the flight pattern. At Ealing Broadway he bought his ticket from a Jamaican and boarded the Underground, which was a misnomer since the tracks ran above ground until somewhere near Hammersmith. Haroun often wished they did not since trains passed immediately across from his rooms and for his first few nights on Craven Street he had been jolted awake every half hour.

Several Sikhs boarded, white turbans immaculate, silky black beards braided and folded under with a knife-edge and totally superhuman neatness. One glanced at Haroun's bowler hat, and they ignored him. A middle-aged woman with a pink caste mark on her forehead harangued five wide-eyed children whose obedience was silent and total.

The train began filling with the students and tourists who occupied every bed and breakfast this time of year. A broadfaced man in Tyrolean hat dropped into the seat across from him. A man and woman in skintight blue warmup suits with zippered legs scooted into the next seat.

Haroun glanced up to see the man in Tyrolean hat glaring. A broadfaced woman stood crowding uncomfortably close. Haroun glanced at the empty seat across the aisle and back out the window. Now the broadfaced man was smiling like a politician and asking with a confidence that would brook no refusal if Haroun would not care to move so his Frau might enjoy the window seat.

When Haroun ignored him the question was repeated with some iron in the smile. Haroun smiled back politely and suggested that the broadfaced man do something with a camel. From the titter at the other end of the motionless car he knew somebody understood Arabic even if the man in the Tyrolean hat did not.

"*Sale boche!*" the woman in the blue warmup suit muttered. The man in Tyrolean hat glowered for a moment, then lunged to his feet and dragged his wife off to the next car toward standing room only.

Haroun studied the ready-to-rain sky and tried to concentrate on what he must do today. The train began moving. They passed the crenellated walls and turrets of a medieval keep in reinforced concrete. Haroun had ridden past that castle daily for almost a year before discovering why it was not on the list of tourist attractions, that in spite of threatening walls and turrets, prisoners of late had been leaving Wormwood Scrubs at their own convenience and not the warden's.

Still he shuddered now each time he saw it. No matter how the British might boast of humane methods, to end up in a foreign prison was not to be desired.

The train went underground and everyone blinked even though there had not been that much daylight on this blustery morning. Haroun tried to concentrate on what he had to do today but his mind kept wandering, absently counting the stops.

They came to the Marble Arch and most of the knapsacked young Americans got off. The rest got off at Oxford Circus, presumably to transfer down to Piccadilly. At Holburn a busker in battered tophat boarded. Haroun wondered if he was getting an early start or was on his way home. The one remaining American, a determined lady of middle years, left the train at St. Pauls. The East Indians remained aboard heading for Petticoat Lane and points east. Haroun was rising when he abruptly knew somebody was looking at him with more than ordinary interest.

For the tiniest of instants he thought of sitting down and getting off at the next stop. But there was nothing illegal in what he was about to do. Nor would riding a stop farther fool anyone. He got off at Bank Station and made his way up, onto Threadneedle Street, still aware of someone's attention. But there were only runners and tourists as he rounded the corner onto Old Broad Street. He went nearly to the Roman wall, remembering with a faint nervous twinge that the narrow passage from the end of the wall over to Houndsditch was called Wormwood Street.

There was nothing illegal in what he was going to do today. Why couldn't he stop thinking about Wormwood Scrubs? He glanced behind as he turned into the stock exchange. This time nobody seemed to be following. Haroun pulled the list from his pocket and began lettering a sell order in the vertical semi-italics his fingers found easier than to struggle with cursive scripts that run from the wrong side of the page. He glanced up and there was Yassir over beyond the Rothschild pillar. Yassir gave a barely discernible nod.

Business began. Each time Haroun sold, Yassir, or one of a half dozen other inconspicuous men, bought. Each time they bought Haroun sold more. By the time Haroun was ready to buy it all back a nervous pall had spread across the floor. Outsiders who had struggled to buy were now floundering frantically in their efforts to get out before Dampier dropped through the floor or—heaven forbid—trading was suspended.

Haroun stepped out for a quick bowl of couscous and coffee and saw the gathering reporters. He sighed, knowing it would not be possible to go home this evening the same inconspicuous way he had come to work. He made a call.

An hour later the last outsider had been shaken out of the market. Even the large operators, who had a pretty fair suspicion of what was happening, knew also that whatever was happening had a limitless flow of petrodollars behind it and that when things of this nature occurred it was the duty of every prudent man to take cover and make bloody well sure he was not caught short.

Haroun could compound a fraction of a percent unto the tenth generation but he had trouble with time zones. He knew, however, as he ran the gauntlet of reporters and dived into the Daimler that as he was leaving the London Exchange, the one on Wall Street was either just opening, would open in an hour from now, or had already been open for an hour. It made no difference. Haroun's day's work was done. He rolled up the window, cutting off the slight drizzle and almost doing likewise for an insistent reporter's head. He settled down for the ride out to Heathrow.

By the time the limo reached the airport there were no reporters following. Haroun paid the driver, stalked across the marbled halls of transport, and rode the escalator down to the Underground. Fifteen minutes and one transfer later he was in his lodgings in Ealing—home in time for prayers.

In New York City on the Street called Wall there was need of prayer, but God casts a suspicious eye on sudden conversions under the bright edge of a falling market and in any event, these men were too busy to pray.

"Quit worrying," M'Meath reassured Dr. Johnson for—it couldn't possibly have been but it seemed at least the thousandth time. "It's just a temporary readjustment."

When the senile doctor still dithered, M'Meath had attempted to explain basic economics. "It's only paper," he lied, secretly knowing it was his life's blood imbued with his immortal soul. "The value's still there. After all, we sold Omar the jets. Nobody can take that away from us."

But Dr. Johnson had come by his senility honestly. In his life he had seen as many things taken away by stroke of pen as by stroke of apoplexy. "It's divine retribution," he warned. "I listened to your serpent's tongue tell me it was time to put Gus out to pasture. This wouldn't have happened if Gus were back in charge."

M'Meath struggled not to put his hand to his cramping midsection. It cost him almost as much effort not to snap, "Well, he's not in charge!"

M'Meath suspected he was undergoing a crisis quite apart from all the things that were happening around him. He had always been a slow, careful worker. Thorough. Lately he had fallen into deep reveries from which nothing could arouse him. It was one thing to know he was coming apart. It was quite another to be able to do anything about it. He supposed the trouble had all started with Tina. But surely it was not her fault.

She had never charged out into the world like some bra burner to do battle with every man. All she had ever asked was to live in her own home, have a husband she could be proud of, and raise her children. M'Meath had thought himself an ideal candidate. How could he have known his marriage and his wife would turn into a battleground over which he and old Gus charged, never once heeding the effect all this warfare was having on the terrain?

He supposed it might have been easier for her had he been guilty as charged. But M'Meath was much too busy. Christ, he hardly ever saw his wife! He spent evenings at the office. Whole nights. When he had finally spent a weekend in uninterrupted struggle to keep ahead of the wave of excrement that threatened to envelop the company she had hired a private detective.

M'Meath had almost told her that company security had warned him immediately that he was being followed. Later he was thankful he hadn't. Nor had he ever allowed her to learn that . . . Well, it was not that he really believed anything was happening but a man had to take simple precautions and look to his own interests if it was going to degenerate into a property and child custody squabble.

To M'Meath's chagrin it had turned out just the opposite from what he had expected. Her detective had never caught him doing anything less honorable than working himself to death. His detective had delivered telephotos and reports on the pudgy young poet whom Tina had fixed upon to while away her empty hours.

M'Meath felt guilty. If he'd been able to find the time to stay home and take care of his own house it never would have happened. She had gone back to school, taken a few extension classes and one thing had led to another. He could even guess what the pudgy young poet would have talked about. They would have lolled in some by-the-hour motel room eating and drinking the best room service could provide while the poet pontificated on the unimportance of money.

M'Meath was not quick but he thought things

out. And he had been married for ten years to the
same woman. She might be lonely but it had not
taken her long to dump the pudgy poet. He tried
to console himself that she was not a total fool.
What could he do to repair things between them?
He fiddled with his desk calendar and made a
note to buy flowers.

He could imagine how she must have felt when
she learned that she had only suspected her husband of what she had actually done. But in a way
he was glad they had both hired detectives. His
and hers had independently discovered and re-
ported something more disquieting than casual
infidelity.

"Maybe it isn't my business," M'Meath's man
had said, "but did you know there's a tall dark
man watching your house?"

M'Meath had known a moment of desolation.
One adventure he could take but if she was going
to turn into a roundheels . . .

"Doesn't seem interested in Mrs. M'Meath," the
investigator continued. "But that tall dark man
seems to be keeping a very accurate track of your
children's comings and goings."

M'Meath pulled himself back from the wrench
that afflicted him every time he relived that moment. He had to do something *now*. Something
about Dr. Johnson and all the others who were
losing confidence in the company. He had told
the old man that Gus Dampier was *not* in charge.

But was he? M'Meath couldn't fathom what had
gone wrong. The market was acting as if somebody was dumping Dampier stock. But who
would do that? M'Meath still held proxies for the
rest of the family. Held Dr. Johnson's too. The only

other stock was Gus's and Albert's. Cross off Albert. That old fool would do whatever Gus told him. But Gus was nearly broke. It would make no sense to dump his own stock when all he had to do was wait until they tied up the loose ends with Sheikh Omar and he would clean up. Not even an angry and vindictive old man would throw ten million away just to spoil M'Meath's breakfast.

What could he do?

Nothing, he guessed. Hang on and ride it out. After all, the company was sound. Once this hurricane blew over M'Meath would still hold the proxies, would hold the company. And if somebody was dumping the few odd shares he didn't know about it might be a good idea to buy them up now while the market was rock bottom. He asked Miss Jepworth to call his banker.

"You're going to *what*?" his banker demanded.

"Buy up some loose shares on the cheap."

"Rots of ruck." The banker's name was Yamamoto and he was a native of Denver. When M'Meath made appropriate sounds of mystification, Yamamoto added, "I'll scrape up the cashier's check if you really want it but I'd recommend a heart-to-heart talk with your stockholders first."

"Dr. Johnson?"

"Among others."

M'Meath felt something cold and hard sliding into a place where he was warm and soft. The only others were family. How long had it been since he'd had a real talk, a night out—anything with Tina?

Miss Jepworth buzzed. She had always been uptight but since his disastrous slip the day he had been interrupted on his way to see Philps

Averill . . . so what? A warm personal relationship with the angular Miss Jepworth was not among M'Meath's needs at this moment. "Yes?" he snapped.

"A bonded messenger," she said icily. "Nothing less than your signature will do."

M'Meath toyed with repeating the "screw him" that had originated this estrangement. Then he realized Yamamoto might for once be doing his job properly. A cashier's check already? "Send him in."

For a bonded messenger the boy didn't look old enough for all that responsibility. M'Meath started to sign, then grumblingly produced a driver's license and an accordion of credit cards before the boy would surrender the envelope. It was not a bank envelope. Suddenly the knife was going deeper into M'Meath's tender parts. He tore it open, saw Dr. Johnson's letterhead, saw a notary's seal. But all he really saw was the line in capitals across the top of the letter. *Subject:* REVOCATION OF PROXY.

M'Meath could understand intellectually what the old man was feeling. But he was just not old enough for a visceral understanding. Dr. Johnson was. The old man remembered 1929, the speculative Armageddon that had reduced members of the Exchange to OTC trading in apples. Get out now and he might salvage half a million. Not much but it would keep an old man off food stamps. M'Meath wondered if he could dump the family stock for enough to save the house. Then he remembered it was Tina's house. Would she let him in tonight?

Suddenly he remembered Philps Averill. He

punched a number—and got a machine. He gave Miss Jepworth a list of the numbers Averill had given him and began inventorying his assets. As if he didn't know he'd tied up every dime just to get control of enough stock to force old Gus into retirement.

Eleven minutes passed and just when M'Meath was beginning to decide Philps Averill was one of the strangers who were doing a number on him Miss Jepworth informed him that Averill was on the line. "What in hell's going on?" the man with the Ivy League voice asked.

"I was about to ask you the same question," M'Meath said.

"But why are you dumping your own stock?"

"I'm not."

There was a moment of silence. "Then who is?"

"Well, for openers I just received a notarized revocation of proxy from Dr. Johnson."

"You should have ushered that fossil back into the tar pits years ago."

"Years ago I was in no position to usher him down the middle aisle of the Roxy. And in a few more hours I won't be able to raise cab fare home—assuming I still have a home."

"Things are tough all over," Averill said.

"How tough?"

"You haven't heard about our problems? No, I don't suppose you would have, not with everything breaking loose at your end."

"What's happening to you?"

"This line's tapped."

"But what have you done?" M'Meath was unaware of the non sequitur as he continued. "What'm I supposed to do?"

"What floor is your office on?"

"The eleventh."

"Don't go near any open windows."

"Is this the same hotshot who was going to give my career such a boost?"

"No. But I'll buy you a drink if you'll just get off this autogenitic PA system."

"I haven't the time just now."

"Neither have I but I think we'd better make some. Same place?"

M'Meath was crossing the street when he saw Philps Averill parked in a surprisingly ratty Mercury. He beckoned and M'Meath scooted in. There seemed to be nothing wrong with the engine. "Where are we going?"

"Hopefully, out of range of any parabolic microphones."

This turned out to be a couple of kilometers across town on a park bench where Averill produced a radio. He tuned it to loud, thumpy music. "Now," he said.

"Now what?" M'Meath demanded. "I've played straight, done everything you asked. And don't tell me you don't know what's happening. If you can screw up a sale to Sheikh Omar and then unscrew it within half an hour, then there's no reason why you can't stop whoever's playing with the market. It's time somebody got investigated for rigging. It's time trading was suspended. It's time Nader's Raiders struck a blow for the little man. Now you get on your phone or radio or whatever and put a stop to it and *then* we'll talk."

"I'm sorry," Averill said. "I didn't think it would come to this."

M'Meath wondered what demon had taken

over his tongue. Until he started yelling these
random accusations he had not even known the
ideas had lain festering in his subconscious ever
since that funny business with King Omar. But
Averill's reaction told him he was on the right
track.

"And why didn't you think it would come to
this?" he asked witheringly. "Did you think the
old man would take it lying down?" As he said it
M'Meath knew he was right about that part too.
He didn't know how Gus had done it but nobody
else had any reason to ruin M'Meath. People
might dislike him . . . despise him, he knew with
a sudden sickening insight. But it was only worth
one man's time to ruin him. And he had fixed
things so that angry old man would have all the
time in the world. How had he ever imagined Gus
Dampier would take up golf?

"All we wanted to do was scare him; get him
mad enough and maybe he'd blow the whistle on
the big ones."

"The big ones?" Then M'Meath saw it all.
"You'd ruin an honest man just to get evidence
against others who aren't! And this is the agency
that's looking out for the little man?" He was
abruptly reminded of Brother Isaac's endless ex-
cursions into Ethics I. Was the end supposed to
justify the means or was it the other way around?
If Brother Isaac hadn't been such a dehydrated old
drone perhaps M'Meath could have remembered.

And at that moment the last thing he needed
was Averill to remind him that M'Meath had
jumped at the opportunity to help ruin an old
man.

"Ironic in a way, I guess."

M'Meath did not rise to the bait.

"I mean about Nader's Raiders being investigated." Averill sighed. "Now I know how the boys in the CIA must have felt. Man does his job, goes by the book, and the next thing he knows some self-righteous SOB is throwing that book at him."

"You spread the rumor that Omar was going to buy from the French?"

Averill shook his head. "Nothing that elementary ever works. Sheikh Omar had to learn over his own intelligence net that there might be delays in delivery, that spare parts might not be there, that service and instructors would be lacking—that the Jewish lobby might not be strong enough to kill the sale but they could make sure no tinhorn Arab ever got a minute's flight time out of all those petrodollars."

"I see." M'Meath had gathered these same bits and snippets through his own company intelligence but he had assumed it was just normal business practice—the same way he had reminded every Arab of the way the French had once contracted and even collected from the Israelis for jet fighters that were never delivered.

"We didn't intend to kill him," Averill continued. "After all, what use would he have been to us dead?"

"Kill who?" M'Meath had not heard about the various attempts on Gus and Albert. Then he began to put things together: the mysterious helicopter crash up at Edwards. And his father-in-law's equally mysterious message to Tina that evening: "Just tell him I'm alive."

M'Meath had wondered. Now he knew that old

Gus didn't just despise him for the proxy business. Gus thought M'Meath was trying to murder him. He felt the knife twist in his bowels again. "Why shouldn't I stand in front of any open windows?" he demanded. "I'm not planning on sky diving."

"Glad to hear it. Then all you have to worry about is which of Gus's loyal employees is standing behind you, or which of Omar's marksmen is focusing the crosshairs in front."

It took M'Meath a moment to digest this. "What'd I ever do to Omar?"

"What did Gus Dampier do?"

"Mr. Dampier never welched on a deal in his life!"

Averill sighed. "Really, M'Meath, you should make some effort to understand human nature—especially as she is lived in the Middle East, the Eastern Seaboard, and other exotic places."

Something elementally Irish began to rise in M'Meath. He had admired old Gus, worked and struggled to win the old man's approval. Gus was about as demonstrative as an Egyptian effigy but there had been times when he had thought the old man's opinion of him had gone beyond mere tolerance. And now, thanks to this Ivy League phallus with the double-ended name M'Meath had done exactly what his mother had always warned him about, what Brother Isaac and every instructor in every school had ever warned him about: he had fallen in with evil companions.

Now old Gus thought his son-in-law was behind all the efforts to murder him. And in a way he was. M'Meath managed not to groan. "It had to be done," he muttered.

"Things that have to be done are never easy or popular," Averill said sententiously.

M'Meath swallowed something pungent and Irish. Instead, he looked around. This was not the place. There could be binoculars or telephoto lenses in one of those apartments across the boulevard. A hundred meters ahead across the greensward was a public toilet. "Let's go," M'Meath said. "I've something to show you."

His stomach was no longer cramping. The only thing that troubled him at the moment was how far to go. Should he break one leg or two? Then a cool breeze of ancestral wisdom dampened his rage for a moment. *Never leave an enemy alive.*

He was astounded at the unsuspecting way Philps Averill got to his feet and walked beside him. Couldn't he feel the hate that boiled within biting, cutting, eye-gouging distance of his doubleknit elegance? M'Meath studied him from the corner of his eye, afraid to look directly lest he telegraph what was to come once they were within the merciless concrete of that tiny shelter.

M'Meath was so glazed with rage that he didn't even see the dog-do. Otherwise he would never have stepped in it. His foot slipped and then he was sitting in it. "If there's any justice," he grated, "that filthy beast's owner will spend ten thousand years in line just waiting for a vacancy in hell."

Still blithely, WASPishly unseeing, Philps Averill risked creasing his suit as he bent to help M'Meath up. Then abruptly Averill's calm shifted to blank surprise. A microsecond later M'Meath heard the shot. Blood began to ooze from Averill's thigh. His bending-over continued until he fell awkwardly atop M'Meath who still sat in dog-do.

M'Meath had never known such violence could dwell within him. He had never been a fighter, never seen combat. Yet he knew instantly that some diarrhoetic cur had saved his life. The bullet that creased Averill's thigh had been aimed at M'Meath's head. And now that Ivy League son of a bitch was on top of him, pinning him down right here in the open.

M'Meath was abruptly on his feet, Averill still draped over his shoulders. He sprinted, zigzagging frantically for the blockhouse, wondering if the next bullet would go clear through Averill or if that WASP elegance would finally serve some useful purpose. Even as he neared the concrete building he knew it was no shelter. He was going to die. He supposed he ought to be thinking about Tina and the children. But all he could think of was that some son of a bitch had robbed him of the joy of maiming Averill. He would have been willing to die for that.

Averill was still draped over his shoulders and starting to complain. M'Meath dropped him onto the cold concrete and felt un unholy joy at the sound of bone cracking. How had he ever managed to carry the bastard this far? Just terror, he guessed. Amazing the strength it could give a man.

To his surprise he was inside the concrete building and still alive. They hadn't even fired a second shot at his shield who lay on the concrete going "Ow-ow-ow!"

This facility had no doors but the entrances were shielded by the sort of wall that in China keeps out evil spirits, who cannot turn corners, and in America forces voyeurs to turn an inconvenient number of corners. As he cowered next to a urinal M'Meath wondered whether bullets would splat against the concrete or ricochet. As he waited to find out, the fine edge of his rage dulled and his critical faculties were sharpened by the knowledge of what waited outside—was probably closing in at this moment. He wondered if a kick in the head would encourage Averill to stop that racket.

Then he heard sirens. Within moments the place was alive with cops and M'Meath wondered if they were in on it, if he was going to be shot while 'trying to escape', and then he was riding down to Headquarters in the back of a black and white and with each moment the cops turned more deferential and finally a very polite and sympathetic detective was taking his statement and before he quite realized what had happened M'Meath was on his way home and no one had even thought to ask him if he had ever considered murdering his park bench companion. In fact, Averill seemed under the delusion that M'Meath had performed a heroic rescue.

His wife did not know whether she was more surprised to see her husband home early for once, or to see him delivered by police car. "What happened?" she asked.

M'Meath lurched past her and poured a slug of Jameson's. He had swallowed it before he remembered he did not drink. But surprisingly, his stomach did not rebel. A warm Irish glow began to suffuse him. He sat down.

"What happened?" Tina repeated. Then her nose wrinkled. "What's that awful smell?"

"It's dogshit and I just tracked it all over your rug. Go tell your father they're shooting at me. Now maybe he'll believe I'm not the one shooting at him."

"Are you hurt?"

"Not where it would show."

Tina stood squarely in front of her husband. "Why should Daddy think you'd want to kill him?" she demanded. "I thought you'd already done that."

"Go curdle some milk."

Tina's reply was interrupted by the door chimes. She turned automatically. M'Meath brushed past her, grabbing the fire tongs on his way. He peered through the one-way glass and it was another bonded messenger.

At least it looked like one. He waved Tina away. She glared for a moment and finally understood that this was more than a family argument. She disappeared. M'Meath was signing for the envelope when Tina returned with a shotgun. The messenger looked from her weapon to the fire tongs under M'Meath's arm and hastily reclaimed the clip board.

"Now what was that all about?" Tina asked when the door was bolted.

"Board meeting tomorrow."

"Coming awfully close together these days, aren't they?"

M'Meath shrugged. He knew what was going to happen. Really no point in going. But he had written the tune. Now he would face the music. The strange thing was that, now that he had lost, he knew he didn't really give a damn. Perhaps once he was out of it all they would stop shooting at him. Even that was not important. "Do you really like this house?" he asked.

"If you want something bigger to impress your friends I'll need some live-in help."

"I was thinking of something smaller."

Tina's eyes widened and he saw that finally she understood.

Albert was back at his old stand polishing the coffee urn. Gus was beaming, doing his walrus-mustached Esquire turn. M'Meath sat wooden at the far end of the table, wondering who the Mexican-looking stranger with the old school tie would turn out to be. Dr. Johnson doddered in, toothbrush mustache screwed into an I-smell-even-more-excrement expression.

"Well," Gus began, "it looks like we're all here. Mr. M'Meath, if you'd care to call the meeting to order I believe our first item might be to select a new chairman of the board."

"Amen," Dr. Johnson said fervently.

Gus raised his eyebrows. "You here?"

"Have I ever missed a meeting?" the old man bristled.

"No," Gus conceded. "But I'd be willing to swear there's something in the by-laws about a board member having to own some stock."

Johnson's mouth gaped. It had completely slipped his mind that in the every-man-for-himself scramble he had sold his—and just at rockbottom before some bunch of strangers quietly started buying it all up. Suddenly he knew what had happened. "You dumped your own stock!" He looked at Gus as if the old pirate had been taken in adultery. "Your own company! What kind of loyalty do you call that?"

"My company?" Gus was bland. "I didn't own it any more. Nor am I here today for any lectures on loyalty. I'm afraid, doctor, that this meeting is limited to board members."

"Looks like you're retirin' before ah am after all, suh." Albert held out Johnson's topcoat. The good doctor's mustache was twitching as he exited the board room.

"Now shall we get back to nominating a new chairman?" When nobody objected, Gus nominated himself. Albert and the dark, Latin-looking stranger promptly voted for him. M'Meath sat in stony silence. What a risk they had taken! Dumping their own stock that way; any stranger might have snapped it up. Then he saw that from Gus's viewpoint it was no risk at all. They had been out in the street. They had flogged their shares and forced the market down. Johnson had panicked and dumped his. Now Gus and Albert and possibly this stranger had bought up everything on the cheap and the only minority stockholder, even with Tina's proxies, was M'Meath.

My own fault, he thought. Never dreamed a man in Gus's position wouldn't cut his losses and play it safe. It had taken more courage than M'Meath could ever have. He got up from the table and began putting on his coat. Nothing more to say. Then, with his hand on the knob he knew there was. "Take care of yourself, Mr. Dampier. They're shooting at me too now." He closed the door and walked out.

Gus, Albert, and Mansour remained alone in the board room. Albert drew three cups of coffee and sat down. He looked inquiringly at Mansour.

The Arab raised his eyes to heaven. They both studied Gus.

"I was almost rich enough to be able to afford a conscience when he pulled the rug out from under me," Gus said. "But we have the company and the plant back now. Who gives a damn about him?"

" 'Cept maybe his wife and kids?"

"I've taken better care of my children than they ever have of me," Gus snapped. Turning to Mansour, he added, "We've got to defuse your brother. Another week like this and I could turn as paranoid as he must be."

"My life and my effectiveness both hinge on Omar's well-being," Mansour said. "Nor am I suited for the life of a sheikh."

"Either he calls his dogs off or we kill him. I'm going to be too busy buying equipment. I'll not waste more time playing James Bond games."

"Sure makes a difference when you've got control. How you planning on getting past all the bodyguards and doing the foul deed?" Albert inquired.

"The way everything else is done: with money."

"No!" Mansour protested. "My brother is a good man."

"So am I. Perhaps your brother and I will kill each other with kindness."

"What have I done?" Mansour mourned.

There was a hiss as elevator doors opened down the hallway, then a rattledeclang and angry voices. Within the board room there were hasty checks of weapons systems as the door banged open. Through it came an electric wheelchair driven by the droopy-skinned remainder of a man. White hair stood out at all angles as if he had just lost a third game of backgammon. But that was not Dr. Sumter's game. "Welcome back," he growled at Gus. Sumter's voice reminded Albert of a skilsaw hitting a nail.

"Back where?" Gus asked as he patted his pistol back into its shoulder holster.

"Back where you belong. How much have you got to spend and how much time have we got to spend it?"

"We?" They stared at this apparition in a wheelchair.

"You do want back into space, don't you?"

Mansour turned to Gus. "You asked with whom I discussed plans," he said acidly.

"You'll be the one with the money," Sumter said, cocking his white head parrotlike. "Very slick the way you did it." He turned back to Gus. "Shall we discuss blue sky bullshit or state-of-the-art?"

"I—think I'd best leave that to you, Doctor," Gus said. How on earth had Sumter gotten onto them so quickly? How many others knew? The world was smaller than Gus remembered. Nowadays it seemed as if everyone knew his plans before he did. Abruptly Gus felt very old.

"Who is this man?" Mansour demanded. "What is he doing in a private meeting?"

"I'm your new technical director," the man in the wheelchair barked. "Man in my position doesn't care where the money comes from—as long as it comes. If the government's going to disband then a professional survivor gets funding somewhere else."

"You talk like everybody knows all 'bout what

we're up to," Albert said from behind the coffee urn.

"Hello, Albert. As long as you're masquerading as a waiter, how about giving a poor old man a cup of coffee with cream, no sugar, and let's get to work."

"Coming up," Albert said with a sidelong glance at Gus.

"Told you it was time to quit that nonsense," Gus said. "The kind of people you fool don't count anyhow." He turned to Sumter. "All right, what put you onto it? So far you're the only one knows and we both know why I know that."

"They'll all be there with their cameras when you go downstairs," Sumter cackled. "But they won't ask the right questions."

"Who is this man?" Mansour repeated.

"He's one of the old timers," Albert said. "Way back before Von Braun was popping things off for Hitler, our Dr. Sumter here was pouring gasoline for Goddard."

"And not once in all those years did I ever waste a dime buying some wornout old rocket and setting it up in the park so children could finish vandalizing it." Sumter bulldozed a place at the table, plowing chairs right and left with a spin of his wheelchair. "Thank you, Albert." He sipped the coffee and grinned at Gus.

"All right, so I bid on some surplus shuttles." Gus sighed. "The government's not using them and the way things seem to be going, nobody would have lifted a finger if the Russians had decided to buy them."

"Why should they? They've had years to inspect them at their leisure."

"But this is impossible!" Mansour protested. "Russians inside an American aerospace facility?"

Dr. Sumter grinned at him, then gave Gus a shrewd look. "You do know where those shuttles are stored, don't you? Or didn't you read the fine print?"

"What difference does it make?" Gus asked.

"Quite a bit if you thought you were going to land an uncertified vehicle back on Earth. But there's still lots of life in those clunkers as long as they never have to take a full g again."

"Should have counted on you to see through that," Gus said mildly. "But then I thought you'd booked onto that Great Shuttle years ago."

"Nearly did," Sumter cackled. "Gravity down here's really hell on old hearts and old bones."

"You've been living someplace where it's better?" Albert asked. "My feet been killing me lately."

"Nearest I've come to heaven is a waterbed," the man in the wheelchair said. "Nearest I'll ever get too, unless somebody's willing to spend a dime and get us back into space."

"Mohammed's coffin!" Mansour exclaimed.

The others stared.

"Nothing," he murmured. "I just thought of an argument when the imams gang up to tell me it's against God's will. If the Prophet's coffin remains suspended midway between heaven and earth as the Book says, it must obviously be in a stable orbit."

"And that's exactly where Gus's shuttles are parked," Sumter said. He ticked off the possibilities on his fingers. "The moon's tied up in lawsuits; the planets are useless. Do you know how many thousands of tons of chemical rockets you'll have to lift out of a four thousand mile gravity well before you can nudge even the tiniest asteroid?"

"We know," Albert said mournfully.

Dr. Sumter squinted up at Gus. "You don't give two hoots in hell for pure research," he said. "How are you going to get your money back?"

Gus shrugged. "Never know what a prospector's going to turn up."

"The problem isn't turning it up," Sumter snapped. "It's bringing it home. I don't suppose you found any used mass drivers for sale?"

"Hardly," Gus agreed. "Do you think those things will ever work?"

"No reason why not. There're any number of ways to go now that chemical rockets have reached their limits. From anywhere off planet you could use an ion rocket."

"Do you have one in the engineering stage?"

"Or you could put together a slingshot or centrifugal mass driver to push your way through space. Makes a handy garbage disposal too."

"How soon?"

"And there are possibilities with controlled fusion rockets," the man in the wheelchair continued.

"Goddammit, Sumter, you're older than I am. I want something *now!*"

"That's why I'm saving the best for last. Now if you've got the money, I've got the laser elevator."

"Say again?"

"Fifty percent efficiency," Sumter cackled. "How do them figures grab you?"

"About 44% more tenaciously than a chemical rocket," Gus said. "But will it work?"

"You better believe it."

"When?"

"When is divisible into how much." Sumter glanced at Mansour.

"What is a laser elevator?" the Arab asked.

"Just another kind of rocket. But any opaque liquid serves for reaction mass. Since we're fairly sure of both ice and carbonaceous chondrites out where you're going, the obvious choice is water with a little carbon black or somesuch mud so the laser can't shoot a beam right through it." The man in the wheelchair paused to see if Mansour was understanding. "The opaque liquid traps the laser's energy, immediately boils, and the steam is reaction mass. It'll take relatively little engineering to get exhaust velocities much faster than chemical rockets. The efficiency should be good enough to get the whole business on a sound economic basis."

"How much money would it take?"

"Around 20 or 30 billion."

Mansour called the hundredth name of God.

"Been nice meeting you, doctor," Gus said.

"Chicken?"

"Ain't got," Albert said. "Ain't never gonna have that kind of money."

"I thought you Arabs had all the money in the world."

"I am not Arabs," Mansour explained. "I am one Arab."

Dr. Sumter fixed his parrotlike gaze on Mansour. "I have heard Saudi Arabia described as the only family-owned business with UN representation."

Mansour gave a sad smile and turned to Gus. "Is it safe to tell this man who I am?"

"You're Mansour ibn Jezail," Sumter cackled, "younger brother of Omar the Beloved, born in Trucial Oman. Let's see . . . been a change there, hmmmmm . . . United Arab Emirates now, isn't it? In any event, you took something better than a gentleman's 'C' at the Harvard School of Business. Always wondered what turned you into a playboy."

"Someday perhaps you'll meet my brother."

Sumter darted that parrotlike glance again. "Of course! Are you working for him or against him?"

Mansour sighed. "There are times when it seems as if I never left home."

"Well, how much money have you got?" Sumter demanded.

"I'm afraid we haven't enough to afford you."

"Look, Gus, we're both old men. It's the only game in town."

"If anybody gets wind of what we're up to," Gus said, "you can count on the government ex-post-factoing us right out of business. And, unlike the government, we have to do it on the cheap. Persons unknown are shooting at us. You work for nothing and if you publish you're first to perish. Do you still want in?"

"I'll sign with blood if Albert'll just give me enough coffee so I can get some flowing."

There was a buzz. Gus picked up the phone, wondering what could have induced Miss Jepworth to break in on a board meeting. "Mr. M'Meath," she said distastefully. "Promises to be brief but it's a matter of life and death."

"All right, put him on." Gus saw three pairs of eyes on him and shrugged. He switched the phone to conference mode.

"Gus?" M'Meath's voice was tinny.

"We're listening."

"Watch out for ECPAD. Those sons of bitches are the ones boring holes in your woodwork." His voice went higher. "They talk about patriotic duty." There was a choking sound and abruptly the line was dead.

Albert looked at Gus. "So what else is new? Those numbskulls think if man was intended to come down out of the trees he'd be born with shoes on."

Gus shook his head in disbelief. "Why couldn't they have just *asked* me?"

"Oh, dey never asks us minorities. They always know what's good for us."

Mansour began to suspect some of the subtleties of American dialect might be eternally beyond him. "Mr. Dampier is of a minority?" he asked.

"How many of us millionaires you think there are in the United States?"

Omar had heard rumors of complaint from foreign oil men but he was unable to understand why anyone should object—unless it were for religious reasons. And the multinational, rootless men who followed the oil were unanimous only in their faith in the almighty petrodollar.

He awoke as anyone would awaken to the sound of an old and friendly alarm clock. It was still dark and the screech that carried over the square mile of palace and government buildings was midway between fire siren and a rooster passing a stone. To foreigners, at least.

Omar drew comfort from the prolonged "*Salaat!*" He rolled off his couch and landed on hands and knees before the actual prayer began: "*Bismillah ar-Rahman, ar-Rahím.*"

In the name of the Merciful and Compassionate, Omar touched his head to the marble floor of his chamber. He was a balding, middle-aged man. High on his forehead was the slightly darker spot that results from a lifetime of banging one's head on the ground, the concrete, the sand or *sabkha* —wherever a True Believer finds himself when the five-times-a-day *salaat* comes shrieking over the PA system.

Morning prayer ended and he finished dressing. He was adjusting his *agal* past the brown spot on his pate (which was sore this morning in accordance with some minor facet of God's plans) when a huge black man came into the chamber. "*Gah-wah,*" the black said cheerfully, and proceeded to pour it. Omar wondered if he was imagining too much white of eye as the slave left the pot and several newspapers.

He sipped thick black coffee and could taste nothing strange. Just nerves, he told himself. In any event, his life was in God's hands, his fate already written. *Maktoub.* He skimmed the local papers to learn what else was *maktoub.* There was another complaint about public drunkenness. Omar sighed. There were too many illicit stills these days and the godless operators were making such an obscene profit from their *munkar* that nothing short of another public execution was going to slow them down.

He put aside the local papers and consulted the big one which, for a man who reads only Arabic, is *Al Ahram* and was delivered daily the 1500 airline miles southeast from Cairo.

OPEC had not even raised prices yet to make up for the latest drop in the dollar and already those ravenous rascals in Egypt were screaming for more money. Omar sighed again. When he had gone to Cairo as a boy he had been amazed at the magnificence of that teeming city. It had never occurred to him then that his own scattered and starving people would one day send the British packing just as Nasser had done—and would end up feeding Egypt as neither Nasser, Sadat, nor even the Merciful and Compassionate seemed capable of doing without continual transfusions of Arab dollars and American wheat. There were times when Omar almost doubted the wisdom of God's having put all the people in Egypt and all the oil in unpopulated and unwatered corners of Islam. But these days the tankers brought so much clean ballast on the return run that some of his faithful were learning to bathe with water instead of sand as was traditional. Then abruptly on the third page of *Al Ahram* Omar discovered he had not been imagining that whiteness of eye in his servant. Someone had gone over a subhead with a yellow marking pen. Lest he miss it, the entire article was circled:

FRIVOLOUS KIN OF UNITED EMIRATES SHEIKH AIDED IN PURCHASE OF JET FIGHTERS. There was no Arab word for playboy, but Omar had only one relative who might be considered frivolous. He sighed for the third time this morning. After all the pains he had taken, all the money he sent, continued to send, was Mansour still going to meddle in things which didn't concern a younger brother?

Cursed be the day their father had sent the boy to learn foreign ways. What was the point of foreign ways? True, the oil money was helpful, but how could there be any true good in the land without submission to the will of God? Someday the oil would be gone. Then the foreigners and their machines would go too and his people would no longer be tempted by munkar.

Foreign filth . . . nowadays they even had a new word for it. Omar sighed for the days when sadíki had truly meant my friend. Now it meant moonshine. What was he going to do about those distillers? What about Mansour?

It wasn't the boy's fault he had been sent off to drown in munkar. Their father had seen the first tentative invasion of the oil men and had known the old ways, piling sacks of gold in odd corners of the palace and keeping count with an abacus . . .

> "—though weakened by recent events, and unable to circumvent the sale of modern jet fighters to the victims of their territorial aggressions, the Zionist lobby was still powerful enough to promise future mischief. Faced with the possibility of a hostile Congress delaying delivery of the jet fighters or delaying spares or maintenance personnel, Sheikh Omar was ready to settle for a slower, but more politically reliable aircraft. Now, thanks to a hitherto undetected diplomatic talent, Mansour ibn Jezail has outmaneuvered the Zionist oppressors. US-made Dampiers are on the way, with ample spares and the necessary foreign experts."

Omar threw the paper down. What was Mansour up to? Currying favor with the military? Planning another coup? There had to be some hidden reason for it. Omar called on the secret, hundredth name of God. Then he picked up the paper again, knowing what it was that really annoyed him. *Necessary foreign experts.* Arabs had conquered the economic world. Why couldn't they keep a jet fighter in the air?

Perhaps he should have brought Mansour home. It was all *munkar* but if one wanted the jets, the oil, the modern weapons, the foreign filth came with them. But Mansour was too soiled by it all. His very presence in a *djemaa* would be a defilement. He had lived outside the True Faith. He had married a *farengi* woman. When Omar suggested he send the child home for a proper upbringing his brother had not even replied. He tried to remember the boy's name. Sharif? Jarfi? Only the Merciful and Compassionate knew where the boy was now. His brother had put aside that Frankish woman at least twenty years ago. *Bismillah*, how the years did slip away!

The huge black man oozed carefully into the room, testing Omar's mood. "The minister is waiting outside," he murmured.

"Later," Omar grunted, then changed his mind. "Tell the *wazír* to round up those distillers of *munkar*. Select three of the worst offenders and behead them."

The black man bowed and hastily left with the coffee things. Omar sighed again. And now if he could just decide about Mansour.

Jarfi ibn Mansour was blond, more Nordic looking than most of those *pieds noirs* who shivered through French winters while their children grew up with a receding memory of the glory that had once been Algerie. But neither a French mother nor the best schools in francophone Switzerland had ever managed to convince him that he was French.

Maman had taken more interest in art—or at least artists—than in her child. Holidays away from school had usually been spent with Papa who spoke every language with only faint traces of hesitation. But the domestic staff spoke Arabic. By the time he was twelve Jarfi's French was Parisian, his English public school, his German passable. His Arabic . . .

Amid every language and culture is one dialect which represents the standard. Affluent Africans and Canadians struggle to sound like poor Parisians. Austrians trade their Gemüttlichkeit for hobnailed Prussian. Honest Arctic Swedes want to sound like Stockholm. Okinawans dream of Tokyo, Sicilians of Rome. American actors spend a year's pay learning to imitate London. And Arabs . . .

In their great days Arabs were as culturally imperialistic as the English. From Morocco to Indonesia, with outposts from Cleveland to Buenos Aires, people speak a language which originated in a small peninsular piece of the world. Jarfi's was the accent in which the Koran was dictated, the elegant and classical tongue which provokes cultural orgasms among those less favored. But he spoke it with a twelve-year-old's vocabulary, not able to quote a single sura from the holy scripture—unable even to read the cursive, flowing script.

At home nowhere, believing nothing, he snorkeled his way into scuba, finally plunging so deep into inner space that he had signed aboard old Cousteau's *Calypso*. A year bunking next to an American diver had erased any public school trace from his English. He watched Cousteau, sensed his terrible earnestness about the imminent end of Earth, and wondered if The Prophet might not have been a bit like this.

But Mohammed had seen a future for man in Submission to the Will of God. This beaky old prophet saw no future for an overcrowded planet where people dumped all their wastes into the ocean, poisoned their only hope to feed the next generation.

Jarfi listened as the old man held forth evenings in the galley. Cousteau was right. The planet was on its last legs. A couple of generations from now all those little annoyances in Israel, in Lebanon, in North Ireland—what difference would it make who was in the right when they had all starved?

But he was grateful for that year aboard the *Calypso*. Thanks to the American diver he could now cross another border without any tiresome flashing of passports. He liked Americans in spite of their shortsighted optimism—even if they all seemed to think a name as common as Jarfi could belong only to some mighty-thewed hero of a Burroughs epic. But any boy who goes off to school in another country learns early on the value of camouflage. He encouraged Americans to call him Jeff.

He lived in a condo on Malibu where older residents still twitched at the mention of Manson.

He had money, youth, nordic good looks, and a
scarred tomcat of ancestry as mixed as his own.
He liked to look at girls. The watching, poolside
or beach, was good around Malibu. He petted the
cat who had adopted him—and waited for something to happen in his aimless life. What was it
about all these girls that, on second and closer
look, turned him off? Was it the girls or was something wrong with him? Would he always be a
loner?

Really ought to look in on his father oftener. But
life was short; he was busy and so, apparently,
was his father. He had not recognized the voice
over the phone. *"C'est bien toi, Papa?"*

*"Oui, c'est moi. Mon fils, je ne sais pas si j'ai le
droit de te demander ceci, mais tu as plongé assez
souvent. Est-ce que c'est la même sensation que
celle de vivre sans gravité dans un satellite ar-
tificiel?"*

Jeff gave a shrug which the phone did not
transmit. How was he to know if life in space was
anything like diving?

"C'est dangereux, n'est-ce pas?"

"Pas plus que la vie elle-même." As he
shrugged off the danger Jeff abruptly sensed what
his father was trying to say. Son of a bitch! A job in
space! A chance to shoot a seedpod away from
this dying planet! He was abruptly so excited he
forgot which language he was speaking. *"Aiwah,
abúya! Ce n'est pas dangereux. Minfádluk.
Please, Papa, get me off this stinking planet before
I get run over."*

So Mansour promised and then Jarfi remembered that he had a dependent who would not be
able to go into space with him. It was awkward.
He would not have hesitated to ask his father for a

million dollars but . . . when finally he had explained his problem Mansour had been both touched and hurt. "You do not remember that I too love cats? Of course I'll take good care. He can live with me."

So with the problem of Lion of Judah solved, Jarfi-Jeff did his homework and mostly it was just the same kind of common sense that made a man pay attention to his equipment and air supply before going down, only this time Jeff went up and he had never tried to sleep in zero g before.

It was not easy. He had never gotten seasick even when the old *Calypso* was disconsolately corkscrewing the wrong way around the roaring 40s. But for the first few days up here it had required firm concentration on other things to keep his stomach in its proper place. Sleeping . . . Finally he had stuffed every loose item of gear—clothes, sweaters, spacesuit, the removable cushion from the pilot's seat—into the net to surround him and give at least the illusion of hanging snug in quiet safety. Even after all this time he still had recurrent dreams of falling.

He had read the literature and knew what to watch for. Even so, he tried to ignore it. Might just be something in his personal metabolism. And there was plenty to be done here in the high orbit station and not enough people to do it.

But continuous nausea had left his clothing so alarmingly loose that before there was time even to get a good start on everything old Gus and that madman in the wheelchair had listed for him to do he had been forced to call a halt. "Maybe a touch of solar flare," he had guessed. "But I'm just too sick to eat."

He had gone down on the next shuttle. And

after a week of eating and exercise his blood count was back to normal. He had lifted back up again, breathing a silent prayer that this time he would be able to stick it.

At least once an hour he cursed the economics that had put him in a superannuated shuttle instead of some vessel designed for protracted residence. It was several orders of magnitude beyond living in a car—with the rest room oscillating between four and twelve thousand miles away. But there was still life in these creaky vehicles. Enough thrust to lift out Earth's four thousand mile gravity well would strain eroded rocket nozzles past the limits of practical engineering. But out here, high above the sporadic low-orbit, low-budget construction, he had space pretty much to himself.

There had been vague press releases about linking the three shuttles together for zero g metallurgical experiments. Jeff hadn't paid attention since it was all just bull and he had enough to do without spending his days *en chantant la pomme.*

The space shuttle's pressurized cockpit was rather like an airliner's, save that the seats can be made to slide back and forth a respectable distance. There might once have been excellent reasons for this, but in zero g people seldom sit. What catnapping one achieves is usually crammed into a net in foetal position.

He pushed the seats out through the airlock. Where possible he used nuts, bolts, pop rivets, epoxy glues—anything to avoid welding inside which contaminated his air with sublimated metal dusts.

Gus's engineers had eliminated stone age oxyacetylene or hydrogen welding. The torches would burn in vacuum but gas got into the melt and without gravity metal boiled. A dingleberry, as any scarred old welder knows, is a drop of hot metal that exits the weld pool with the sound and velocity of shrapnel, and burns through leathers and often skin before cooling. A man in a thin spacesuit prefers to avoid dingleberries.

Up here Jeff used bare wire instead of Earthside welding rod with its flux coating. Thus his weld beads did not require "Tomahawking" to clean them. But there were other disadvantages to zero g welding. If the Russians had solved them they were being characteristically closemouthed.

Each shuttle had once carried a primitive pottie, now long gone. Now Jeff struggled with the contraption that some optimists still called a zero g toilet. It could only be plumbed through-hull by welding. As he wrestled with the mutual incompatibility of space helmet and welder's hood he wondered why somebody on the ground couldn't have thought ahead. Finally he was finished, cabin evacuated to blow out dust and dingleberries, and once more pressurized.

He emerged from his clammy suit and surveyed the third head he had installed. An hour later cabin pressure had dropped half a dozen millibars. No valves leaking. Jeff sighed. Where metal boiled and outgassed like beer, a nonporous weld was hopeless. He squeezed a ribbon of silicone. Six hours later the vinegary stink was strong but cabin pressure was unchanged.

Jeff's internal pressure had changed. He scanned valves and pressure regulators a final time and mounted the contraption. Someday a valve was going to fail. Pressure would glue him to this throne and squeeze him like a toothpaste. He was getting morbid, for which there was no time if he was to have at least one orbiter ready on schedule.

Unsqueezed, he suited up and pushed out through the airlock. No matter what he had told his father, outside was not at all like diving. Water had body—the comforting viscosity of a prenatal environment. Here he could not swim. Though the mind accepted Newton and the impossibility of falling out of orbit, his strength was wasted on subconscious hanging on lest he splatter down onto that streaky blue-white planet below. No matter how many lifelines, each time he went adrift, Jeff struggled with primal terror.

While horsing all this metal around, there were infinite possibilities to go adrift. On Earth, weight kept a man in place. Here the wrench stood still and Jeff turned. He would wrap a leg or hook a heel for leverage but as time and air ran short he would hurry—and there he was again at the end of his rope watching a nut or bolt float irrevocably away, not moving in the natural parabola of a missile subject to gravity. Each time an unsecured part made a beeline for infinity Jeff's hands ran compulsively over the snaps of his lifeline. Someday he knew he was going to forget.

Highway flares were supposed to push him back if ever he went adrift. Half a gram's worth of thrust seemed unable even to overcome the kinks in his lifeline. Finally he had radioed a careful message: "Experiments satisfactory but behind schedule."

When he was over LA again the reply came:

"Labor-saving device next launch window." The crated labor-saving device was Armand Fortin, who spoke neither French nor Arabic. Jeff studied Army in the light of Mansour's impassioned sermons on the need to get Arabs in space.

The first week Army vomited almost as much as Jeff had. Between bouts of nausea the gangling young black worked. "But I never learned to weld," he protested.

As Jeff raised his eyebrows heavenward he realized that without gravity to orient him he might be raising them toward Earth. "Why'd they send you up here without any training?" he asked.

"I guess there wasn't time."

"What can you do?"

"I'm an expert at computer fraud. Lately I've learned how to run delta vee equations."

"Learn to weld."

"But how?"

"Imagine you want to join two pieces of wax. You heat the edges with a candle so they flow together. Wherever there's a gap you dribble candle wax in to make it up."

"I can't even dribble piss up here!"

That was the problem. It had taken Jeff countless hours to get the hang of striking an arc, holding it long enough to melt a puddle, then flipping the drop off the end of his electrode into the puddle where surface tension could take over—all the while holding an arc and making sure dingleberries were not puncturing his space suit. "Practice as if your life depended on it," he suggested.

Within days Army was flipping his drop into the puddle. Slowly, they converted shuttles designed for hours of low-orbit flight into pushers with padded fenders over the bows, with food and air to keep one human alive for years, with solid fuel boosters to get out there and back. Any shuttle would have used up 99% of these rockets just getting off Earth. But out here, skimming the 4000-mile lid of the gravity well, a tenth of a g for hours on end could work wonders with the numbers. All it took was money—and advance warning about solar flares.

There had been debate over piling all the cargo on one side vs. centering the shuttle. Experts thought improved shielding from an angry sun might be outweighed by cosmic rays from all directions, plus the problems of pushing a lopsided load.

"What about coming back?" Army asked.

"What about it?" Jeff said flatly. Once the orbiter completed its swing halfway out and retro fired, the boosters would be jettisoned, cargo nearly gone, the pilot naked and committed. If arrival coincided with a solar flareup . . . Return would be hard, fast, and dirty. So would the pilot.

Their working space was coming to resemble some whirlpool where débris collects but the resemblance was superficial. Everything not tied down would drift sooner or later beyond recovery. Down in the closed-off section of Dampier's hangar Jeff and Army had assembled parts of this rig. Up there they did not have to strain with weight but the mass was still there. It just took as much grunting to start a ton of metal moving. It took more to stop it.

They were hampered by the need to keep shuttle crews in the dark. And Army, who had come up as freight, had to hide until they were gone. "I have to stay this high up," Jeff had improvised, "because there's just enough magnetism in the Van Allen belts to screw up my steel-aluminum mix." He wondered if such things would ever really happen. Probably. That nobody could mix oil and water had not impeded the development of mayonnaise.

Finally the last load was up, the last shuttle down and they could stop pretending. They discovered that holes drilled to perfect alignment on Earth would not mate where there was no gravity to warp beams the way God intended the works of man to sag. They learned that going adrift was tame compared to a hung-up electric drill that flung them spinning like patent fish lures on the swivels of their lifelines. To vomit in a suit is above and beyond the normal filth where bits of the undigested and the totally digested drift lazily toward a clogged air filter.

"Too bad we can't use that external tank and the main engines," Army groused. But the shuttles had been built during trying times for astronauts —when any politician knew the one important thing about the space program was to grab some of that shrinking appropriation for his own district.

The solid rocket boosters were made in Utah by a manufacturer who knew how to deliver rated thrust for the proper number of seconds. The shuttle was built within spitting distance of Gus's plant and this whole story might never have happened if Dampier Industries had gotten a fair share of the subcontracting.

Its three main engines carried no inboard fuel. Their bulletshaped tank was longer than the orbiter. Burning 100 tons a minute, it took a whole tankful, plus a pair of solid fuel boosters, just to get off the ground.

"What I can't figure," Army groused, "is, when one single SRB has three times the poop of the hydrogen-oxygen engines, why did they bother with a liquid fuel system at all?"

"Have you ever tried to turn off a solid fuel rocket in mid-burn?" Jeff asked.

Army had not. The complex liquid fuel system had less push, but it had a throttle, which can be handy to make final adjustments into low orbit.

Gus had talked of using the main engines but nobody knew how to keep oxygen or hydrogen liquid for more than a few hours. Now the shuttles had only strap-on SRBs for big thrust and Orbital Maneuvering System engines which ran on a hypergolic mix of monomethyl hydrazine and nitrogen tetroxide. These are harder to spell than oxygen or hydrogen, but they store as easily as kerosene.

When Army could be trusted outside alone Jeff put him to stripping frills off the Solid Rocket Boosters. The black worked the duration of his air supply cutting off nose fairings and skirts. "Why did they have to ship all this weight up here?" he groused. "Couldn't they have cut it off down on Earth?"

"An SRB without streamlining or chutes is obviously never coming back down through Earth's atmosphere," Jeff said. "You ready to explain why to NASA?"

Army was not. "But how do we shed them after burnout? The separation motors are in there too."

"We go outside and kick them away."

Army stared for a moment, then realized it could be done. "You don't want to save anything?"

"The chutes. We can always use the line in the shrouds."

They never had enough. There was graphite strapping, twice as strong as steel, for lashing boosters. But hacking and butching, struggling to hang onto parts that refused to stay put, there was always need for more line. And it wasted minutes worth of oxygen every time they struggled to tie one of those complex knots that keep slick nylon from coming apart. They needed more velcro, more billhooks, more snaps, more time.

Labor-saving device next launch window.

Jeff managed to get rid of the shuttle crew and they forced open the crate before the labor-saving device could run out of O_2. Even enclosed in packing material, breathing apparatus, and spacesuit, it was obvious that this was a different model. Jeff was so startled he emitted an *"Ah lah, mien el bint?"* which Army unknowingly paraphrased: "My God, who's the girl?"

They were young men. They had been up here several weeks. As Army and Jeff saw a contour that not even a spacesuit could conceal, a hint of straight blond hair inside that helmet, each man was abruptly overcome with a wave of nearly uncontrollable lust. They looked away, determined not to admit it to one another and, if at all possible, not even to themselves. As for the girl, whoever she was, each made a private vow that She Must Never Know.

But of course Sin did, as women always know. Once she had time to think about it she realized old Gus could not possibly have devised a more foolproof way to protect her virtue. There was no privacy, but the watchers were too busy keeping tabs on each other to give her much trouble. And within days the long hair was gone, the golden tan going, and the tired, pallid face in the spacesuit was of less interest than another working pair of gloved hands. Nevertheless, the schedule that cynical old man had set up called for Sin to blast off first. She would never have to spend an hour alone with either of them.

And now, well into the asteroids, her orbit was one-third completed, calcium equally depleted, and Army was burning fuel as if the GSA were paying for it, smoking a trail of head-long pursuit of her cold motors. He had left in such a hurry that he hadn't even had time to remove the chute packs from the noses of the extra SRB's he had strapped on in hopes of catching up with her. "Say again," she said.

It took less than a minute for him to reply, which meant he had gained considerably on her—must be within three million miles—only a dozen times as far as Earth to Luna.

"I said, how are the old bones holding out?"

"As well as can be expected," she said glumly. "I'm so afraid I'll break something I hardly move."

"How are the batteries?"

"I'm going to shut down now. Let me know when you're visual." Then, before she flipped the switch Sin remembered to ask, "How are your bones?"

"I can feel some change," Army said. "But I begin to suspect my genetic package carries some unexpected advantages."

It took Sin a moment to work this out. Then she remembered that from what little she had seen inside a suit, Army was probably black. And no matter how the equalizers might quack and flap, there *were* differences: The fontanel closed earlier; frontal and parietal bones fused solidly in mature blacks. In whites those sutures never quite come together—which gives blacks a reputation for hard headedness and whites the puzzling aspect of some organism arrested in mid-development. Could all of a black's bones be harder, less apt to decalcify? Why hadn't NASA let a few of them up in orbit and found out? But she knew the answer to that one. If it were to turn out that only blacks were fit for space, that Earth was to be the white man's ghetto, who would ever vote another dime for any space program?

She wondered what Army had in mind once he got here. No doubt he was miserable too but if they were going to die midway between Mars and Jupiter, what difference did it make? After all, everyone dies alone.

There was a buzz clearly audible above the murmur of fans and pumps, the cricket chirring of expanding and contracting metal as her ship drifted through its ten minute roll. Sin unwound from a foetal ball of misery to study the CRT display. The spike was interesting. She punched the keyboard for a moment, put in a **GOTO** instead of a **GOSUB,** gritted her teeth when the screen said **TILT,** and started over. It was definitely a possible. The orbit was almost Earth—intersecting and with a few thousand newtons of encouragement, could be persuaded to cross the same part of Earth's orbit that planet would occupy in six years or, for 2-½ times as much thrust, only 18 months.

The mass-volume ratio made the asteroid almost surely a 14-Irene type. Unless she was being misled by the narrow end aspect of something long and capsule shaped instead of spherical . . . but as she watched the spike moved slightly down, then back up. It was rotating with little change in diameter. That ball had to be 95% iron unless the stony content was balanced out by even heavier metals. Had anyone ever found gold or lead or uranium in a meteorite? She made a mental note to run through her library of floppys. But not now. Now was time to gather every possible bit of data before she got too far past that chunk of iron.

If only she had the strength and gumption to get out and chip off a sample. But the batteries were low and she was afraid even to put her back into pedaling or cranking the generator lest she shatter a bone. Should have installed larger solar collectors. The inverse square law was really raising hell with battery charging this far out. That compulsory exercise machine hadn't been such a good idea after all.

She had stopped using lights long ago, except for the odd moment when she just had to find something. Every ten minutes a reflection of distant sunlight off an SRB cylinder gave enough illumination to remind her that she had not already evolved into one of those unsighted creatures that frequent caves.

Finally she had every measurement that radar, optical scanning, gravitometers, and magnetic detectors would give her. In the hours this material had been piling onto a floppy she had glanced occasionally at the asteroid through the six inch refractor mounted in the bow—until the chunk was so far to one side she could no longer twist the scope around to look at it.

She ought to send all this telemetering home but she couldn't spare the power; and to keep emitting a weak signal would only call attention to her without giving Dampier Industries anything worthwhile. But she was running low on floppies and would need this one again. She compromised by erasing a cassette of music she was thoroughly sick of, and putting all the asteroid's secrets in its place. If she lived—if Army had some brilliant idea that was going to save both their lives—or if only black men were destined to survive. . . . She waited for the every-ten-minute blink of sun and found a marking pen. On the cassette she printed "Army." Then she went back to her slow, careful pedaling and cranking. She had to give it the old college try or there was even less hope of being alive when Army finally caught up with her.

She studied the meter. Putting out less than a watt. Not even keeping up with the barest minimum of pumps and fans. She took a deep breath and began pedaling faster, spraying sweat from every pore as she tried to keep up with the linked-together hand cranks. Slowly the power began climbing past the break-even point. Jesus, what a way to live! She remembered woodcuts from Victorian books—orphans and other poor unfortunates climbing a treadmill for endless hours.

On Earth, people who talk to themselves are often regarded with a certain whiteness of eye.

Out here Sin felt she had to, lest she forget how. Also, it helped to drown out the chuckles of pumps and relays as the ship's parts shared jokes at her expense. A chain link or sprocket tooth had chipped in her exerciser-charger. Now each turn of the pedals brought a thump followed by a series of clicks. She had tried at first to ignore them, later to put a cheerful interpretation on that rhythm. But no matter how she Pollyanna-ed, each turn of the pedals brought a rhythmic repetition that assured her, "You ain't gonna make it; ain't gonna make it; *ain't gonna make it.*"

She gritted her teeth, then remembered not to. They were loose. The batteries were taking a charge. If she could just keep this up for two or three hours maybe she would feel well enough to finish up tomorrow. Then she felt a funny little snap in her right forearm. The pain that began to grow was neither funny nor little.

Army's bones were in better shape than Sin's but he still felt lousy all the time. Most maddening was the fuzziness that affected his thinking. He had to do everything several times and even then stupid mistakes kept cropping up. Sooner or later one of those mistakes was going to kill him.

And then, his gangling body had stretched four inches. His thin waist had shrunk correspondingly, then shrunk still more from the monotony of food concentrates and the queasiness that still afflicted him in zero g. He pedaled his charger, slowing occasionally to wipe his face. If only the sweat would run off somewhere instead of just piling up. . . .

In spite of decalcified bones and semistarvation

he was putting a steady eighty watts back into his batteries. He stopped to wipe himself down again and waited for the surface charge to dissipate. A minute later he decided the fractional voltmeter was not lying, that he had really pumped up as much energy as could be stored. A final wipedown and he began struggling into his suit. If he didn't stop growing the damned thing was going to rip and then where would he be? But he had been putting off housekeeping since the last burn.

In anticipation of this job he had been living dangerously for a week, gradually lowering cabin pressure and keeping the air breathable by increasing the O_2—a practice universally eschewed since a couple of astronauts had burned to death on the pad.

He made a final check to see how many things were not tied down. Last time he had lost a floppy with some particularly juicy telemetering. He rigged his fine mesh sleeping net over the airlock, gave his suit a final check, and forced both sides of the lock.

A whoosh of escaping air swept his cabin clean. A notebook, an empty food tube, and his lost toothbrush ended up on the net. He put them away. An hour's vacuum would draw the moisture from filters and save him the job of changing them. The CO_2 absorber would also surrender its load and be ready for another round. He removed the net, unsnapped one end of his lifeline, and pushed out through the blocked-open airlock.

The lifeline was Army's improvement and he was rather proud of it: a billhook on each end. The line passed freely through a belt swivel that was too small for the hooks. When possible, he fastened both ends but having them interchangeable, he could stairstep from one anchorage to the next without ever being totally adrift. Since thinking it up he had been sleeping better.

Jesus, how he was sweating! He would have to turn the clammy suit inside out and wipe it before he could stand to don it again. Was it resorption or radiation that was doing him in? Maybe he shouldn't throw away the shielding around his tiny orbiter.

But if he hoped to see Earth again . . . He hooked up outside, kicked himself aft, and fended his billiardlike passage off orbiter and SRB surfaces until he had reached the end of his tether. He fastened the other hook to an eye on an OMS pod, then trolleyed back to unhook the opposite end of the line.

Unlike Jeff, whose suit radio emitted an eternal mumble of trilingual blasphemy, Army very seldom talked to himself. He backtracked out past the inner ring of SRB nozzles and began unstrapping the two he had emptied with the last burn. It took an hour and a bottle of air to free the aft ends of both boosters. He went back to the cargo bay for another bottle, then out again to tackle the forward ends. Finally, he braced his shoulders on the inboard SRB, put his feet on the empty, and began pushing.

There was some background noise in his suit radio. Gradually it cleared up and he could hear voices in some language so nearly like English that he was almost understanding. Suddenly he remembered how far away he was from any chance transmission. He double checked and of course his suit radio was off—been off since he had parted company with Jeff. The noise faded. If he didn't watch it he was going to start taking these hallucinations seriously. Just loneliness. Had to be. "They're gonna get you," a voice had said clearly.

Several minutes passed since he began straining at the SRB and he was beginning to suspect that in spite of all his rechecking something was still holding it to the ship. Then he saw that his straining legs had moved at least a centimeter. Slow as an hour hand, the booster began swinging. He scooted down amidships and began pushing again. His second air bottle was nearly gone before there was a visible interval between the orbiter and the second SRB.

Army was totally gone. He wondered how Sin had ever kicked her empties loose. Or had she? He went back inside, pressurized the cabin to the barest of breathability, and unsuited. He didn't mind dumping old, used up air but it horrified him to waste even the tiny amount of new air that was inevitably going to escape with each opening of the airlock.

He wiped down and got into his spare suit, then locked through outside carrying the one he had worn. Outside, he turned the clammy, sweatfilled suit inside out. He brushed frost and grime loose, then airlocked back into the cabin. It would be a few days now before he had to go out again. He began bringing his cabin air back up to normal.

The recorder emitted a beep. There were two immense spikes on the screen. "Now they're really gonna get you," the voices chorused.

Army felt a moment of panic—not from the

voices, but from the proximity of two immense rocks that were going to clash him between them like Scylla and Charybdis. How could they have gotten this close without warning? He was punching frantically at the computer for an evasion maneuver that he already knew was too impossibly late when suddenly sanity returned and he knew what the radar blips were. He was looking at the boosters he had just kicked away, now a hundred meters to each side of the orbiter.

They promised to linger for weeks, drifting away at a meter a minute. He would have to program the alarm to ignore them and still warn him if anything interesting came close. A week from now when it was time to start another burn each dead booster would still be only ten kilometers away.

Popular fiction has asteroids grinding together like ice floes in a polar sea. Army was nearing the center of the belt, which is not sharply defined: some asteroids intersect Earth's orbit, looping well beyond Jupiter on the other end of their ellipses. So far he had not come within a half million kilometers of anything large enough to be worth examining. Every three or four days the orbiter would clang from the impact of a sandsized meteorite pounding into one of the SRBs but his chances of being holed were on the order of being hit by lightning—and considerably less than being hit by a car.

If only he didn't feel so lousy. But at least he was better off than the girl. Was it race? Sex? His antenna was pointed in her general direction. He corrected the vector since his last transmission. "Turn on your transponder for a second," he said.

She was low on power and the radar-enhancing transponder would let him fine tune on her position without a lot of battery-consuming chatter. He waited for his transmission to reach her and a radar echo to return. A half hour later he was still waiting.

And that's the name of that tune! Any key he played it, Army had screwed up. He had ripped off a couple of Jeff's SRBs so he could chase out here to rescue the girl from sure disaster—and he had come too late. Why hadn't he taken all of Jeff's boosters and gotten here in time? This way he had just managed to ruin the whole damned project: leave Jeff behind and crippled, with a few SRBs but not enough to power his swing through the asteroids.

Meanwhile Army had ignored his own sector to go haring off after the girl and now she was dead and if he didn't get there soon and get her remaining rockets to burn off all the velocity he had piled on to catch her . . . But what difference did it make? He couldn't come back emptyhanded—not after his burst of impractical gallantry had managed to bankrupt Dampier Industries even more surely than ever he could have with a paltry million dollar computer ripoff. And Albert had been decent, tried to keep him out of prison.

"They're gonna get you, boy."

"Like hell they are!" Army snapped in one of his rare vocalizations. "They already got me."

He was sweating profusely even though the cabin temperature tended to hang near 21°F. Did he know how to run a blood count? Probably the information was somewhere in his stack of floppys. But why bother? He pushed over to the

exercise machine and made a halfhearted attempt
to pump up the batteries again. It was just because
he'd spent so much time working outside, he told
himself. Tomorrow he would feel better. He'd better.

Sin was not being stoical. She was just too sick
to give a damn. At least she hadn't snapped both
bones. It felt like a simple fracture of the radius.
This was odd since she had been pushing on the
crank handle when it happened—which usually
results in a fracture of the olecranon at the head of
the ulna. But her bones were so cheesy anything
could happen. Somewhere in the darkness was an
inflatable cuff for temporary splinting. To keep it
on was an open invitation to gangrene. If she were
feeling better she could devise a cast out of glues
and resins in the spares locker but the fracture
didn't really seem to be all the way through. More
like a crack. Flounder around trying to fix it and
she might end up breaking it the rest of the way.

Army would be here in a week. He must be in
better shape than she was. If she lay perfectly still
and cut her O_2 needs to a minimum . . . She felt
her way to the sleeping net, crawled in, and began
shallow breathing. She would have twisted her
legs into the lotus position but she didn't want to
break them too. Slowly, she felt herself slipping
into a dreamy, trancelike state. It seemed easier
here alone with the chuckle of blowers and
pumps. As long as she didn't move the arm didn't
hurt too badly. She caught herself calculating O_2
consumption against cabin volume and willed
her mind back to blankness.

Which, of course, didn't work. Couldn't she do

anything right anymore? Her mind was going even softer than her bones. She began chanting rhythmic mantric nonsense.

Augustus Dampier had been forty-five before he was out of debt and owned a small chain saw company like a dozen others with one minor exception: Gus's saw worked. So had Gus. He had matured in an era when one did not lightly take on responsibility. But few men can wait forever. Though it was still risky, he took a bride when he was only forty-five.

As marriages go, it went—until Clara presented him with a daughter and promptly died. Gus had been desolated, but the frantic jockeying of ladies in competition to provide a home for that poor orphaned little girl and her not-at-all-poor father had cured him of any thoughts in that direction.

By now he had enough money. There had to be more to life than collecting chips and keeping score. He spent the next five years with his daughter, whiling away the hours she was in school by perfecting his own neglected education.

Which naturally took time from his business. Abruptly Gus found himself broke, his company taken over, assets stripped. At fifty he decided it was time to learn the rules of the game the big boys played. "I'm sorry, Albert," he said. "I should have listened to you."

" 'Tain't too late," Albert said. "But next time we've got to be a little more careful."

"Chainsaws are penny ante. But I learned things along the way about casting light metals. What do you think we ought to try?"

"You learned something about making the

lightest horsepower-to-pound engine on the market too," Albert said. "And down as far as we are, there's only one way to go."

"Up?" To Gus it was the obvious comment. He did not take his partner's full meaning.

Albert nodded. "Now, at the moment we're fresh out of wars and the gov'ment's running out of moving targets. But I do suspect the only real way to learn how to shoot down an airplane is to shoot down an airplane."

"Gets expensive if you don't have an enemy furnishing them."

"Maybe if you was to start making little engines like was in them chainsaws, only put 'em in little airplanes—say somethin' about ten-foot wings and a couple of hundred mile an hour, I bet you'd find somebody's air force ready to buy 'em."

And thus were target drones born back in the dear dead days when the aircraft industry was beginning to toy with a name that sounded visionary and even silly . . . but Gus liked the sound of aerospace. He liked it even better when patience taught him how he had been leveraged out of his company, and what he should have done.

He smiled on the wolves who had raided him, accepted their congratulations on his marvelous comeback in aerospace, and when the chance came. . . . They had casually milked his little company, closed it down, gutted the pension plan his employees had helped pay for, and then gone off for a drink at the end of another day's work.

When Gus bankrupted his tormentors he did not relax. He kept up a steady, unrelenting pressure and saw them in court, in handcuffs, in prison. When financial reporters had asked publicly if this was not a technical violation of the rules (After all, it's just a game.), Gus said, "They should have left that pension fund alone."

But of course it wasn't really that and Gus knew it. He knew even better that a Robin Hood reputation would do him less damage than to be seen as a once-burned man.

He should have been prepared for next time. Was, as far as that went. Most of them were out of prison now, their fangs drawn. But they had family, friends, all the connections. Old Money could be patient and wait. So could Gus. But years had passed, he had mellowed, and never had any great opinion of his son-in-law's intelligence. That had been the trouble. M'Meath could be blamed no more than one blames a shark for obeying the single instinct its pea-sized brain can accommodate.

Which was why he had dithered so long. First time was their fault. Second time was his own. In spite of Albert's attempts to pump a little gumption back into him, Gus had almost believed he was too old—until Mansour came along.

Mansour, Albert, and Gus sat drinking coffee, having finally gotten rid of the mad old man in the wheelchair. "He is as good as he thinks he is?" Mansour asked.

"Almost. I like the idea of a laser elevator but whether we can afford it or whether it comes in time . . . You know the fix we're in."

"Perhaps if you were to run over it quickly."

"We playin' penny ante bluff in a five dollah game," Albert began, then shrugged an apology. "It used up most of your half billion just to outfit those old shuttles. What do we do if they come home emptyhanded?"

"But I thought this was exploration only—that we were to expect no return from this first run."

"Have you ever wondered what I do around this outfit?" Gus asked. "Albert's the brains. You're the money."

Mansour's gentle Semitic eyes waited for the answer.

"I'm not even an engineer," Gus said. "I had a good instinctive grasp of mechanics back in pre-computer days. But now my function is mainly PR."

"He the con man," Albert said.

"I'm the one who exudes the calm confidence of a commissar with a Swiss account," Gus explained. "Your half billion was seed money. You realize we're in direct competition with governments—whole countries?"

Mansour did.

"Either we create the impression that we're onto something big, that now's the time to get in on the ground floor, or there won't be any second trip."

"But we will have acquired valuable experience," Mansour protested.

"Make me an offer for a lifetime's worth."

"Spain and Portugal had experience," Albert elaborated. "England got profits."

"Innovators go broke," Gus added.

"But we are not innovators," the Arab said.

"Glad you noticed that. In spite of Albert's best finagling, the government has taxed me unmercifully for over fifty years. The same government bails out every Old Boy incompetent, but has

never lifted a finger to help me. This is why my
gratitude to NASA is—tempered.

"Still, we reap the benefits of a government
financed technology. Other taxpayers will scream
for my blood. To digress for a moment, the oil
companies have explained to these citizens that
you Arabs are all suicidal fanatics out to scuttle
your own dollar investments. The oil crisis is all
your fault so when some reporter blows the whistle it's obvious that Dampier's already sold out to
the enemy."

"But we Arabs did not form OPEC," Mansour
protested. "It was the oil companies who insisted
that prices remain at par with inflation and de-
valuation."

Gus shrugged. "You and I know it."

Albert took up the argument. "We're cutting it
too thin. Nothing goes wrong and we might make
it. One slipup and we're screwed, blued, and tat-
tooed."

"What more can I do?" Mansour asked.

"You're closer to your brother than we are."

Mansour winced. "Too close."

"We got enough problems without some nut
shootin' at us," Albert said. "How do you think
it's gonna look if one of us had to—? There're
people in this country would pay to see old Gus
hung for murder."

"I do not know what I can do," Mansour said
woodenly. "But Omar is a good man. Do not kill
him."

"Will you let him kill you?" Gus paused, then
added, "I managed a plant with the Pan-Islamic
News Service about how Zionist elements nearly
crabbed the sale of those jets; that only your heroic

and patriotic intervention ironed things out."

Mansour's dark face turned gray. *"Inshallah,"* he muttered, then shrugged. "Now I start to think like my brother."

"If it be God's will," Albert said pointedly. Turning to Gus he added, "But you have put Mansour on the spot. Now King Omar gonna just *know* he's sharpenin' up the knife."

"You understand us," the Arab said.

"I hadn't planned on leaving it at that," Gus said.

"Will we never emerge into the 20th century?" Mansour wailed.

"You're there," Gus snapped. "The difference is you accept it and the West tries to pretend that's not the way things are."

"Islam means submission to the will of God," Mansour growled. "An excellent religion until science and medicine gave man some measure of control over his life."

"What you need now is some kind of Dislam," Albert offered.

"We look backward toward a perfect past. If all things are written, how can there ever be change? Yet my people see themselves outgunned, surpassed in every way by Infidels. Is it any marvel that in trying to reconcile God's will with our stagnation we grow mad?"

There was an embarrassed silence. "Perhaps you do need a new prophet," Gus conceded. "One who raises his eyes to heaven and his middle finger in the same direction."

Mansour smiled sadly. "All religions teach man to accept pain, injustice, and death. But Albert, in your struggle for liberation, why take the worst possible choice?"

"Beats me," Albert said. "I guess Malcolm X wasn't old enough to remember who raided the interior and dragged us out to the ships."

"Officially," Mansour said wryly, "we abolished slavery in 1954. What can one do with a faith that permits complacence in the midst of evil?"

"You could change it. God helps those who help themselves."

Mansour sighed. "We have no happy proverbs. Ours are all toward acceptance. Now it is God's will that my brother kill me."

"You see no other way?" Gus asked.

Mansour shrugged. In spite of Bond Street suit and conservative tie, he looked totally biblical.

"I told you I hadn't planned on letting it go at that," Gus said. There was a knock on the door. Three hands went into three jackets.

"Startin' to act like mafia," Albert growled.

"Who is it?" Gus asked.

A young, longhaired man stuck his head through the door. "Ready for that conference call?" he asked. Without waiting he began wheeling in a small TV pickup with an oversized monitor.

"Who we calling?" Albert asked.

"King Omar."

"No!" Suddenly Albert and Mansour were out of their chairs. Then Mansour controlled himself. He sat down and waited.

Moments later the screen was alight and Mansour felt a wrench as he recognized the room behind his brother and a thin young man who was probably an interpreter. At that moment the sheikh must have seen Mansour along with Gus and Albert on his screen. There was an instant of blank surprise, then those eyes so like Mansour's narrowed.

Gus was beaming as he rambled through greetings, compliments, inquiries about the health of the royal family, everything except what was on everybody's mind. Beside the sheikh, the young man emitted occasional spurts of monotone.

Just as it seemed he would go on forever, Gus finished. Now it was the king's turn. After Omar's first burst, Mansour and the thin young man both began interpreting, hesitated, bowed nervously toward each other, and finally Omar's man began the ritual inquiries. There was a sudden silence. "He asks about your health," Mansour prompted.

Still beaming like a benevolent walrus, Gus said, "Lousy. I may die any moment."

Mansour and the interpreter exchanged a wild look. Even Albert was startled. Omar growled something which was obviously, "What the hell did he say?" The young man told him. Then the king wanted to know what was wrong with Gus.

"I'm spending so much time dodging bullets that I can't tend to business. Tell Omar I'm doing my best to get those jets delivered on schedule but if I die or have a nervous breakdown—"

Another brief question in Arabic and then the thin young man was saying, "His Highness asks if he can do anything to protect you from the Zionists."

"They all look like Arabs to me," Gus said.

"His Highness will also do whatever he can to protect you from the PLO or other disruptive elements."

Albert and Mansour glanced at one another, then Mansour was facing the camera, speaking with rapid earnestness to his elder brother. The interpreter fidgeted and obviously wished he were somewhere else. Gus felt sorry for the young man but sorrier for himself for never having taken time to learn Arabic. Then he remembered that Albert's look of wooden incomprehension did not mean he wasn't taking it all in.

The colloquy between brothers went on even longer than Gus's opening harangue. Finally Mansour sat back. He seemed stunned. He said no further word while Gus rambled through ritual assurances that he would struggle from his death-bed to deliver those jets and spares as per your agreement. When the screen had gone dead and the longhaired young man had removed it the Arab still seemed dazed.

Gus glanced at Albert.

"The king gave a pretty good imitation of a man who's not even sure what he's being accused of," Albert said.

"Perhaps," Gus said drily. "But now he knows what it'll cost him if he doesn't lay off."

"He didn't know," Mansour said.

"Oh come off it! Surely you can see through another Arab."

"I accused him of trying to kill me. He was so surprised that he blurted it right out."

"What'd he say?"

Albert laughed. "The king said, 'How can you know when I'm still making up my mind?'"

Gus was silent for a long moment. "If your brother isn't," he asked, "then who the hell is shooting at us?"

They sat another moment. Finally Albert sighed and got to his feet. "Be interesting to see if anybody still is."

But Mansour was still sunk in his chair.

"Americans," he muttered. "Who else would have thought of something so direct and simple?"

"Uncle Remus was an American too," Albert said. "Anyhow, it isn't going to work."

"No," Mansour agreed. "Like any Freudian, my brother will brood and analyze and never cease hunting the hidden meaning. Nothing will ever convince him that I do not wish to be sheikh— only wish him to pull his head from the sand and see the long range needs of our people. When the oil is gone—or once the West remembers there is oil everywhere, that the real shortage is only of those willing to live downwind from a refinery—what good will it do our poor people then to have acquired a taste for foreign luxury?

"*Munkar!*" Mansour almost spat. "If I take a foreign wife or drink whiskey I harm only myself. What will our people do when they learn to bathe, when their toilets flush with water—and one day the tankers no longer come?"

"Ever ask Omar that?"

"A few minutes ago," Albert said.

"And what'd he have to say?"

"Nothing. He seemed rather thoughtful."

Albert sighed. "Well, who wants to be first downstairs and out the door? Be interesting to see if anybody's still shooting at us."

M'Meath had twisted enough official arms to have police posted around the house. After a personal check of doors and windows he had stalked off to bed. Now he drank coffee in the kitchen— half a spoonful of sugar and enough cream to feed his ulcer. Tina came in with the *Times* and poured herself coffee. The silence between them had lasted nearly twelve hours.

"It says you're a hero."

M'Meath sipped coffee.

"Carried your wounded companion to safety without regard for your own danger."

M'Meath almost laughed. He wondered what Tina would have to say if he were to tell her the only reason he'd kept that son of a bitch draped over his shoulders was so Averill could stop the next bullet. But he wasn't going to tell her. As soon as he finished his coffee M'Meath was going to pack an extra pair of socks and walk out—leave the driving to Greyound, and see if he could get on again stripping loins at the packing plant. Somewhere he was sure he still had his card in the meat cutter's union, a relic of pre-Gus, pre-Tina days.

"That old uncle Seamus or whoever he was must have been a real cross to bear."

Now what in hell was she getting at?

"Coming around drunk, starting fights, spoiling every family gathering."

M'Meath refused to rise to the bait.

"Yet no matter what an inconvenience drunken, brawling old Uncle Seamus was, he had a place to go right up till the day he disappeared."

M'Meath had taken a single drink last night: his first in years.

"What is it with you?" she demanded. "Are you so superior to us lesser breeds that you never make mistakes? Have the children done you dirty? What's so horrible that decent people can't discuss it?"

He had never caught her talking Irish before. Must have picked it up from him. Did he really sound like that after being born and raised in this country?

" 'Tis not another woman you've left me for."

Been checking up?

"Nor is it lazy y'are. You work enough for two men. Have I spent more than I should? Is it for me and the children you're workin' yourself to death?"

M'Meath put down his cup and went to his study. He began rummaging through drawers. Where was that motherless Meat Cutters' card? Tina stood in the doorway. "Try the top shelf of your closet," she suggested.

He went to the closet and found an overnight bag. It was packed.

"Ironed them myself," she said. "At least I can show the world my husband was well cared for whenever he let himself be. But if ever I leave you," she added, "I'll be kind enough to tell you why."

It was a reasonable request. The only problem was that M'Meath could not find an answer. "It's not that I can't support you in the style to which you're accustomed," he finally said. "I can't support you at all. In a few days the police will decide the danger's over. Then I won't even be able to protect you."

"So you'll leave us to take care of ourselves?"

"It's not you they want. If the scandal is big enough and the fight loud enough, then they'll know they can't reach me through you."

"Who is it? Why are they after you?"

"If I knew that I could do something about it."

"You don't know?" Tina was incredulous. "I've tried not to get involved in your battles with Daddy. But when strangers hang around the neighborhood and keep track of our children, do you still expect me not to take sides?"

"I'd better leave right away."

Tina's eyes narrowed and he saw tears for the first time. But it was not pity. "Is suicide the best you can do? Do you think you'll fool your god by letting somebody else pull the trigger?"

"What do you suggest?"

"Get off your noble, self-sacrificing ass! They want to kill you; kill them first."

"What about you—the children?"

Tina was punching a number into the phone. "Daddy? Oh. Albert, your company problems are spilling over into my home. Could you come around and pick up the children?

"No, just the children. But you might bring a couple of pistols. Remember the kind you taught me to shoot? Yes."

My God, M'Meath thought. Ten years married and this's the first time I ever even knew she could shoot!

But who was shooting at him? He went back to the kitchen and poured another cup of coffee-and-cream. And half the answer came. He didn't know who but he knew who ought to know. That spalpeen probably still thought M'Meath had saved his life. He went to the wall phone in the kitchen. After some demanding of names and ranks he was finally connected to a hospital room. "This is your companion in misfortune. How soon will you be ambulatory?"

Averill was drowsy with sedation. "Be a while," he said. "They hit the bone."

So that was why he had fallen so heavily. "We've got to talk. How?"

"Not much choice," Averill slurred. "Bring some flowers and a radio."

"I'll be right—"

Tina was semaphoring from across the kitchen.

"Be there as soon as I can make it," M'Meath amended.

"You're not going anywhere until the children are off safe with Daddy and Albert," Tina said. "And whither thou goest I go."

Funny. He had always thought of her as a clinging vine.

Finally Albert and the children had departed in the venerable Mark V. The day was raw and windy by Southern California standards, though it would have been considered balmy anywhere else. M'Meath had foregone a business suit in favor of a hunting jacket that made his shoulder holster less obvious. When he parked in the hospital lot people stared at the man in hunting jacket and his elegantly caped and muffed companion.

There was a guard by the door. For one mad moment M'Meath thought Averill was under arrest, then he saw it was only rent-a-cop. The uniformed man rose from his chair.

"I'm M'Meath."

"I don't care who you are—" The guard's eyes widened as he saw the diameter of the barrel that peeped from Tina's muff. "Please don't be tiresome," she snapped, and brushed past. The guard heard Averill's, "Well, hello there," before the door closed. He sat down and tried to pretend it had not really been a gun at all he had seen in that muff.

The hospital was one of those modern, round edifices with pieshaped rooms so that one nurse could keep an eye on every patient on her floor. M'Meath taped a piece of paper over the window in the door in case she went in for lip reading. He decided the squawk box at the head of the bed was the logical point for any bug. He put the pocket radio there. Tina captured a chair and sat with her back to the wall opposite the door. M'Meath drew close to the bed where Philps Averill lay with his leg in a cast dangling from a trestle of weights and pulleys. "Who did it and why?" he asked.

Averill was slightly dopey. "Don't know," he slurred. "Don't even know why anybody'd want shoot at you—much less me."

It took M'Meath a fraction of a second to see that the elegant Ivy Leaguer had still not realized that but for the grace of some diarrhoetic dog that shot would have gotten M'Meath instead of the man in the hospital bed. "Well, it's not Gus Dampier's people. And I've never done anything to offend Sheikh Omar."

"Maybe it's the PLO. Maybe it's the Jews. Maybe Iranians. Or how about the Russians? The world's full of people who'd be just as happy if the sheikh didn't have a modern air force."

M'Meath considered this. Somehow it just didn't seem Jewish. Unless Gus was planning a sellout of King Omar . . . and that didn't sound like Gus. He checked the radio near the intercom and decided it was loud enough. "Your agency started the ball rolling."

"What is his agency?" It was the first time Tina had spoken.

In his doped condition Averill seemed to have forgotten she was here. He raised his eyebrows.

"There will be no more secrets," Tina said. "You dragged me in so you can learn to wear an albatross."

"The lady has spoken," M'Meath added. "He's with ECPAD."

"Is that the Nader's Raiders agency after they went straight and joined the establishment?"

Averill managed a nod.

"Ralph Nader is Arab."

"So's Danny Thomas," Averill said tiredly. "Maybe St. Jude's is behind it all."

The door burst open and a dark young man with almost kinky hair tore the wrapping from a huge bouquet he was carrying. "*Bismillah!*" he shouted as he began aiming the burp gun.

Two careful shots emerged from Tina's muff. As the echoes reverberated from uncurtained hospital walls M'Meath wondered if he would ever hear again. Tina sat without moving or blinking. The young Arab gave a look of mixed reproach and surprise. The burp gun clattered to the floor an instant before he did. The door burst open again.

The guard's fly was still unzipped within a hair's breadth of indecent exposure. "Oh Jesus!" he moaned. "There goes my job!"

"If you don't learn to knock first you won't need a job," Tina said.

M'Meath wondered how he could have lived ten years with this woman and never known her. "Get out of here," he snapped. "And when you come back with the lieutenant of the homicide squad, make sure you identify yourself." As the guard flapped off down the hall with his fly still ajar M'Meath pushed the burp gun to the far corner of the linoleum. Uzi, he noted. But weapons could be bought, sold, captured. An

Israeli-made gun meant nothing. He pulled the young Arab's hands away from his abdomen. "You're still alive. Now who are you? Where do you come from?"

The stranger's eyes were glazing with shock. It occurred to M'Meath that he might not speak English. But he wouldn't know Irish or Church Latin either. M'Meath fumbled in his pocket for a knife, then saw a large one sheathed on the Arab's belt. He pointed the tip where the would-be assassin had been gripping his abdomen. "Too bad you don't speak English. We'll have to fish for that bullet without any anaesthetic."

"Jesus Christ, M'Meath, do you know what you're doing?" The excitement had lifted Philps Averill out of his drugged fuzziness.

"No," M'Meath conceded. "I need some on-the-job training." He turned back to the young man. "Does it hurt?"

The Arab nodded in mute agony.

So he did understand English.

"Good. With any luck we can keep you hurting for months. And then when you're better we'll turn you over to the Jews. And if they've no stomach for it there'll be some in Belfast could give lessons. Now who was it sent you?"

No answer. M'Meath slit the trousers open and exposed a surprisingly small red-rimmed hole in the young man's abdomen. He glanced first at the Arab, then the knife he had taken from him.

The Arab gritted his teeth with pain. Then abruptly he was gasping, choking. Belatedly M'Meath realized the gritting had not been teeth. He had bitten down on something that was rapidly turning his whole body cyanotic.

"*Nunc dimittis*," M'Meath said. After a moment he added "Shit!"

"Jesus!" Philps Averill gasped. "Whatever got into you?"

"Ask her."

Tina sat with her hands in the muff. Apart from exchanging a partially empty clip for a full one, then reloading the other, she had not moved. "It has something to do with separating a mother from her children," she said. "Both glandular, and highly inadvisable." There was a clatter of footsteps outside. This time somebody knocked.

"Where'd you put them?" Gus asked.

"They're in Watts, being tutored by a Harvard man."

Gus raised his eyebrows.

"Alumni always used to sponsor one just to show how enlightened they were. Matter of fact, this one works for us."

"Does he know who they are?"

"He thinks he's helping one of our data processors in a child custody squabble. I'm not totally innocent."

Gus grinned. "If the news is accurate, my son-in-law must rapidly be shedding that quality."

Albert shrugged. "Personnel manger saw something odd in the morning readout," he said. "And since we're all a little antsy about infiltration, he chased down the actual application. What do you make of it?" He handed the form to Gus. The attached photograph was M'Meath's.

Gus flipped through the form. "Data seem accurate. If somebody wanted to slip in a ringer they could pick somebody a little less obvious."

"Looks to me like your son-in-law's tryin' to apologize."

"How do you figure that?"

"See what he put in 'position applied for'?"

"My God!"

M'Meath wanted to be a janitor.

Gus crumpled the form.

"You sure you want it that way?" Albert asked.

Gus picked up the phone and asked Miss Jepworth to call Tina.

"Where are the children?" his daughter demanded.

"If you don't know then nobody can force the information out of you." While she was digesting this he added, "If your husband's there perhaps he'd like to exchange a word with me."

Moments later M'Meath was on. "Still have a company scrambler?" Gus asked.

"Yes."

Gus waited until squeaks emanated from the phone. He switched in his own and M'Meath became intelligible again. "I'll have to recommend against your application," Gus said. "You're overqualified."

Though they were not on a picture phone the shrug was obvious in M'Meath's reply.

"But there is something you could do. I'm afraid it may turn out worse than sweeping up."

"You want me in space? Hell, I'll go!"

"You're old, encumbered, and underqualified."

"Look," M'Meath said. "I thought I was doing the right thing. You were losing it. I wanted to keep it in the family."

"You're out now—publicly and notoriously. Stay out. Stay mad. Stay open to offers."

"From whom?"

"Just once in my life I'd like a man inside the enemy's organization instead of theirs in mine."

"I never thought of that."

"By now you know they're not playing with rubber bullets. If they ever learn you're communicating with me . . ."

"I'll do it," M'Meath promised, and broke the connection.

"Now what are you grinning about?" Gus snarled.

"Not one single thing. If he lives he might turn into a man after all. By the way, you got any idea where Mansour is?"

"He went home to talk things over with his brother."

Albert's eyes widened. "Has everybody gone crazy around here? Old Omar gonna kill him sure as hell!"

"Mansour's old enough to do what he wants."

"You sure you didn't con him?"

"Albert, you know me better than that."

"I do. I can see you maneuvering a born sucker like M'Meath . . . but Mansour—that man must have a death wish."

"Why don't you ask that old hot rodder in the wheel chair? Our partner spent several hours yesterday in earnest converse with our technical director."

"And you don't know about what?"

"All I know is our schedule's been turned into a Chinese fire drill since that Army kid grabbed more than his share and went tearing off in the wrong direction. If we can't send Jeff out we might as well let him come back down."

"Can't we get any more SRBs?"

"It seems that NASA needs every damned solid booster in production for the next six months."

"I'll have to look into that," Albert said.

"Do you have a pipeline into Utah?"

"Can't figure why anybody would want to join a church where it took congressional arm-twisting to convince the elders that all blacks aren't descended from Satan."

"A black Mormon?"

"He's a bishop now. He's also a junior accountant with Thiokol Chemical."

Gus managed not to laugh.

"They ever identify that dude Miss Tina shot?"

Gus shook his head. "No documents, naturally. And no prints on file with the FBI or Interpol. The latter agency sometimes tells the truth."

"Circumcised?"

"In his early teens according to the examiner."

"Then he's Moslem and not Israeli."

"Stomach contents were lamb, eggplant, and rice."

"You can get Arab food anywhere. Anything odd about the poison?"

"Just the usual HCN."

"If every kid had a funny tooth to bite down on whenever the world disappointed him, prussic acid could solve our population problems in one generation."

Gus gave an unbelieving look. "This from the man who singlehandedly struggles to save Watts?"

"Ah, I'm just tired. Us ol' men get that way. But

Mansour isn't old. That man must have a death wish."

Gus sighed. "I suppose you realize that if he's dead, so are we."

Albert knew.

Army's zero g nightmares were usually of falling but this time he struggled up from a maelstrom of even greater than usual confusion. He knew it was just fatigue plus aggravated solitude but he seemed to be holding conversations with some examiner who asked those pointless questions Army had come to associate with psychological testing.

Did you love your mother?

Where are you from?

Do you have a girl friend?

Where are you going?

Is money more important than friendship?

What are you doing?

Do you like to steal?

How long do you want to live?

Why?

Not a shrink. It was more as if he was being plagued by some articulate four-year-old. He'd had the dream several times before. Ought to mean something but his waking hours were too busy to maunder over Freudian jungles and Adlerian jingles. He untangled himself from his net. He checked the batteries and the scope.

Every instrument told him he was on course but he was still insecure enough to wish for the additional comfort of a fix from Sin. It would be nearly thirty hours before he had to start retrofiring but with no blip from her transponder he would have to do the final approach visually.

Not that he wouldn't be able soon to find her on the radar but—within the last couple of days business had picked up. He had come within a few thousand kilometers of several spaceship sized rocks. It could be embarrassingly fatal to lock onto one of these instead of Sin's rockets.

He ran the shaver over his head and decided it was time to do the rest of his body. Meanwhile, he tried to remember what he had left undone. Since kicking the burntout SRBs away he had been inventorying his cordage. Not much. But two of the SRBs he had appropriated from Jeff had not yet been pruned of their nose fairings or separation motors. There ought to be drogue and main chutes inside there somewhere.

Thanks to the extra thrust he had misappropriated, he had nearly caught up with Sin but now he had an extra load of velocity that had to be burned off if he were not to go past her like several multiples of the Wabash Cannonball. He suited up and wondered if it was imagination or if his gangling body was still stretching.

SRBs had been designed to fasten to an external fuel tank which this shuttle had not seen since departing Earth some years ago. This was why he had been reduced to kicking them loose rather than use the explosive bolts and separation motors originally built into Solid Rocket Boosters. But Army's attachment of the extra rockets had been even more hasty than most 10th-g construction. Had he fired them in the first burn they would have torn loose. Now he had to go out and horse them around into the slots where he had kicked two burnouts loose. It took nearly ten hours and before he was finished he had to go back into the cargo bay to recharge all his air bottles.

But finally they were in place and he was ready. He went through the airlock and peeled off his clammy suit. Nineteen hours till burn. It was, of course, possible to fire at any time but in rocketry proverbs about the equivalance of time and money acquire extra meaning: fire at the proper moment or use several times more fuel than he had.

He gave the radio the old college try, hoping Sin would hear now that he was closer, but it was a forlorn hope. In the weeks they'd been able to talk while catching up, Army had finally connected up the wan hairless girl in the space suit with that leggy tanned blonde on all the NASA handouts. Had NASA known space would do this to women?

The alarm beeped and for an instant he thought he was closing too soon on her. Then he saw it was just another chunk of—couldn't be rock. He checked the readout again. He took radar bearings, then struggled for a visual with the six-inch refractor.

The asteroid was a near perfect sphere and had an abraded surface—almost as if it had been water-and-gravel eroded. Density . . . Must be some lead or other heavy metal in it. Solid iron would weigh less. He checked his magnetometers, gravitometers. Everything was recording. He went back to the refractor. It was slightly out of the ecliptic and would pass less than a thousand kilometers in front of him. But radar dopplering also told him that even if he didn't have to concentrate on matching velocities with Sin, this heavy metal was coming up too fast for him ever to get more than a glimpse as it whizzed by. He ran the numbers for Earth intersection. Hopeless. But it was interesting to know there was something heavier than iron out here.

Interesting because iron was the breakoff point for any natural stellar breakdown of hydrogen into helium ad infinitum—infinitum being iron. The heavier elements were all formed by some planetary core process that Army had read about but couldn't remember. So were the asteroids a broken-up planet after all, instead of one that had never formed? He would have to give this one a close scan for radioactivity.

Meanwhile back at the ranch, it was seventeen hours till burn. To be a half hour late could be as disastrous as a half hour early. He swallowed a tube of some gagsome gruel and squeezed into his sleeping net. Halfway in, he heard a clang like a dropped manhole cover. Immediately pressure was building inside his ears.

He dithered for a microsecond hunting his spacesuit. Ought to learn to sleep in the clammy thing. Then he saw the bullet hole in the thermal window pane, just below the refractor. It could have been worse. He could have been squinting through the scope when that pebble hit. Air was shrieking through the hole. He was fumbling for something to plug it when a welding glove followed the rush of air and clapped itself neatly over the hole.

Army released another belch. His ears were aching. He wondered if he was going to have a nosebleed before he could get into his suit. He gulped air and squeezed his chest down on it as he had been taught. His vision cleared and he felt the cabin pressure start to rise. He rummaged about for a patch. Ought to replace that thermal pane but he didn't have time until after the burn and anyhow, to replace it would mean dumping the rest of his cabin air. He found a patch of fiberglas cloth impregnated with silicone and peeled off the backing.

He slid the glove off the star of radiating cracks and the patch plopped down neatly over the hole. Air pressure would hold it until the silicone cured. Sixteen and a half hours till burn. He ought to be resting but first he had to go through this motherless cabin and see how many irreplaceables that pebble had destroyed on its way through. Of all the goddam times for a statistic to hit him! But it could have been during the burn.

It didn't take him long to discover the second thing the meteorite had destroyed. The CRT on his computer was shattered. He sighed and cinched down the locks on his space suit. Spare picture tubes were all stored in vacuum out in the cargo bay. He had already lost half his air. He shrugged and forced both sides of the airlock open. The whoosh removed most of the shattered glass. Once he had a readout he could pick up the rest of it with masking tape—if there was time— and if the pebble had not holed something else.

The shuttle had originally had three systems: one to use and two backups. But computers were slightly more reliable since this orbiter had been built. He had started out with two and one of them had turned balky. He wondered if he was going to spend the rest of his months up here patching

computer circuitry, then knew he would not. If he
screwed up on this next burn he might as well
take off his suit and open an airlock.

There were a dozen spare picture tubes out in
the cargo bay, thoughtfully stored in separate lo-
cations. He found one and pulled himself back
through the open lock. No use building up cabin
pressure until he knew how many more times he
would have to go out for something else. He fumbled with gloved hands to replace the CRT.

When he finally had it plugged in and the yokes
slid into focus the computer ran through its
checkout without glitching. He made the machine check as many other systems as it could
while he drifted about the evacuated cabin trying
to see whether the pebble had shattered or if it
had managed to exit through another bulkhead.
Nothing else seemed damaged. Probably, the
meteorite had turned into dust and been puffed
out along with most of the broken glass. But
clammy or not, Army suspected he would never
be able to sleep outside of a space suit again.

Thirteen hours till burn. He was sure he had
enough fuel. If he didn't get some sleep he would
be in no shape to do anything. Cabin pressure was
down a couple of millibars. He tried to convince
himself it was just from opening the airlock, then
remembered he had not opened it since repres-
surizing. Somewhere there was still a tiny leak.
He was about to light his first cigarette in several
months and follow the smoke when he had a
sudden inspiration. He found a shard of glass
imbedded in the inside airlock door gasket.
Twelve and a half hours till burn.

Was that the only leak? To hell with it. He

checked pressure again. Down a few millibars from what he had bled into the airlock. He was about to call it quits when he realized his brains had turned to peanut butter again. Was it radiation or zero grav that was doing this to him? When he had come inside, the inner door had closed last—which had to mean the airlock was at full cabin pressure. For pressure to drop there must be something stuck in the outer door seal too.

Thank Thoth he was still in his suit. He pulled himself into the airlock. Sho' nuff! Pressure was dropping even though both doors were closed. He braced himself against the draft and opened the outer hatch. This time he could find nothing. He ran his finger over the gasket and its mating surface. If there was any irregularity it was too fine for his gloved hand to feel.

Army sighed and closed the outer door. He pressurized the lock and waited. Twenty minutes later pressure had not dropped. Since the airlock was smaller than the cabin, any leak should have shown up by now. He decided whatever it was must have blown away when he opened the outer seal. He locked through into the cabin and made sure the low pressure alarm was turned on. It was eleven and a half hours till burn when he crawled back into the sleeping net, still in his clammy space suit, with his helmet tucked beside him like a teddy bear.

And now if he could just go to sleep . . .

His collectors did their sunflower best to keep him alive but these ships just would not stay still. Every time collector plates rotated into shadow the tracking would stutter to a halt, then spin to face the dawn that came every ten and a half seconds.

Army knew that by now he ought not even to be hearing that rhythmic clack and whir. But he did. The ship was continually telling jokes that pumps and relays found hilarious even though Army never got the point. It had taken him months even to decipher what the solar tracking was trying to tell him. Then one night half asleep he had suddenly understood. The damned machine was quoting the custodian who had found Army working out in the gym of his lilywhite suburban school: "What the hell you doin' here, boy?"

There it went again: "What the hell you doin' here, boy?" Then something was buzzing.

Army jerked awake and realized it was not the cabin pressure alarm. He turned on a light and pulled himself to the newly replaced CRT screen. Probably the wobbling orbiter had turned far enough to pick up one of the SRBs he had kicked away days ago. Then he saw the spike was too small. He did the numbers. It was where Sin ought to be.

Cabin pressure had risen a millibar, which was roughly equal to the amount of CO_2 he had traded for O_2 in the last six hours. He pushed toward the six inch refractor and tried to see what was causing the spike on his radar. It was too far to be more than a point source of varying light. It could be a spinning ship—or a spinning asteroid. He went back to the CRT. The spike had changed shape and was larger.

God damn! He had actually done it! Army knew there was nothing miraculous about it but he also knew how many zeros there are behind every calculation out here. A needle in a haystack was—a bowling ball in its bag compared to the job his instruments had just accomplished: more on the order of selecting a single electron from an auditoriumful of air. But the changed shape of the spike also meant something even more important. She was still alive!

Then his joy sagged as he realized what had really happened. Sin would have programmed her transponder to give him her batteries' dying gasp as soon as he was close enough to need a fix.

He still had five hours to kill. He was slept out. Didn't feel too bad this morning—if it was morning. But he knew he was not thinking with the old clarity that had let him steal Dampier blind. At least he was alive. To stay that way Army decided he'd better put on his helmet and go outside to see how many things he had crossconnected or otherwise screwed up.

He hoped Sin had done her numbers properly. She was supposed to be orbiting on a minimum fuel trajectory. It would take all the fuel he had liberated from Jeff—and then some just to burn off excess velocity and match speed with her. If one or both of them lived long enough there would still be the problem of not plowing back into Earth at some whitehot meteoritic velocity.

This time the airlock worked smoothly, so he guessed he'd flushed out the crud. The rest of it would be in his air filters by now. Should have taken them outside with him for a shakeout. He snapped his lifeline and, checklist in hand, began going over what he had done yesterday.

He could not find a single mistake. An hour later, barely minutes ahead of his air, he locked back into the cabin and tried to shake off the feeling that he was forgetting something. Nerves, he told himself. It was time to pedal some life back

into the batteries. Pedaling, he remembered the
inquisitor in his dream.

He was sweating profusely but either he was
having a good day or perhaps he had reached
some kind of plateau in his gradual disintegra-
tion. He didn't feel any worse than a week ago.
Lousy—but no worse. By the time he had pumped
up the batteries and wiped down for the last time
he was actually hungry. He finished a good tube
and it was two and a half hours till burn. With full
knowledge of the human body's perversity, Army
knew that now with everything close he could
easily fall asleep after the long strain of waiting.
He punched a wakeup call into the computer and
scrunched back into the net.

Minutes later he was out of the net again, drifting aimlessly about the cabin trying to find what
he had forgotten. The patch was holding. He took
another bearing and aimed the refractor. Sin's
ship was turning slowly, making about ten minutes per spin. He was spinning faster and in the
opposite direction. At first it had nauseated him
to try to see in a field of rotating stars but he had
grown used to it and begrudged the fuel to correct
the spin.

But for the girl the problem would be more
acute. Solar collectors track on the sun but the
plane of her spin must be occulting them half the
time. No wonder she was low on power.

These ships just would not stand still. At first
he had thought it was some tiny residual inertia
he had not been able to cancel out with the Reaction Control System verniers. Then he had finally
realized that this slow roll was the inevitable
Newtonian reaction to his hours of cranking and
pedaling.

He had run the numbers a week ago to line up for this burn but now that she was visual Sin seemed to be a couple of degrees off. He lined up the crosshairs in the refractor and measured the angles from her ship to a couple of reference stars. While the computer was deciding which other stars would align him 180° around he fired an RCS vernier. The orbiter began rotating around another axis and Sin drifted from view. It took the next hour to cancel out the remaining wobbles and get his OMS nozzles pointed toward the girl.

Still an hour till burn. He rotated the antenna and cranked up the power. Surely she could hear him from this distance.

"Sin! You all right? Let me know if you're there."

"What the hell you doin' here, boy?" his tracker replied.

He hadn't really been expecting an answer from Sin. Still plagued with the idea that he was forgetting something, he rechecked switches and programming. He closed his eyes and tried to breathe himself into calm. If he could just stop thinking for a while maybe he would remember what his irradiated, decalcified, peanut butter brains were . . .

Solenoids clacked and valves opened and an instant later came the whump of hypergolic fuel igniting. He felt heavy and awkward after months of weightlessness. In spite of all his housekeeping something small sailed past and clunked on the aft bulkhead.

Army climbed laboriously from his net and almost fell before he remembered to grab a stanchion. He tried to ignore the sudden need to urinate as acceleration reoriented liquids and pressed down on sphincters gone lazy with weightlessness. Only a tenth of a g, he reminded himself. Now where was whatever had sailed past him? He ran his hands along the edges of the air filter and then he saw it. The sphere was about a centimeter across and highly polished. Looked like a ball bearing.

There were ball bearings in some parts of this ship but neither he nor Jeff had ever taken any of the rocket motor gimbals apart. He tossed it and a tenth of a g brought it to a sedate repose in his palm. The burn seemed to be progressing properly. He climbed to the bow and the refractor's crosshairs were still on the proper reference star. Sudden inspiration made him hold the polished ball next to the magnetometer. Nothing. He dropped it in sudden panic, then remembered that fuel pellets were not polished. He let himself back down to the aft bulkhead and recovered the ball. A minute later he knew it was not radioactive.

Some former pilot's queeg ball? How had it survived so many housecleanings? He tried different wavelengths and found no fluorescence. It was just a highly polished sphere with a slight brownish cast. Something changed in the sound of the rocket engines.

Army pocketed the ball and hurried into his net just in time to avoid being caught in the almost half g as two SRBs ignited. He lay in the sagging net and waited. Fifty-five seconds passed and the thrust abruptly reduced by one third. It made no sense up here but the SRB propellant grains were all shaped to reduce the strain during the worst part of a liftoff.

Seven minutes passed and then the g forces

halved as one SRB burned out. OMS engines gim-
balled their full 8° limit as they struggled to correct the unbalanced thrust. Then the other SRB
burned out and he was back down to a tenth of a g
as the Orbital Maneuvering System burned val-
iantly away realigning the ship and putting the
final touches to velocity matching. He got out of
the net and fidgeted in front of the CRT. He could
see nothing through the fog of exhaust. The OMS
rockets stopped firing. Weightless again, Army
checked his alignment. He searched for Sin's blip
but the exhaust cloud was moving right along
with him. He knew from previous burns that it
would take several minutes to dissipate.

He struggled to control the antsy feeling that he
was going to plow into her. By the time he could
rotate ship for a visual the crud would have
cleared away and he would most probably only
have to turn around again for a final velocity-
matching burn.

"You there? You alive?"

No answer. If there were the slightest hope he
would have turned around and accelerated. But
he had better uses for his fuel. He suited up and
locked outside to cut the empties loose.

He had not had time to remove the separation
motors from this pair of stolen boosters. Nor did
he want them slamming into Sin while he was
docking. He spent nearly an hour making sure
everything was free except for a couple of wires.
Then he went back inside and fired the separation
motors. It sure beat trying to kick 85 tons away.

He punched the weight of the empties into the
computer. When the OMS engines came back on
he wondered if he was imagining the change in

acceleration now that he was pushing 170 tons less. The burn ended with Sin twenty kilometers away, closing in one hour.

Sin's ship was rolling, presenting its bow every ten minutes. He struggled to time his docking so they would meet at just enough angle to cancel out her roll. To Army's mild amazement his docking hook latched on the first try and they were mated. He secured systems, donned his helmet, and locked out. He was not looking forward to what he would find.

But in a suit he would be spared the ordeal of smell. He opened her outer hatch. He was forcing the inner door to whoosh out the worst of it when some obscure instinct warned him. He locked through and felt his way. A light switch achieved a faint red glow in an underpowered filament. He switched on his suit light. She was in the net, eyes dull and unfocussed.

"Christ!" Army wheezed, "I almost let your air out." Then he realized that with his suit on she couldn't hear him. He took off his helmet. Even after the gaminess of his own cabin it was something else.

"Broke my arm." Her voice was gritty from lack of use.

Army gritted his teeth and managed to control himself. "Know where the splints are?" He was already rummaging through a medical chest that was in the same place as his. Moments later he was wrapping her arm. "Got to get you into a suit."

"Where are we going?"

"I haven't time to pump up your batteries. Besides, we've got to make other arrangements unless you want your bones to finish turning to mush."

He sensed coming argument but she said nothing. He helped her splinted arm into the sleeve of a suit and found a bottle with enough air to manage the transfer. Once he had her in his sleeping net and nipping at a tube of high calcium broth Army went back outside and got to work.

He had pondered ever since committing himself to this pursuit if his abstraction of Jeff's still unstripped SRBs had been a lucky accident or subconscious planning. Either way, those drogue and main chutes would augment his supply of graphite cordage.

There was much to do—and little time. Given his druthers, Army would first have stripped Sin's ship of solar panels and everything else useful. But if the near-dead girl were not to continue her downward slide he had to get some calcium back into her bones.

He thought he knew how. What he did not know was what any engineer considers essential: the strength of his materials. The cordage from one chute would support one empty SRB in normal gravity. How many multiples of 83 tons were there in his and Sin's orbiters and their surround of cargo and extra boosters? How much gravity could the weakened girl stand without collapsing? How much did she need to get her calcium deposition working properly again? Where in hell was NASA when he needed them?

He had been doubling and splicing for months. Now, struggling to join one end to the docking hook of Sin's ship, he felt the approach of the moment of truth. He wanted to go back inside to separate the ships with an RCS vernier but he didn't want to come up with a jerk, nor was he enthused at the thought of incinerating a loop of his makeshift cable in a blast of rocket exhaust. He braced himself between the two orbiters and began pushing. It was slower and harder than pushing away an SRB but finally the ships were moving apart with all the deliberate majesty of drifting continents. He locked back inside to change air bottles. "Feeling any better?"

Sin nodded a valiant lie but he could see that she was close to vomiting the broth he had given her.

"Hang in there," he said. "I'm working on it."

By the time he was outside again the ships had separated two meters. The cable loops were just beginning to separate. He waited. Slowly the cable began spiraling out like a telephone cord until, near the end of his second air bottle he decided it was past the possibility of any snarl. He locked back in and unsuited. He spent half an hour pedaling batteries back up, then wiped down and pulled himself forward to look out through a thermal pane. Sin's ship loomed dead ahead fifty meters, the line between them nearly taut. He swam back to the control panel and gave a final glance rearward to make sure Sin was in the net. "Get comfortable," he warned. "We're going to have some g." He fired bow and stern Reaction Control System jets. The ship began moving sideways.

Minutes later there was a slight jerk as the line came taut. The ship yoyoed up and down for half an hour and finally the oscillations dampened just when he knew he was going to be sick and Sin already had, but finally his ship and Sin's were spinning at the ends of fifty meters of cable and damned if he didn't feel like a ton even if the accelerometer said it was only a tenth of a g.

Sin was scrunched up in the net. Had to get her out before she broke another bone. He found an inflatable mattress and got her stretched out on the aft bulkhead. "Feel any better?"

"Got to pee."

So did Army now that they were back in some kind of gravity again. "Can you—?" Of course she couldn't. She was barely able to move. He dithered a moment, then turned out the lights and helped her over to the throne. "Angle's funny," he apologized. "Later on I'll try to hang this ship so we can stand on the decks instead of the bulkheads."

She was wretched and starving, with a half inch of blond hair sprouting from pink scalp and still Army was so womanstarved he was afraid to touch her. He prayed she would be too preoccupied with her own misery to see the naked need in him. He climbed toward the bow. Going to have to get used to fulltime gravity again.

The line was holding. He wanted to get some of the more irreplaceable items from Sin's ship over to his, in case they broke apart, but he had worn himself out. Have to sling a net up here by the window now that he could no longer float. He studied the pane where the meteoritic pebble had come through.

As soon as Sin felt up to donning a suit again for a couple of hours he would have to replace that thermal glass. The cracks were no worse but there was a centimeter diameter hole there with nothing separating him and vacuum but a silicone patch. He thrust his hand into his pocket and found the polished ball bearing. It was just the size of the hole.

Army considered this most unwillingly. For it to have punctured his window meant the ball had to have come from outside. He studied it again. Slightly brownish metal. But hard compacted. This was no drop of condensate or melt. It took machinery—a well-developed technology to make a polished metal sphere. Was it a weapon? A bucketful of these with enough speed differential would go through a ship like buckshot through a goose. He worried the pellet about in his hands and recalled that French farmers were still occasionally blowing themselves into orbit as they plowed up WW-1 shells. Had he been hit by a stray bullet from some aeons-old war out here? What else was he liable to run into?

Mansour ibn Jezail was not sure whether he would be allowed off the plane. And if he were, would he be permitted to live? He had sized up passengers on this final stage of the journey, trying to see which had been detailed to keep an eye on him. But he would not be able to tell until he tried to leave the airport.

In preparation for this he had shed his Bond Street suit in Cairo and now wore *agal*, *kuffieh*, and *bornús*, as did every other man aboard except for a quartet of Norwegian drillers who monopolized the lounge and kept insisting to the stewardess that their bottle of akvavit was cough medicine. Mansour searched his memory and prayed *munkar* had never tempted him into pub-

lic displays. The old man in the next seat was
trying to ignore them but his beads passed ever
faster through his fingers. The trilingual seatbelts
sign lit up and gave Mansour something to do
with his hands. "If it be the will of God," the old
man muttered.

"*Ah-man*," Mansour echoed, though privately
he had more faith in regular maintenance and
inspections. Engines throttled back and flaps
came down. The plane and his stomach hesitated
for several heartbeats, then they were sliding
through bumpy, heat-thinned afternoon air
toward the runway.

In spite of high rise buildings in the distance
the deplaning and baggage areas were as aridly
infernal as he remembered. Doubly so after the
air-conditioned jet. A harried immigration official stamped his passport without a second
glance. Passengers stampeded toward buses,
limos, and taxis. Mansour was mildly surprised
when none lingered to see which way he would
be going. He lugged his carry-on bag to the head of
the taxi stand. "*Is-saráya*," he said. The driver
opened the door with the blasé air of a man who
has hauled many passengers to the palace.

"Why did you come?" his brother asked when
finally Mansour had penetrated protective circles
of guards, advisors, and hangers on.

"I came to live or die as my god and my brother
will decide." When Omar did not reply he added,
"Also because we must discuss family matters
without proclaiming to every troublemaker that
we do not see eye to eye."

"We do not," Omar said flatly. "Your life is half
over. If ever you made your *hajj* I have not heard of

it. Nor do I suppose your *farengi* son even knows
the meaning of the word."

"My son travels alone on a more distant and
perilous journey than to Mecca. Has another of
your subjects gone halfway to the moon for the
greater glory of Islam?"

"*Munkar!*"

"Is God then, who created the heavens and
Earth, also foreign filth? Did not the same God
who gave us the oil also provide the foreigners
with their machines to dig it, burn it, turn it into
gold for us?"

Subconsciously, Mansour had been preparing
this speech ever since his first year at the univer-
sity. While Omar floundered in theology he drew
a breath and continued, "My brother, you speak of
foreign filth. Yet God created the water, just as
God creates the alcohol when grapes ferment on
the vine. When does it become *munkar?*

"Does God's water become *munkar* when the
ballasted tankers haul it to our land? The things of
God are eternal. Are the oil tankers eternal? Our
people bathe with *munkar*, flush filth from their
houses with other, foreign filth. When the tankers
no longer come and our people have grown soft
and cannot remember the old ways, will God
scourge them and not the sheikh who led them
into evil?"

"No gold sticks to me," Omar snapped. "I am a
river unto my people."

"A Frankish wise man once said the road to hell
is paved with good intentions."

"And can you do better?"

"Even if I could, you are my sheikh."

"What would you do?"

"Will you go the way of the shah?"

"The Iranians are not Arab."

"They are Moslem. All people are alike—even the Franks. You have given ours piped water, automobiles, telephones, air conditioning, TV. After a taste of munkar will they return to bitter herbs?"

"I knew you were planning revolt."

"I am trying to prevent it."

Omar sat silent, studying Mansour with sad, Semitic, brother's eyes. He pulled the cord and somewhere a distant gong sounded. When the slave stuck his head into the room Omar said, "Gahwah."

The slave bowed and disappeared. They waited in silence until he returned with the tray. The black poured tiny cups of the thick brew for Omar and Mansour, then an even tinier one for himself. Mansour picked up his, then saw from the corner of his eye that Omar was waiting for the servant to taste it.

Later he would decide that he had been too many years in the West. But at the moment Mansour was only overcome with a sudden rage. Must people still live this way? "If it be the will of God," he snarled, and gulped his bitter brew.

Sheikh and slave stared, then abruptly the black was bowing and retreating. "You tire of life?" Omar asked.

"I have no quarrel with God."

There were sudden tears in Omar's eyes. "I will hear you," he said.

"There is no such thing as half a reform," Mansour began. "And you know what will happen if you try to move backward. Now let us consider how God will send His water when the tankers no longer come."

Gus and Albert were going over some figures in the boardroom when Mansour walked in. "Well now! And how's the Arkansas traveler?" Albert asked.

Mansour smiled. "I have never been in Arkansas. Is that really how you pronounce it?"

"You're alive," Gus greeted. "What induced your brother to grant that favor?"

"I promised him a nuclear powered desalination plant."

Albert put his coffee cup down. "Not from us, I hope."

"There is no reason why we should not make a reasonable profit," Mansour said.

"I'm afraid there are exactly one hundred reasons, collectively known as the United States Senate," Albert said.

"I'm running into some snags just getting export permits for those fighters," Gus explained. "I'm afraid that with the shah gone and several others going there's no way the soverign people would stand for more fissionable materials in the Middle East."

"But the Israelis already have nuclear weapons."

"Chances are several others have. But most of the experts think the PLO doesn't have any so far."

"What has this to do with my brother?"

"You and I know he's opposed to extremists," Gus said tiredly. "Which reminds me that we still don't know who's shooting at us. But have you ever tried to explain Sheikh Omar's position to some biblespouting foreign relations chairman who couldn't tell you within six thousand miles whether the Strait of Hormuz is in the Red Sea or the Persian Gulf?"

"But there must be a way," Mansour protested. "We need that uranium."

"Then you *are* going to make bombs!"

"Not exactly."

"We try to run an honest business," Albert said. "What're you up to?"

Mansour studied them in some astonishment. "You don't know?"

"Why should we?"

Mansour's confusion was growing. "But I naturally assumed he would have told you first."

"Who?"

The door burst open from the impact of a motorized wheelchair. The three of them were reaching inside their coats when they recognized Dr. Sumter. Abruptly Gus and Albert remembered the afternoon Mansour had spent in close converse with this madman. Gus rounded on their technical director. "If you're planning nuclear blackmail," he said, "you might remember that most of our facilities are still Earthside. And most of us will have to spend the rest of our lives here."

Sumter stared for a fraction of a second, then cackled. "Albert, please give a poor old man a cup of coffee."

"Do you want it with strychnine or arsenic?"

The man in the wheelchair faced Mansour. "What in hell's going on?" he demanded.

"I supposed you would have told them about

the nuclear fuel," Mansour said. "You did not tell me it was to be a secret."

" 'Tisn't. Now what's all this about blackmail?"

"Don't you ever read the papers?" Gus asked. "With the Middle East coming apart there's no way you're ever going to get an export permit."

"Who said anything about export permits? Besides, we're not shipping it to the Middle East."

Gus and Albert turned to Mansour. "What did your brother agree to?" Gus demanded.

Mansour's discomfort grew. "There may be some ambiguity in the details of the agreement," he conceded.

"Whether or not your brother's agents have been doing it," Gus said, "I really don't need anybody else shooting at me. Now what have you set me up for?"

"Us," Albert amended.

"We need the fuel," Mansour said.

"What for?"

"Remember what I told you about laser elevators?" Sumter asked. While they stared the old madman in the wheelchair slurped coffee noisily. "Thank you, Albert. Just the way I like it.

"Laser elevators work because the heavy equipment—power supply, the lasers themselves—all stay on the ground. You aim half a dozen of them into the opaqued reaction mass and keep tracking as the rocket lifts off. Single stage; only $10,000 a ton to get payload into orbit. That's unbelievably cheap by today's standards. But there just isn't that kind of power to spare in any commercial grid."

"You need a nuclear power plant just for your laser elevator?" Gus asked.

Sumter nodded.

"How long to get it all together?"

"With any luck we'll have liftoff in three years."

Albert and Gus looked bleakly at one another.

"You did not tell me it would take so long," Mansour said.

"You think Tom Swift cobbles that kind of stuff together in his basement?" Sumter asked.

"Of course not," Gus said. "But we explained the situation to you. Perhaps you only hear what you want to hear."

"I hear you've got a couple of dead pilots up there. Bring the other one down before you make it three."

"We don't know they're dead."

"Nobody knew Columbus wouldn't fall off the edge. I'm sorry for them and all that. If it'll make you happier I'll go up next time."

"We can't hold out that long," Albert said.

"Sell some chainsaws. Sell some jets. Water your stock." Sumter slammed down his coffee cup. "I've seen the reports on what that girl found—before the reports stopped coming. Do you want to salvage one of those chunks or do you want to go bankrupt again? Incidentally, how do you dump that much iron into the economy without wrecking the market?"

"Three years," Albert said thoughtfully. "That's one hell of a long wait for a return." He glanced at Mansour. "Don't s'pose you could get another billion out of your brother?"

Mansour's air grew sheepish. "The sheikh expects that plant to provide water for his people."

There was sudden glacial silence. Albert studied Mansour with the same mournful air he had last lavished on young Army fresh-caught with his hand in the till. "Your own brother," he sighed.

Gus struggled to see a silver lining. He couldn't. "When that desalination plant doesn't arrive, Omar's going to come gunning for Albert and me. But you'll be number one on the fecal roster."

"Like hell he will," Sumter cackled. "You accuse me of not reading the papers."

"All right," Gus sighed. "What do you know that we don't?"

"Can you foresee a time when there will not be trouble in the Middle East?" Mansour asked. "There will be no export permits."

Albert erupted in nervous laughter.

"Blame it on the government," Gus mused.

"The government abandons space," Sumter said. "Let it serve some useful purpose."

"But what about your brother? What about all those people expecting water?"

"I'm sure Mansour intends to make it up to him one way or another," Gus soothed.

"And if not, the sheikh and I are brothers."

"Half brothers," Albert amended.

"My brother sometimes forgets that he is only half Arab." Mansour smiled his sad smile. "I am all Arab."

Albert drew himself a cup of coffee and sat heavily. "I knew it was too good to last."

"Nothing is forever," Gus consoled. "But what else is bothering you?"

"Just getting old, I guess. Been near two weeks since anybody took a shot at me. I was starting to get used to it."

Gus turned to the wrinkled madman in the

wheelchair. "How do you manage return trips with that laser elevator?"

"Small chemical rockets—just enough to break orbit and start gliding down."

"How do you bring a few million tons of payload back from the asteroids?"

"Same way but your rockets have to be a little bigger. You can use SRBs. With the laser lifting them off you won't be burning up nine of them just to get the tenth into low orbit."

Gus remained unconvinced. So was Albert. But it was the only game in town. "I just hope you can keep your brother off us for three years," he said.

"By the way," Gus asked, "has your Mormon bishop found out why NASA can't spare us any more SRBs?"

Albert grinned. "Seems like ev'body's stockpiling boosters they won't need for two-three years yet. It's enough to make a man think somebody don't want us to get our work done on time."

"Or coincidence enough to make you think somebody knows," Gus growled. "Can't you do something?"

This time Albert laughed. "The board members of one comsat corporation spent a few hours searching their souls. They decided an antitrust investigation would be less expensive than their wives finding out what happened when the whole board went off est-ing last summer. We've got ten SRBs parked in orbit."

Gus turned to Mansour. "Your boy's holding up well enough, isn't he?"

"He comes down for a holiday every four or five weeks."

"And it'll be a year before the other two get a chance at anything like normal gravity."

"If they're alive. If I had my druthers I can think of plenty of people I'd've sent up first."

"They knew the odds," Gus snapped.

"Nobody's blaming you. Except yourself."

"Should've asked me," Sumter said.

They turned to stare at the ancient in the wheel-chair.

"Why not?" Sumter snapped. "Cut the legs off a suit and I'd make it as well as any bedroom athlete. In zero g I'll function better than a man who has to lift a pair of heavy and totally useless legs off Earth."

"Get your laser elevator working and I'll put your name on the list," Gus said.

"If the government gets wind of what we're up to we can all lift off. There won't be room for us on this planet."

"Such gloom," Mansour said. "Americans are supposed to be optimists."

"Yup. Albert, have you applied for those export permits?"

Albert nodded.

"Wouldn't hurt to plant something with the media about how we're hurting for money."

"What of our investors? You wish to frighten them away?"

"That wouldn't be half as embarrassing as it could be if some bureacrat just happened to stamp an "approved" on those permits."

"But surely nobody would—"

"Someday I'll compile you a list of the wars that could have been avoided if only people would read things before rushing off to a golf game."

"You know what worries me?" Albert asked. "It's been two weeks since anybody shot at us."

"You should be happy."

"Maybe. But if nobody's shooting then maybe somebody knows something."

"Like what?"

"Maybe we're already dead."

Haroun remembered how he had hated Europe when he followed Mansour into exile. Of all the wet, raw, blustery cities in which he had waited, vegetating in rented rooms, London had been the most dreary.

But now he was used to the weather, had improved his English, and if ever he felt nostalgia for the old ways, there were plenty of compatriots visiting or living here. London had acquired every amenity to be found in an Arab city—plus all the munkar and other delights not to be flaunted in Islam. He would not mind ending his days in his comfortable digs out in Ealing—close enough to Heathrow for any sudden scramble, yet less than an hour by tube to the City.

The only thing that annoyed him about the underground was that part of it was not. Each morning as he rode in to the Exchange he was forced to look upon those ferroconcrete turrets and crenellations. The British were so civilized about most things. Why couldn't they keep their prisons off somewhere out of sight? Or was Wormwood Scrubs intended to be a constant reminder?

In the months since he had initiated the coup that ended with Mansour and Gus recapturing Dampier Industries there had been little for Haroun to do. Mansour's eggs were now all in one basket and if he was determined to sink or swim with no thought of hedging his bets, there was little Haroun could do about it. Except worry.

Each day he studied the Floor and tried to see the hidden currents beneath all that antlike scurry. Each evening he prepared his report, written out in careful Arabic, then recast into an Arabic version of pig latin in which not just every word, but every syllable is repeated with an added consonant until *maktoub*, for example, of "it is written' transmogrifies into *mafaktoufoub*. After completing this exercise Haroun would transliterate the whole report into Roman characters for teletype transmission.

Somewhere in the Foreign Office a cryptographer was employed fulltime to render this daily report into English—which often used up ten minutes of his day to do what any Arab schoolboy could have done in five. The cryptographer had long since concluded that Haroun would never put any real information into this puerile code. It was just the broker's way to provide a government salary for a brother Arab.

But this evening in his Ealing digs Haroun labored over the report. Something odd was happening in the market. He still didn't know what, nor who was behind it. But any mechanic develops a feel for his engine. Haroun could sense the premonitory clanks and squeaks. But how does one put a feeling, an instinct, into a brief report to one's employer?

He put down his Bic and thought a moment. Then he picked up the phone and dialed. Was anybody tapping his line? It made no difference. Haroun was not involved in illegal activities. A woman answered, then a moment later he heard Yassir pick up the extension. "Did you feel it?" Haroun asked.

Yassir did not require lengthy explanations. Of course he had felt it. As well try to ignore the first rumble of an earthquake.

"Who?" Haroun asked.

"The accents were Lebanese."

Those Phoenician finks again! Even before Moses led his people out of Egypt, the European savages were already violent antiSemites, thanks to traveling salesmen with the ethics of crocodiles and the morals of tomcats. It was not enough that they tore their country and themselves apart over squabbles between Christian and Moslem, Israeli and PLO. With Beirut in ashes they still managed to freeze out the competition for Middle Eastern money—and this with banking procedures that elicited dyspeptic eructations of raw bacon and raw onion from the gnomes of Zürich. "Did you know any of them?" Haroun asked.

Yassir did not. "They sounded Lebanese," he repeated. There was an uncertainty in his tone. "But . . . do you believe in things like time travel?"

Haroun wondered if his aide was starting to crack from too long away from home. He struggled for a neutral tone. "Time travel?"

"They dressed well in the British fashion but their clothes were all new. And their speech— They had clean fingernails but they spoke like the peasants in my grandfather's tales of his war against Abdul the Damned."

"Ah?" A suspicion was growing in Haroun. "And did they also speak English?"

"Rather oddly. The locals seemed at times not to understand."

"I see." Haroun ran mechanically through

ritual inquiries about the health of family members and salaamed off the telephone. He crumpled the sheet on which he had been writing.

Several hours later the F.O. cryptographer deciphered Haroun's report without much interest. Most of the commentary could have been lifted from any financial page. There was a hint that some new lot of raiders was about to try what every beginner attempted sooner or later: 3rd GEN US-LEB IMMIGRANTS CAUSING INSTABILITY. SUGGEST INVESTIGATION YOUR END.

M'Meath had enjoyed it at first but after a while a wife's constant company can be something of a drag even if a man is not inclined toward extracurricular activity. Finally in desperation he had given her the slip long enough to put the company scrambler over the mouthpiece of a pay phone. Gus had not been available so he had to explain his problem to Albert. "I know she's a good shot but she's not bulletproof. Could you get the children home and give her something else to do with her time? I know you and I're supposed to be on the outs but there must be some way you can arrange security so it won't be obvious that the company's—"

"Only if you was to move out."

M'Meath sighed. He had been on the point of doing it once. Tina had put a stop to that. And saved his life while she was at it. "I tried," he said.

Albert laughed. "Miss Tina got a mind of her own."

A whim of iron was the way M'Meath would have put it. "But what'm I going to do?"

"Don't go home. I'll get the children back and

I'll explain what you're up to. Once she has time to think about it—''

M'Meath knew. There were not a hundred women on the planet would hesitate when it came to a choice between husband or children.

"You heard anything?"

M'Meath shook his head, then remembered it was not a picture phone. "Been visiting every day," he said. "Maybe without my ball and chain along that bastard'll open up."

But he didn't go that day because he probably would have run into Tina hunting him down. Instead, he waited until Gus and Albert had time to deliver the children and put some more security around the house.

"Where were you?" Averill asked next day when he came in with the usual flowers and radio. It was funny the way any radio he left with Philps Averill always seemed to have been tampered with the next time he went to turn it on in front of the squawk box. He had wondered for a time if it was Averill's ECPAD people or if there was a third party buried deep in the hospital staff. "Shaking my bodyguard," M'Meath said. "Now that we're alone, how're you feeling?"

"You couldn't ask me that in front of your wife?"

"I might ask it but could you answer?"

Averill shrugged as best he could with his leg in a cast suspended from pulleys. "Doesn't hurt any more. Lately I've been spitting out the sleeping pills."

"So who did it?"

"Really, M'Meath, I've not had much freedom of movement. I'd think you could've learned more by now."

"You must have some suspicions."

"Well, naturally any organization with as much clout as ECPAD makes a few enemies."

"Arab enemies?"

"They're taking a larger rôle in world affairs."

"But what have you done to them?"

"What have you done?" Averill countered. "They were shooting at you."

M'Meath managed to conceal his surprise. He had known. He hadn't known that Averill had figured it out. Or had he? Could he have known all the time? M'Meath tried to remember whose idea it had been to go to that park, that bench.

"Perhaps King Omar decided to tie the can on you for botching the delivery of those jet fighters."

"Haven't they been delivered yet?"

"You know how long it takes to get anything through Congress," Averill said.

"But everything was on rails when I last heard about it."

"That was when you were in charge. Surely you don't care if the company runs into a few of the usual snags now that you're out on the street."

"I guess not." M'Meath didn't want to overdo the righteous indignation bit.

"See the paper this morning?"

M'Meath had been too preoccupied with finding a hole where he would be safe from Tina. He picked up the paper that had fallen from the bed. The headlines were about another sex murder.

"Here." Averill pointed at the lower corner of the page.

ISRAELI ENVOY RAPS SALE OF FISSIONABLES TO ARABS

"What do you think of them apples?" Averill asked in precise Ivy League tones.

"I'd be just as happy if nobody ever invented the damned things," M'Meath snapped. "Given a second choice, I'd have them all safe at home and the rest of the world slinging plowshares."

"Keep reading."

M'Meath did—right on down until he learned who was handling the sale and applying for export permits. "Jaysus, Mary, and Joseph!" he muttered.

"Not exactly my phrasing," Averill said, "but my sentiments."

"It'll never go through," M'Meath prophesied. "I wonder whatever made him think he could get away with it."

"Indeed," Averill said thoughtfully. "His enemies have accused Gus Dampier of many crimes, but to the best of my knowledge nobody has ever called him stupid."

There was a thoughtful silence. "Obviously, Mr. Dampier has something totally different on his mind," Averill said. "Be interesting to speculate on what it might be."

Abruptly M'Meath remembered that he had come here to pump Averill, and not the other way around. "I'll see what I can find out," he said, and made his escape before this slick bastard could worm any more information from him.

But as he walked down the hall and out of the hospital M'Meath's calm returned. What could Averill have learned from him? He didn't know what was going on. But he knew that he had somehow been maneuvered, that Averill had won this round. It was not the first time in his life that M'Meath sensed the limitations of his cleverness. But what could he do about it? One thing he could do, he finally decided, was not make a beeline to the nearest phone booth.

There was something odd about the car. He was halfway in the seat and stabbing a key when suddenly he sensed it. Hastily, M'Meath scooted out. When the car didn't blow him into orbit he studied it from a distance. Finally he peeled off his jacket and wormed his way beneath the chasis. Caked mud from last winter's rain was undisturbed. He dirtied hands and sleeves feeling around behind tires and found nothing.

He screwed up his courage and raised the hood. Still alive. He wasn't much of a mechanic but he could see no obvious signs of tampering. The light coating of oily grime lay undisturbed. Imagining things, he decided. He forced himself back into the car. Before he could change his mind he stabbed the key into the ignition and twisted it. The car started. He was still alive.

He drove carefully back toward the room he had rented, wondering if he shouldn't have copped out and gone back to meat packing after all. A man could only take so much of this. What was old Gus up to? There had to be something not quite kosher about those zero g metallurgical experiments he'd tried to put a stop to during his brief tenancy in the old man's office. Was the old man making bombs? There had been purchase orders for enough SRBs to lift half of Southern California into low orbit. Suddenly M'Meath found himself wondering if he had ever mentioned any of this to Philps Averill. That smooth spalpeen could have wormed it out of him without M'Meath even knowing he was being pumped.

He sighed and thanked his saint that he really

didn't know what old Gus was up to. If he knew,
M'Meath knew he would blow it as well as himself if ever the enemy should learn he was in
secret communication with Gus and Albert.
Funny how in all the years he'd been with the
company he'd never really noticed how large a
rôle Albert played. But it had been the old black
man who brought the guns, took the children
away, was taking care of Tina now.

The car was running just as always. Was it
bugged? Hardly necessary. If they wanted to
know where he was hiding they had more resources than his wife. They could follow him.
Superstitious mick, he told himself. But even superstitious Irishmen are sometimes right. Jesus,
Mary, and Joseph! He had not even looked in the
trunk!

He drove another two blocks before he found a
place to park. When he found one he considered
just abandoning the car and renting another. But
born poor is always poor. M'Meath shuddered at
the expense. He got out and gingerly opened the
deck lid. When nothing happened he studied the
jack and spare tire, the half bag of charcoal that
had lain there for a year, the long outdated confidential report he had never gotten around to reading.

"I'm not made for this kind of life," he muttered, and slammed the deck lid. He got back in,
disappointing an old man in a porch rocker who
had been preparing to evaluate M'Meath's tire
changing skills. He was nosing out of the parking
space when abruptly M'Meath knew what had
been bothering him. He crunched into reverse and

craned his neck into the back seat as the car tried to climb the curb.

May the Almighty and merciful Lord grant me pardon, absolution, and remission of all my sins! He had put it on the back seat. Should have hidden it. But damn it, he had locked the car! It had still been locked when he came out of the hospital. Not that it made any difference now. The scrambler was gone.

There was a mom and pop grocery store on the corner. Several youths lounged in front of the phone. He locked the car and walked toward them. The boys studied him speculatively, not offering to step aside from the phone. M'Meath hunched and let his jacket gape just enough to show the butt of the pistol. The phone was his. *Exactly what I was not going to do,* he reminded himself as he dialed the private number.

He would keep it brief, not identify himself or divulge any more than necessary over an open line. "Security breached," M'Meath said. "Scrambler in enemy possession."

"All right, Francis," Gus said tiredly. "I'll take care of it. I don't suppose you'd happen to have another?"

"This is an open line!"

"It's time we had a talk anyhow. Where can we meet?"

If the old fool was going to broadcast his name, what difference did it make? "Company cafeteria?"

"Send word when you're there."

M'Meath hung up and walked back to the car. He might not be smart but he knew he was no longer undercover. It took him a while to realize what Gus must have seen right off—that if somebody knew enough to steal a scrambler from his car, there was little point in playing gumshoe games.

Gus sat, barricaded from the world by Miss Jepworth's angular efficiency. He was struggling for just the right tone of gentlemanly anguish in a publicity release which dealt with the way Dampier Industries paid exorbitant taxes, boosted the economy, improved the balance of payments, had never once been bailed out of incompetence by the government, nor caught with its hand in the till—in return for which Dampier had been unfailingly pushed aside for aerospace contracts. Albert walked in.

He glanced over Gus's shoulder and smiled. "Laying the groundwork?"

Gus nodded and continued writing.

"I wonder how much time we have before you have to go back and testify."

Gus put down his pen. "Well, thank god we're not doing Mr. Bones this morning," he said. "The Israelis are screaming. In a few days the whole damned Third World will be on one side or the other, depending on whether they hope to get nuclear arms too. The papers haven't really tuned up yet here. The Swedes still aren't bleeding their hearts out. I'd say we have five or six weeks before we get investigated."

Albert chuckled. "And then you pour on the charm."

"Like hell I will! I'm going to come over like the fruit of an unnatural union between Ronald Regan and Howard Jarvis."

"We might's well bring Mansour's boy back down. No use of Jeff gettin' cooked or whatever happened to the others." Albert sighed. "Always had some hopes for that Army."

Gus remembered the girl. It wasn't as if Sin hadn't known the dangers. Still, he had talked her into it. Now she would never do the things that lithe body was built for. He winced at the memory of how she had accused him of wanting to make blue movies.

Mansour burst into the office several steps ahead of Miss Jepworth's announcement. "You have seen the news?" he demanded.

Gus shook his head. Albert went to the wall and opened a panel so he could backtrack the recorder.

"They granted our export permits!" Mansour blurted.

Army had shrunk an inch and gained it around his waist, which made his space suit fit better. He had been working incessantly since linking up with Sin. The ship now swung from a cradle that put the decks down for a change. And he had stopped spin long enough to attach graphite strapping, then reinforce it with every bit of nylon parachute shroud he had been able to splice and braid. The trick was to make the nylon reinforcements exactly 12% shorter than the graphite so they would stretch to their maximum and share the strain. Now they spun on a longer arc and the coriolis effect was not so nauseating nor did they have to allow such fantastic Kentucky windage when pouring. Gravity was up to 25%.

Sin was still delicate but her recovery had been

faster than he dared hope. Her arm was splinted but she handled routine chores inside, kept track of their scanning equipment, even had a hot meal of sorts ready whenever Army came staggering back in through the airlock after a hard day of cannibalizing.

First, he had gotten Sin's solar panels over to his orbiter and attached them opposite his own. Now, even with the inverse square law working against them at this distance from the sun he did not have to spend so many hours pumping up batteries. He spent them transferring SRBs, food, air, everything usable from Sin's ship to his.

Until he had everything on this end of the tether he could not relax. If that hybrid graphite-nylon cable were to snap and send half of everything spinning off at an unpredictable tangent. . . . And this tangent would be impossibly expensive to intercept since they were spinning at right angles to the ecliptic. Dangerous, but it gave the solar collectors more exposure and gave Sin a better view of what was coming up while he was out there dodging meteorites.

So far they had not been forced to alter course. To do so promised to be several times more complicated than to move a single orbiter.

Army worked himself into a stupor. Had to if they were to have any margin of safety. But even if there weren't so much to do he would have spent most of his time outside in an orbital, asteroidal equivalent of the cold shower.

Sin was looking better each day. He had hoped familiarity might breed contempt but it did not. He had bathed her, carried her to the pottie, cleaned up after her. And still his whole being yearned and burned for carnal knowledge of that reviving flesh.

They were holed again. This time he interrupted work long enough to get her suited up, then replace that patched thermal pane as well as fixing the second hole. "So what on Earth's this?" Sin asked when they had air in the cabin again.

"We're not on Earth," Army grunted. It was another polished, slightly brownish metal sphere. He fished around and the first one was still in his pocket. "While you're resting maybe you could run a spectrogram and tell me just what these things are."

"That polish must've come from some kind of machinery."

"Little green men?" He suited up and went out to lash up another netful of supplies. At ¼ g he couldn't move the prodigious loads he had been used to kicking around. It was a weird feeling to pull himself across the tether between their ships, climbing up out of a gradually diminishing gravity past the null point, then sliding downhill into growing g forces as he reached the other end. And each time he transferred cannibalized parts from Sin's orbiter the axial null shifted closer to his own ship.

"It's manganese and iron with something else to harden it," she said when he came back in for a bottle of air.

"Seems to be a lot of it out there. You suppose the company could use it?"

"In another ten years the only exploitable ores left will be in Gabon and someplace I can't remember in South America. The steel makers are starting to worry."

"What about sea floor mining?"

"That," Sin agreed, "is the joker. They're extracting trace metals from those nodules and dumping the manganese back into the ocean just to keep the price from collapsing."

Army shrugged. "Nice to have simple, clearcut choices. I just hope there is a company when we get back."

"But it still looks manufactured." She wore the same one-piece jumpsuit that Army wore whenever he was not rigged for going outside. On Sin it bulged in all the proper places. He looked away and hurried through changing his air bottle.

"How much longer before we get home?" she asked.

"Search me." He dogged down his helmet and pointed at the CRT while heading for the airlock. The shuttles were still spinning at right angles to the ecliptic but they had orbited around until the flat-side aspect of their spin no longer faced squarely toward the distant sun. One set of collectors was occulting for part of each revolution. Which meant he was going to have to maneuver the ships around and, thanks to immutable Newtonian laws the damned orbiters were going to precess and—he wondered if he could find time to set up some kind of program. Could it all be done from one ship or would he have to go to hers and/or string wire to fire both ships' verniers at once? Still had to get a couple of SRBs from her ship to his. There was no way he could winch 600 tons across, even if he was only fighting ¼ of a g.

Sin was much improved now—even vivacious at times. Could she stand a few days of zero g while he finished transferring everything? That way there would be fewer problems starting up the spin again at a new sun-facing angle. Why had she asked how many days till home? Feeling well enough to be sick of his company? Anyhow, she could have been less obvious and asked the computer. Why did she have to bulge so enticingly? Maybe he ought to make her stay in a spacesuit. After all, they had been holed twice. To keep the girl suited up might save her life. It could save some of the constant strain on Army's bulbus cavernosus. What had he come out here to do?

Nothing, damn it! He had done everything that could be done until he killed spin and got those SRBs across. He was hiding. They still had several months together. He couldn't spend all his time out here soaking up radiation. What was he going to do?

He had dithered away half a bottle of air without doing anything. It was wasteful to be continually exhaling half-used air when he could just as well be inside breathing into the absorbers and recirculators. But the orbiter was small for one person. How long could he face the bulkhead without the girl beginning to wonder if he'd been too long in space? "*What the hell you doin' here, boy?*"

Army jerked out of his reverie. His suit radio was on, now that there was somebody in the ship. But that masculine growl was not Sin's. It was the voice of the solar tracker, which he could not even hear out here in vacuo. Jesus! He had been in space too long. He locked back in and took off his helmet. "You know," he began, "we've been holed twice and it looks like there may be more of those ball bearings around. Don't you think you ought to stay in your suit and keep your helmet handy?"

"One hundred eighty-six days," Sin said.

"What?"

"We've got that much more time together."

"So?" Army was instantly defensive.

"If I ever get this splint off we could separate. Cover twice as much ground that way."

"You'd just start coming apart again."

"Not if I keep some g on me to hold that calcium in place. Why not fasten onto a rock instead of counterbalancing each other?"

Only seconds ago Army had prayed to be free of constant temptation. Now he was pleading lack of cable, all the time to refit her ship with solar panels again—

Sin smiled a secret little smile. "Actually, I was thinking about supplies."

"Plenty of food—if you call it that. Enough air and water too. But I used over half my rockets getting here."

"So we're stuck with each other. What kind of g will we face getting home—after we cut my ship loose?"

She knew the answer as well as he did. "Not over half a g," Army said. "And from low orbit down to the ground, NASA shuttles are just like landing an airplane."

"Funny about those supplies," Sin mused. "I thought old Gus had covered everything but there's one thing he forgot."

If she says hair straightener I'll kill her.

"That's why I've been counting the days," she continued.

Army looked around desperately but there was nobody else to play straight man. How was he ever going to survive all those months trying not to look at—?

"Of course Gus had it worked out so that I'd never be left alone with either of you. He didn't think it necessary. Or maybe the medical staff thought I'd have enough metabolic glitches without the Pill."

Army was hallucinating. She had to be saying something totally different. "Must be the pressure differential," he lied. "My ears popped when I unsuited."

Sin gave him a crooked grin. "You're hearing me. Do you think I want to spend a hundred eighty-six days with a man who'll end up trying to kill me or himself?"

"Should have let Albert send me to the Joint," Army muttered. "I wouldn't've ended up any loonier."

"I've been up longer than you."

Army began to believe he was really hearing her. "Never work out," he began. "We're too different."

"Who cares about working out? We're together in this sardine can. Six months is about 69% of the way through a normal fullterm, so, even assuming bullseye on the first try, why not relieve some of the worst of the tension?" She began sliding the zipper down the front of her jumpsuit. Like Army, she wore nothing underneath.

This was really happening! Suddenly Army's perpetual rut crescendoed until his ears were ringing. His whole body was ringing.

It was the goddamn alarm bell that was ringing!

"Was it for the jet fighters or the nuclear plant?" Gus asked.

"Congress has granted export permits for both!" Mansour wailed.

"Oh mother!" Albert chorused.

"How can your Congress do a thing like that?"

"Next time, make sure it's an election year," Albert said.

"Some would be understandable," Mansour said. "But a majority? There is, after all, a strong Zionist lobby."

"What was the vote?"

"Almost unanimous."

"We have the best government money can buy," Gus said. He crumpled the press release he had been writing. "So what do we do now?"

"When that stuff doesn't come through Omar's going to kill you."

"Me or Mansour?"

"All of us. 'Ceptin' me. I jus' drives de car 'roun' here."

The intercom buzzed. "Mr. M'Meath sends word that he's waiting in the cafeteria." It was obvious that Miss Jepworth didn't care how long M'Meath cooled his heels.

"What's he doing here?"

"I'd forgotten. The nincompoop managed to lose a scrambler. Now we'll have to change all the codes again."

"But what's he doing here?"

"It was the only thing stolen from his locked car while he was visiting that other nincompoop who managed to get himself shot."

"Who?"

"How should I know? Ebberly, Avery, something or other. You two geniuses see if you can find a way to save the company while I go see if I can save my son-in-law. I try to believe he thought he was saving me." Before they could offer more comment Gus strode out of the office.

M'Meath sat sipping heavily creamed coffee at a corner table. Company brass avoided him like some new species of biological warfare. There was sudden dead silence when Gus entered the room. When he went straight to M'Meath's table the silence lasted another half beat. Then suddenly everybody was discussing baseball scores.

"I screwed up," M'Meath opened.

"Oh come on, nothing's that bad. Anyway, how did you screw up?"

"Left it in sight in the back seat."

"Was the car locked again when you came back?"

M'Meath nodded.

"Then somebody was onto us already. The question is, who?"

"I've been wondering . . . what was the point?"

Gus was startled. It was a good question. Why steal a scrambler if its loss would merely alert the company to change all the codes? It would have made more sense to gut the thing with an electronic profiler and leave it there for the unsuspecting. But . . . everybody knew computers could unscramble a handheld cuisinart so no real information ever . . . Gus was about to ask how many people knew when he realized anyone could assume that M'Meath might have kept a few pieces of company equipment to accompany him on his fall from grace. "How're things at home?"

"OK, I guess. I might as well go back now."

Gus had been married long enough to realize

that even the best of marriages can founder when
an unemployed husband spends a week under-
foot. "We'll have to find something for you to do."

"Like what?"

At least M'Meath understood the problem. Gus
managed not to look at his watch. He wanted to
get back upstairs and see if Albert and Mansour
had any ideas on how to keep the world from
coming to an end. But this poor dumb bastard
was family. M'Meath seemed to have some so-
cially redeeming qualities for Tina and the children. What was he going to do with him? He
remembered Albert's question and used it to fill
an awkward silence. "What's the name of that
fellow whose life you saved?"

"Averill."

The name meant nothing. "With Nader's Raiders?"

"They prefer to call it the Environmental and
Consumers' Protection Administration."

"Oh yes, ECPAD."

"Economic Chaos, Panic, and Despair."
M'Meath was struggling too. They managed
smiles which were duly noted at other tables.

"What were they trying to get out of you?"

M'Meath shrugged. "They wanted me to turn
you."

"Me?" Gus knew what he meant. He just
wanted to hear M'Meath's interpretation.

"You'd been passed over dozens of times on
contracts because you weren't one of the Good
Old Boys. ECPAD thought you might be mad
enough to help put some of them behind bars."

"Why couldn't they have just asked me?"

M'Meath shrugged. "I didn't take them seriously until they hung up the sale of those jets and then unhung it within half an hour."

Gus raised his eyebrows but his mind was not really on it. What was going on upstairs? Had Albert and Mansour taken up skydiving? The jet fighters were no problem. Fill the extra tanks and ferry pilots could nonstop them straight to Omar. But a nuclear desalination plant? Even if Mansour had the money, how could they possibly jawbone two of them? "Uh, sorry. Think I need a new battery in this damned thing."

"I said it's a matter of public record that you put one batch of scoundrels behind bars."

"That was a long time ago."

"Twenty-five years this month."

Gus sighed. Did everybody have to remind him how time was getting away? M'Meath had done his homework. How could a brain so handy with facts and figures be so lacking in judgment? He remembered how he had written "overqualified" on that application. There had to be some place where M'Meath could feel useful and still not be a danger to company survival. What to do with him?

What about that export permit? It would be explainable if peace had broken out but . . . if he lived Gus was going to dedicate himself to ending some Congressional careers. Take his last million and run for Congress just so he could publicly rub their noses in it. Crooked sons of bitches!

"Philps said you never really seemed to care until they gutted the pension fund."

"Philps?"

"Philps Averill.

"Oh." Gus's coffee was cold and forgotten. Why

was he futzing around here when everything was coming apart? Get rid of M'Meath and get back upstairs—figure out what they were going to do.

"—smart."

"What?"

"I go there to pump him and end up getting nothing."

Gus had a sudden inspiration. "Seen the news today?"

M'Meath had been much too busy.

"Our troubles are over," Gus exulted. "ECPAD can go picnic on an anthill."

"I don't understand."

"Congress either saw the red light or handled the green. We got our export permits. Without them we'd've been in bad shape. Now there's nothing anyone can do to us."

"You sure?"

"Don't go crowing to your friend in hospital about it." Gus was on his feet, clapping M'Meath on the shoulder and promising lunch next week before his son-in-law quite realized the interview was over. They left the cafeteria together but as Gus went up the executive elevator M'Meath went out the back door and home toward a waiting Tina.

Albert was behind Gus's desk talking earnestly into one phone while Mansour spoke Arabic into another. Albert had shed his plantation dialect and was talking—well I'll be damned, Gus thought. Wonder how many times he's imitated me over the phone. Mansour salaamed and hung up. At that moment Albert broke off too. "So how's it going?" Gus asked.

"Bargain day at the Wailing Wall," Albert said.

"Now fear the fire the unbeliever saith is not," Mansour quoted.

Gus explained what misinformation he had attempted to plant through M'Meath. "Too late, I suppose. But we've got to give it the old college try."

Gloom hung undiluted. "By the way, Albert, does Philps ring a bell?"

"Who's Philps?"

"Philps who," Gus corrected. "His last name's Averill."

"Course it rings a bell," Albert snapped. "I got to make some more calls."

"That's the name of the ECPAD agent my son-in-law's been visiting in the hospital."

"But he's young—" Albert hesitated.

Mansour interrupted his dialing. "What is it?"

"Arabs are not the only ones blessed with family problems," Gus said.

"He is related to you?"

"Twenty-five years ago there was a Mr. Philps among those who bankrupted me. I put them all in prison. Now that I reflect upon it, there was also an Averill among those thieves."

"Sure is touching the way old money sticks together."

"At least it's nice to know who's been sharpening the shaft."

"Little late for that," Albert said.

"Would it have made a difference had you known earlier?" Mansour asked.

"Probably not. Now what are we going to do?"

"Just stay away from open windows."

"Who've you been calling?"

"News media."

Gus pondered a moment. "Wouldn't you be more at home twisting politicians' arms? Mansour and I can handle the media."

"Suits me," Albert said. "Got to get back to my own office anyhow." He scooted out of Gus's chair.

Even as Gus began preparing the statement he knew it would be of little use. There was no way he could argue openly against the export permits his own company had applied for. And using fronts—The Jewish lobby would need no encouragement to scream over what Congress had done. But the more he thought about it, the more Gus understood that for someone to pull the rug from under him in this particular fashion meant that somebody had detailed knowledge of what he was up to. But if somebody knew he had a couple of pilots unreported in the asteroids, why sour their chances for reelection by giving nuclear arms to some tinpot dictator? He was going down the spout without any help. Perhaps it was just a fishing expedition to see how he and the company would react.

Haroun was nervous. It was a brilliant sunny day, which was not that unusual now that London was warmed with North Sea gas instead of coal. But Haroun's mood was wintery with foreboding. Those third-generation US-Lebanese spoke fluent American but their Arabic was the same peasant dialect their grandfathers had exported from the Ottoman Empire to the steel mills of Cleveland. They fooled no Arab; but no Arab seemed to care, save Haroun. The British were thoroughly bedazzled at the prospect of still more petrodollars converted into pounds sterling. Perhaps they knew too. But what was morality when it came to pumping a few pence back into the pound?

As near as Haroun could make it out, somebody was gunning for Mansour—personally. Why else would they concentrate on buying up every stray share of Dampier? Already the stock had inflated well beyond any real value. Were they planning on dumping all their acquisitions at once? There were so many ways to pull the rug from under the company. He had warned Mansour in his coded nightly cables. There had been no reply.

At the next table from where Haroun lunched alone, an elderly man in native dress was belching loudly after each mouthful of roast lamb and cold eggplant. It had taken Haroun some time to discover that Arab good manners were considered offensive in this country. He considered warning the old man, then common sense told him to mind his own business. He went back to the financial page. The news was always forty-eight hours out of date but he knew the government often used that section to drop hints for those who take an interest in such things.

SMALLHOLDERS DEMAND PROBE OF RIGGING IN DAMPIER SHARES

So that was how those sons of camel turds were going about it!

Haroun gulped coffee and signaled for his check. He wondered if he ought to wait till evening and transmit this in his nightly report. By then, if he was paying attention, Mansour would have learned about it from other sources—which would not be the best possible recommendation for continuing Haroun's comfortable stipend. But should he risk making more waves with a transatlantic call that was sure to be overheard?

He took a quick look in on the floor and sure enough, those Phoenician finks were still pussyfooting around after the odd share of Dampier that cropped up from time to time. They couldn't possibly get control, or even much leverage. But one share gave any troublemaker the right to demand an investigation. Haroun reminded himself that he had done nothing illegal. But once governments started meddling they could make up their own and retroactive rules.

Had Mansour been reading his reports? Probably busy with other things. Haroun decided it was time for a holiday. He would visit Beverly Hills, see Palm Springs. They were supposed to be just like home—even to the same all pervading stench of petroleum. Perhaps Mansour would do something once he had heard Haroun out and realized these finks were more than a minor nuisance. He averted his eyes from the ferroconcrete crenellations of Wormwood Scrubs on the ride back to Ealing.

His bag was packed and he was checking his passport when the phone gave its British double ring. A woman was speaking rapidly, frantically. It took him a moment to discover that it was one of the women in Yassir's household. Haroun made the nonsense sounds one uses to calm women or horses. Finally he discovered what had happened. "They took him away? Were they uniformed police?"

It seemed that they were not. Yassir had known the bowler-hatted pair of Englishmen who called. He had told her not to be nervous, that it was just a routine inquiry. But that had been nearly seven hours ago and still she had not heard from Yassir.

"You have money to tide you over?"

Money was not the problem. What was going to happen to Yassir?

Haroun didn't know. But one does not tell hysterical women that. He spoke more reassuring nonsense while wondering what he could do. The women and children would be all right. As for Yassir—he had enough money to bail himself out if the British were to decide it was a bailable offense. And that would depend on who promised to inject or extract how many ounces of gold from the national economy. Finally he had managed to calm her and get off the phone.

Alone in his lodgings, Haroun's eyes drifted from his passport to the dead phone. Finally, thoughtfully, he opened the trimming attachment on his shaver and removed his mustache. Then he got his other, the Brazilian passport.

On the way out he passed his landlady who gave him an odd look but did not realize what was strange about his appearance. Nobody paid any attention on the Underground. He picked up an abandoned paper and searched the financial page. Nothing new.

Why so nervous? He had done nothing illegal. But neither had poor Yassir. Were they even now pounding on him with rubber truncheons, beating him over both ears with majestic British impartiality?

Haroun got in line at the ticket counter. In the Name of the Merciful and Compassionate, would that silly old sod never stop quibbling over the difference between tourist and first class? How

much time did he have before the next flight?
Could he possibly make it? Finally the line was
moving again.

Every tourist wants to go somewhere exotic and
different—but not too different. Since the dollars
started gushing out of Arab ground, there has
been a growing influx of the Faithful who wish to
see Hollywood, Beverly Hills, Palm Springs—all
the holy places familiar on film. Foreign Office
employees are no exception. The young man who
spent ten minutes a day translating Haroun's
nightly pig latin reports had put in the rest of his
day writing for Arab periodicals, had lived frug-
ally, and now even he could afford one of Sir
Freddy's no frills flights.

He had arrived with an hour to spare and
moped about kicking his bag along the terrazzo
from one boutique to the next. Then he saw a man
he thought he recognized. He was about to accost
Haroun when he hesitated. The man whose picture he connected with those nightly messages
had a mustache. But times and styles change.

It *was* Haroun. This was the man who had
singlehandedly created a job and a government
salary for a brother Arab. He knew from his reading that Haroun was no prude. The least he could
do was introduce himself, thank Haroun for his
joke on the British, invite him to the bar for a glass
of *munkar*.

He gave his bag a glance, decided it would be
safe for the dozen steps it would take him to catch
up with Haroun. "Sir, sir, are you Haroun ibn—?"
He would have spoken Arabic but if the man were
to turn out to be English . . .

Haroun spun wildly, saw the young man walking toward him, and knew someone besides his landlady had seen past a mustache. He dropped his bag and sprinted for the barrier. If he could just get on that plane and into the air before—He was still stampeding headlong out of the building and across the tarmac when a tractor and a string of baggage trucks changed his plans.

The translator remained inside the terminal, wondering if he had accosted some madman or fugitive terrorist by mistake. He stepped gingerly around the bag Haroun had flung at him, then he heard his flight being called. He picked up his own bag and trudged toward his boarding ramp. Three weeks later he learned about the accident. It seemed that the Foreign Office would not be needing his services any more. Two weeks prior to that Yassir had been released only to step in front of a lorryful of carpets on his way home. The Turkish driver had been adjudged not at fault.

Still hanging half out of her jumpsuit, Sin jostled with Army to look at the scope. The alarm was still chirring. Something big was coming up. It was on their path and the velocities were not too different. They could get out and look it over.

Of all the motherless times! Army gritted his teeth and plotted ways to revenge himself on the universe. Sin was punching numbers. She smiled. "We've got an hour. No reason why we can't wear you down to a comfortable fit in a spacesuit by then."

He had quite forgotten that it was supposed to be fun, that people could actually laugh about it. "I've been having a fit ever since you came aboard," he said. But now, with relief in sight, Army suddenly saw something else. "We'll have to wait. Get into your suit quick!"

"What is it?"

"That thing out there's a binary. Any two rocks heavy enough to orbit around each other that fast are going to have one ungodly cloud of gravel around them!" There was a clang as the first grain of sand struck.

Albert had been using various voices and dialects over the phone for several hours as he pointed out to representatives and senators that there was always the possibility, however remote, that voters would someday rebel against the blatant venality of those who offered one bill of goods and immediately sold another. "And there might be enough money floating around," he warned, "for all those soreheads out there to buy some prime TV time. Where would this country be if some real third party came along to dump all you cozy Reps and Dems down the same spout?"

They had all been polite. Politicians are. But they had all politely pointed out that few soreheads have the kind of money it takes to buy prime time. Albert knew they must get dozens of such calls every day: angry voices from Israeli, Moslem, Ecologist, Flat Earther. . . . Without some visible clout he was spinning his wheels. That export permit had been applied for; it had been granted. There was no way he dared any direct complaint now about lack of government cooperation.

He was an old man; tired. But there were times when he was still shaken by a toothgrinding impotent fury. Wreck the government? He had often been tempted. But who would ship the dog food to Watts and Harlem then? He wanted those people off welfare but first there had to be some other way for them to live. He turned off the automatic dialer and leaned back in his chair. How to stall King Omar now?

Mansour was busy creating some randygazoo about design failures and leakage: technical problems that would hold up delivery for a few weeks. But a few weeks were not enough. There had been a couple of possibles in the data Albert had analyzed before Sin stopped transmitting any more. If Jeff could get out there with a million SRBs (but that would take several multiples of a million just to get them in orbit) perhaps they could blast a chunk of metal down.

When they had started this project Albert had thought that was all it took. Only later had he learned that hundred ton meteorites hit Earth on an average of one per day. The thing was, stony meteorites shattered and burned to dust long before they neared the heavy bottom of the atmosphere. It was only the occasional million-ton chunk of iron that managed to leave a track and even that was more often a footprint than a crater.

The million ton Tunguska meteorite had gotten closer to home—only 6 kilometers up when finally it had disintegrated with a flash that scorched witnesses' clothes standing 60 kilometers from ground zero. Thousands of square miles of trees had fallen inward but there was no crater. So it was not enough just to send an asteroid home. It had to come in slow enough not to vaporize itself and whoever was underneath.

Albert left it to the engineers to decide whether

a meteor could be slowed with drogue chutes or rockets. Maybe it would be better to cut it up out in orbit, and send down manageable chunks via shuttle. If only they had a shuttle new enough to stand full g.

Where could he option enough cheap land to keep some opportunist or a cutthroat government from trying to claim whatever landed as a natural disaster—or any of the hundred other ways they could tax or legislate Dampier's legitimate profits out of existence? If only he dared wreck the government. But it would be like cutting off his own head. Any way he looked at it, Albert knew he was whistling Dixie.

If Jeff survived the trip—if they had any kind of propulsion for a real payload—it would still take months for him to get there, more months to prepare an asteroid for moving, and who could say how long for it to get here? It made no difference. Dampier would be discredited, bankrupt long before . . .

Why had he wasted a morning on politicians? Should have known they would never honor an obligation. Not to Dampier, not to God, not to Country. Albert couldn't save the company. But there was one thing he could do. He called Harlem. He called Watts. Then he called the biggest ghetto of them all. Some people around Washington were going to have a brand new servant problem.

It didn't make his tired old feet feel any better. He swung them up on the desk. That old madman in the wheelchair had the right idea. Full gravity was just too much for old bones. But Albert knew that was all just blue-sky someday talk. He was old right now. How many years before space was comfortable or even endurable? Poor skinny black Army must be dead by now. Girl too. He was sorry for her but not so much. At least she'd had her shot at the best of everything when she was alive.

How would Gus take this new setback? He had begun to wonder if he would ever pump any gumption back into the old goat after M'Meath's takeover. What about Miss Tina? Would there be any company left for her bungling husband to ruin? Should have kept Army down here and groomed him to take over. Nothing wrong with the brains in that gangling body. All he needed was a push in the right direction. Why had they gone and turned him into a mule jack? The phone buzzed. He answered with Gus's voice.

"Salvation!" Dr. Sumter crowed.

"Say again."

"You should have told me how much the company had riding on those three rockets."

"We did." Albert had started with Gus's voice. Now he was stuck with it.

"What could you do with a hundred meter sphere of solid iron?"

So Sumter had been thinking about it too. "Wreck the global economy if we didn't handle it right. That's 1/25th of world production the last year we went all out dumping stuff in Vietnam."

"Don't go away. I'm coming up."

By the time the old man had gotten his wheelchair upstairs Gus and Mansour were in the same office. And by then Albert had already guessed the only possible way they could move that much metal without a laser elevator. "You can't blow it home with nuclear fuel," he said. "No country would stand for that. We got 'nuff pollution now.''

"The explosions will be out in the asteroid belt. That's so far beyond Mars that nothing could possibly drift toward Earth even if it wasn't bucking a constant solar wind.''

"I suppose you've done the numbers for all this?" Gus asked.

"Naturally.''

"And you realize that if you set off a nuke to blow that iron into an Earth-intersecting orbit it's going to be radioactive even unto the tenth generation?''

"Oh ye of little faith," Sumter cackled. "You plant the bomb on one side. That side will soak up a little radiation. But when it's time to land, that side comes in first. You burn the first few feet off and the rest of the metal is clean.''

"Feces," Albert said. "You just scatter radiation all over Earth 'stead of concentrating it in one spot.''

"Don't forget the solar wind. A little fine tuning on entry and we can skip it in and out of the upper atmosphere a dozen times before it takes the plunge. Ninety-nine percent of the crap heads for Pluto. The rest isn't normal leakage from one reactor.''

"Assuming you can convince the environmentalists—" Gus began.

"Must we tell everyone our business?" Mansour asked. "Does anyone even know that we explore the asteroids?''

"No need for Nader's Nitpickers to know anything," Sumter said. "What they don't look for they'll probably not find.''

"Sure," Gus said heavily. "What other state-of-the-art could move that kind of tonnage?''

"You're the con man," Sumter snapped. "Cook up something about manifest destiny: the god-given orbit so close to perfect that all it needed was a few newtons of nudge."

"That might solve one problem," Albert said. "But how do we get fissionables in orbit without NASA coming down on us like a ton of tormented tomcats?"

"Personal luggage," Sumter said.

"A whole goddam desalination plant?"

"The plant can rust in peace. All we need is a few kilos of U-235 and some triggers."

"I wonder." Gus turned to Mansour. "Your boy's holding up well enough, isn't he?"

"But he comes down for a holiday every few weeks."

They were silent, remembering how long since any word had come from Army or Sin. "Got to be soon," Gus said.

"I know. My brother has already heard all the stories in the Thousand Nights and a Night."

"Not just that. It's launch windows. Do it within a couple of weeks or else we wait years for everything to line up right again."

"I must go call my brother." Mansour left.

A phone buzzed. Albert picked it up.

"Mr. Dampier?"

"Yes," Albert said.

"You wanted a firsthand look at any data Jeff sent down."

Albert nodded, then remembered the video was off. Playing Gus, he reminded himself. And this time Gus was watching and listening.

The engineer's face was worried. "Suddenly sent a big indigestible mess. It may take us weeks to process."

"That's all right. Just copy it and send me up some floppys." They were still wrangling about how to get fissionables into the asteroid belt when, fifteen minutes later, Albert heard the hiss-thunk of a cartridge arriving in his pneumatic tube. He unrolled the disc and put it in the machine, then punched the code that would sort the tiny bit of signal he wanted out of all those machine code squeaks, clacks, and howls. "Be damned," he muttered. "I thought Mansour said the boy hadn't even been raised Moslem."

Jeff-Jarfi was quoting *suras* from *Ul Quar'ân,* which is sometimes westernized as Koran. The quotations were nonsense.

Albert punched up the original Chapter of the Spoils, first revealed at Yathreb, as it was called before the Prophet's stay gave the town such prominence that it came to be known simply as *El Medîna*—The City.

Jeff was quoting out of context: *Taste now the torment for ye that misbelieved.* Albert wondered how much the boy knew about the inner workings of the company. Must hear some news up there in medium orbit. . . . *Verily, God is with the patient. If there be among you twenty patient men they will conquer two hundred. Eat of what spoils ye have taken, what is lawful and good; and fear God, verily, God is forgiving and merciful.*

Jeff had seemed wellbalanced. If he was turning flaky even with Earthside visits every four or five weeks, Albert pondered what it must have been like for Army and Sin. Had they ever gotten near enough to be able to talk? *Those who believe and have fought strenuously in God's cause, and*

*those who have given a refuge and a help; to them
is forgiveness and generous provision due.*

Mansour came back in.

"What do you make of this?" Albert asked.

"I think I've convinced my brother to fuel the
plant with petroleum temporarily until we can
solve our problems with a 'leaky reactor,' " Mansour said. He picked up the fanfold of printout
and sighed. "Like most holy scripture, it is lofty,
noble, and basically without meaning. This is also
abridged and garbled. Where did it come from?"

"Your boy."

Mansour turned a shade lighter and sat down.
He began studying the printout.

"Is he trying to tell us somethin'?"

"Obviously," Mansour snapped. "So was the
Prophet."

Albert continued poring over the printout.
Gus began reading up from the other end of the
accordian folds. "I hope it's good news," he said.

"What?" Albert demanded. "How'd you work
it out so quick?"

Gus handed him the tail end. Buried among
pages of numbers was a final *sura*: *Behold, I send
you a messenger.*

"When's he due back down?"

"Next week," Mansour said.

"Why don't you get on the radio and ask how
he's feeling? See if maybe he wants to come down
sooner."

"You think he becomes unbalanced?"

"Maybe he has something to tell us and doesn't
want the whole world to hear."

"In the Name of the Merciful and Compassionate, I pray you be right."

Jeff had gathered together the SRBs that Albert had blackmailed out of various hoarders and held them tethered in his floating junkyard until the uranium and trigger could be sent up. He had planned to stow that outside in the push cradle but after carefully vague and allusive messages sprinkled throughout telemetering it had become obvious that he was soaking up enough radiation just sitting here without all that fissionable material parked unshielded next to his living quarters. It would have to go in the rear of the sixty foot long cargo bay. Only then could he lash the SRBs in place around his orbiter. Ever in his mind was the understanding that, nuclear or not, he would be heading out in exactly the same fashion as two previous, and still unreported ships.

His antennae swept Army and Sin's locus incessantly. At least once every eight hours he analyzed the trace. He kept telling himself they were just being closemouthed. It was true that they were not too far away to beam to him without blanketing Earth, Luna, and every working platform in between—should anyone happen to have his antenna facing the wrong way. But instinct told him they were just plain dead.

Until suddenly his usually blank floppy was crammed with the meaningless raw data of telemetering. It had taken him a while to sort the message from camouflaging garbage. It had taken longer to believe it. And then he knew he dared not dream of making waves by repeating it. He hoped nobody would bother to analyze or triangulate on yet more numbers from one of the probes, platforms, and construction crews who filled the bands with bytes. But Jeff also knew

something of the company's vulnerability. He
hoped to Christ and all the rest of the prophets
that Dampier Industries could hold out until he
could get down and tell them.

"Well," Gus observed, "it could be worse."

"We could be dangling by our heels over the
middle kettle of hell," Albert guessed.

"Try looking at it this way: We had two ships
and two pilots unreported, presumed dead. Now
we know they're alive. They seem to have mastered the trick of living in zero g. On the strength
of this alone we could jawbone enough backing
for a proper expedition out there."

"There isn't time."

"My brother's patience stretches thin," Mansour added. "I cannot tell him djinn tales forever.
Had I known that madman in the wheelchair
would need so much time—"

"There's iron on the way. With 1/25 of a year's
world production arriving in a single lump we
should be able to pull a swiftie in the futures
market. Albert?"

"When's it due?"

"A little over a year. I can call up the exact
date."

"It's possible," Albert agreed. "If we can just
keep the government out of our hair. I let the
company be swindled royally on some worked-
out oil wells near Prudhoe Bay."

"We control the land then?"

Albert nodded. "They snickered all the way to
the bank but now we have us an empty piece of
Alaska with nothing but ocean for several

thousand miles in each direction. Good a place as any to bring a meteor in."

"By then we can have a crew in low orbit to cut it up and drop it a piece at a time."

"But what do I tell my brother for the next year?"

"How'll our financial position be once we get that iron down?"

Albert shrugged. "America's priced itself out of the steel market. Depends on whether we bring it in as American or foreign."

"We don't even own a steel mill," Gus said. "And if it lands in Alaska, what choice do we have?"

"That's the problem. Nobody—and especially the FTC, is going to believe us. But as long as there's enough of Dampier for the creditors to cut up they'll all lick their chops and wait. And meanwhile, the FTC won't be able to do anything until delivery day comes and we default."

"I'll see if we can lease an abandoned plant somewhere," Gus said.

"Why?" Mansour wailed. "Do we not have better ways to spend my money?"

"The idea is to let people think we have a secret new process."

"And let spies convince themselves it flopped and we're in trouble," Albert elaborated.

"But my brother—"

"Is he paying full market price for that desalination plant?"

Mansour nodded.

Gus turned to Albert. "When our ship comes in a year from now, can we afford to compensate him for the delay?"

"If it all comes together and we keep the government off our backs, a year from now we could make him a gift of the thing."

Gus smiled. "I told you it could be much worse." He turned to Mansour. "Is your boy taking the stuff out to meet them?"

"He went back up as soon as he'd greeted me and his cat."

"On his way before we'd even finished interpreting the information," Albert said.

Army and Sin were having their own problems interpreting information. "Not as big as it looks," she said. Half a minute had passed since a grain of sand clanged somewhere and there had not been a repetition—yet. Which was no reason for not hurrying into her suit as fast as a splinted arm could be greased into it. His ardor momentarily subdued, Army helped. "All right," she hastened. "I can do the rest. Try the refractor."

Army tore his eyes from the CRT image of two mile-sized asteroids orbiting a common center. There was something weird about them. He scooted through a quarter g toward the telescope in the bow. "Give me a bearing."

"Try forty-seven degrees." By which she meant forty-seven degrees off the axis of their own spin.

It flashed by in the rotating star field. Army punched numbers into the mount and then the telescope was gyrating through twice 47° to cancel out the movement of his and Sin's ships. He was going to have a stiff neck. Then abruptly he knew why the CRT image seemed strange. Just as anyone can watch a ball in flight and know where it will land, he had developed a *feel*. For two rocks to orbit each other at that speed and distance was just *wrong*. Even if he was doing something stupid like adding instead of subtracting his own spin, those rocks should be flying apart.

Sin had suited up except for helmet. She crowded beside him. Army massaged his neck and went back to the CRT. They were within fifty thousand kilometers of the binary, closing at something over 1300 km/hr. Time to kill spin and get set to retrofire. Thirteen hundred kilometers differential was a tiny fraction of one SRB even with their two ships in docking mode. He would have to use the OMS system. "How you fixed for hypergolics?" he asked.

She didn't know. He punched up the numbers and decided to make the burn from Sin's ship. That way they could save his fuel for the day when they might have to . . . He remembered Albert's parting words: "You stay there if you want, but get that ship back."

It took several hours outside kicking and struggling to force the cable into some kind of order as Sin twiddled RCS verniers to kill spin, then nudge the ships together. Finally their docking hooks were mated.

Every SRB and other bit of outboard cargo had, of course, been attached on the assumption that thrust would come from the rear. Docking hooks were in the bows. It had worked well enough while they orbited bow-to-bow at the ends of the cable. He had been forced to beef up everything before he could permit one ship to orbit decks-down. Now his alterations would face the supreme test: when he fired Sin's Orbital Maneuvering System everything attached to his own orbiter would be subjected to a prolonged .05 g from the wrong direction. More. Since his last OMS burn he had jettisoned several empty SRBs.

"What you doin' here, boy?"

Screw the voice. He had company, all sorts of delights in store once this—He asked Sin for the exact g factor. Moments later her voice came tinny over the radio. "Point zero six seven. Will the strapping take it?"

"You can have your money back if it doesn't." He wrestled to lash coils of cable where they would not droop into rocket exhaust.

"Start burn in three hours," she said. "Should I come outside?"

"No way. Give me a nudge from both portside verniers and maybe this cable will fall in place."

Finally he thought they were ready. He was ready to drop.

"Want me to go out and check things?"

Army didn't want her outside alone with a splinted arm. Besides, in the weeks since they had let out the cable he had sensed a gradual dissipation of that fuzzymindedness that had plagued him in zero g. He closed his eyes and began reciting everything he had done.

"Sounds good," Sin said. "But did you notice the spin on those rocks?"

Of course he had. He would have liked another visual but their linked ships were turned and ready for the burn. It was pointless to waste fuel when soon they would be looking at the asteroids without a telescope. But how could two—? They couldn't be as big as they looked in the CRT. Which meant they had to be several times more dense, and highly reflective to radar. Neither made sense.

CLANG!

For an instant he thought they had been holed but cabin pressure held. Just a larger than usual grain of sand. He hoped it would not have chopped a wire or ruined an igniter. Someday a grain of sand was going to penetrate exactly the right spot to light off an SRB in a spontaneous, lopsided, and totally uncontrollable burn. He was mentally calculating the g force while Sin ran checks over their circuitry. "I don't think it hit anything," she said.

They had not run into the cloud of gravel he had been expecting. Belatedly, he realized they were probably inside it but this cloud was only 1300 km/hr less than their own speed. Things coming from the opposite direction could be moving at a measurable fraction of light speed.

"Hang on," Sin muttered. He heard the whump as hypergolic fuel components came together in the OMS motors. After weeks in ¼ g the minuscule acceleration was noticeable only because they kept drifting together toward the bow. "Be more fun if we weren't in space suits," she said.

Army strained to see out but Sin's ship blanked most of the view. Exhaust from her OMS rockets blocked the rest. But those rocks were too heavy. There is a law, whose name Army could not recall, that limits the progressive fusion of hydrogen via helium so that, in practice, *ad infinitum* stops at *ad ferrum*. It takes pressures that happen only in the midst of stars or fairsized planets to form elements heavier than iron. Respectable cosmogony for the last half century has rejected the idea of the asteroids as broken-up chunks of a destroyed planet, preferring to see them as a planet that never quite formed. "It's not radioactive," he muttered.

"Lots of heavy metals out here," Sin said. "But why so much manganese?"

There were, Army supposed, conditions in space that could duplicate the forging, grinding, and polishing that forms a ball bearing on Earth: in zero g, zero atmosphere metal might condense into a perfect sphere with an uncorroded surface. But why would metal in space be hot enough in the first place? High velocity collision? Would their ship someday turn into titanium, aluminum, and stainless steel balls? The burn ended.

They floated back through zero g to the CRT and waited for the exhaust to clear. The binary asteroid was only kilometers away, still orbiting too fast. He would have preferred a visual approach but there was no quick way to separate the ships. He fired another twenty-five seconds to slow their closing rate and while the crud was clearing he studied the recorded image of those orbiting rocks. Nowhere near a mile across. High albedo and density had fooled the radar. They weren't the same size, nor was the largest even spherical. It was a cone with a convex bottom. Suddenly Army saw that it looked just like the working part from a sealed-beam headlight. The apex of the cone faced inward, toward the opposite, much smaller half of the binary. As near as Army could make it out this other half was a sphere. They seemed to be revolving aboug an equidistant point, which would make the fifteen foot sphere weigh as much as the cone. And that cone had to be at least a hundred feet across the base.

It was wrong. The radar wasn't seeing right. Army glanced out to see if the exhaust had cleared away. "Don't go away," he murmured. "I'll be right back." He put on his helmet and slipped into the airlock.

"Can you see anything?" Sin's voice came tinny.

"Yeah." Army's voice was heavy. "I can see it." He supposed he ought to be excited but he was not. He wondered if his name would go down in the history books. Most first contacts made it. He recalled something else that often happened to explorers who achieved first contact. Captain Cook had been eaten by contactees.

He wondered at his lack of excitement. This was an historical occasion—far more important than man's first faltering steps on the moon. Army was looking on something no man had ever seen before. But . . . he had been prepared for it. Prepared for it ever since he had picked up that ball bearing and known in his heart of hearts that there is no natural process for grinding, polishing, and tempering perfect spheres.

He didn't know if there'd ever been a war out here. But there must have been shipwrecks. He squinted. He was numb. Sooner or later he would have to become excited. It was inevitable that it happen someday. But it was not inevitable that it happen to Army.

"What is it?" Sin's voice came thin and anxious over the suit radio. "Can you see what it is?"

"You're looking at it. Radar's just reporting what it sees."

"Then how can they orbit so fast? Why don't they fly apart?"

"Same reason we don't. There's a cable between them."

"Oooooooohh!" Sin's voice was faint. Moments later, splinted arm and all, she had locked out to see for herself..

They tethered to a ring near the OMS pod on the stern of her ship, studying the cone and counterweight. It was impossible to judge distances in space. Each time the big end swung toward them they involuntarily ducked. "I ran some numbers," she said.

"And?"

"Orbital speed and cable length don't factor out to any nice neat fraction of Earth hours or g."

"Little green men," Army muttered. "But even if somebody on Earth was that far ahead, would they use what I think that is for a counterweight?"

"That fifteen-foot sphere's one fiftieth of the total amount that's been mined on Earth since we came down out of the trees."

"Do you suppose we ought to?" Army asked. "There might be anything inside there."

Sin's grin was visible even in a space suit. "Who're you kidding? If they want us, they've already got us."

"I was thinking about Indians and smallpox."

"A while ago I wasn't going to make it. Can you think of a nicer way to go?"

Army considered his first twenty-three years on Earth. He had never lacked for money. It had not bought what he needed. "Why don't you see if you can get the news home in some quiet fashion? Meanwhile I'll—"

"You'll get the tools ready and find some way to tie us up and we'll go in together," Sin said firmly.

"But somebody ought to—"

"Call me Pandora. My desire to enter that is of the same intensity as yours to enter me."

Army knew when he was licked. "But we can't tie on. Two hundred meters of cable at three rpm is a full g. Your bones may take it but our ships can't."

"We could unhook and push against each end." As she said it she knew it was impossible.

"How do you approach either end of that thing without a crunch? Can you make these orbiters circle backwards?"

"So what do we do?"

"I could get over to the null point and hook onto that cable, then maybe rappel out with a rocket."

"Why not latch on with the docking hook and then let the ship creep out to one end. The added weight ought to slow the spin by half. And if we start firing just past midpoint maybe we won't crack the whip."

Army considered. Locking onto that cable would require a careful visual approach. "You stay."

"Like hell I do!"

"You want to pilot yours over, go ahead. I'd like one ship to come back to if I smash up the other."

"All right, so you go. Be interesting to see who comes slithering out when the spin stops."

"If they haven't seen us yet they aren't going to."

"Different metabolic rates? Given time, things that move as slowly as a tree could build a ship. Maybe they sleep or hibernate or just turn off."

"Never find out here." They pulled themselves back inside. While Sin composed the message Army got more air and went back out to undock. An hour later he was back in. "Ready," he said. "Did Jeff hear you?"

"He sent a burst of static on cue. Just came in a moment ago."

"Here goes." An hour later, to Army's mild amazement, the program had gone off without a glitch and he had gotten the spin slowed until Sin could approach with their other ship. She drifted behind the cone and he lost the hum of carrier wave in his radio. Then she drifted back out again and aimed her hook at the slack cable between cone and counterweight. He had chosen the other end of the bolas to anchor Sin's stripped, nearly out-of-fuel shuttle.

"I've been running analyses with the gravitometer," she said. "Could you bring in a sample?" She meant the counterweight at Army's end.

"Is it?" he asked when he had gotten out of his sweat-filled suit.

"Twenty-four karat. I've already asked which end they want."

Army raised his eyebrows.

"Surely you can see what this does to the old ballgame."

"I've been trying not to think about it."

"We could just grab off the counterweight and take it home. Let the other end go adrift for another few thousand years, or at least until mankind's ready for that much new technology in one concentrated dose."

"I've screwed up too many times. I owe the company something."

"So do I," Sin said. "They paid our fare out here. But to whom do we owe the most—the company or humanity?"

"Do you know it's going to turn into pure disaster? There might be cheap food, cures for every disease—you can't guess what's in that thing."

"But knowing humanity, I can guess how the new arts will be applied."

"Then screw humanity. Our obligation is to Dampier."

"If Dampier Industries still exists."

"Why shouldn't they?"

Sin looked at him. "Things were dicey when I went up. Gus told me there was a 50-50 chance of collapse before we could send anything back."

Army had not realized this. He paused a moment. "But if the company's bankrupt, then our real obligation is still to Gus and Albert."

"They paid the bills. And since they're in a bind for some quick money, I asked which end they want first."

Army understood. All the possibilities in the big end of this whirling bolas didn't mean anything unless Gus and Albert could keep their heads above water long enough to see some return—and hang onto the company. And the quickest, surest return was from a fifteen-foot sphere of gold.

"What the company needs right now is a bird in the hand," Sin said.

"The problem is how to fly that bird home. What else did you come up with?"

"That counterweight's not as heavy as my ship."

Army found this interesting but abruptly the accumulated exhaustion was catching up with him. He could feel himself drooping even in zero g.

"Why don't you get out of that suit and eat

something and then perhaps we can both get to sleep," Sin suggested.

He had almost forgotten. But as she began working her careful way out of her snug space suit Army was suddenly less tired than he had thought.

Much later, more at ease than he had been in months, Army could still not sleep. "You awake?"

She was.

"I screwed up. This time I want to do it right."

"Any time, lover."

"I mean with the company. I think we can get both ends of that thing home."

"How?"

"Put that counterweight in your cargo bay and strap on a few SRBs. There's still a little hypergolic fuel for the OMS and RCS systems. When it gets close Jeff can decide whether to orbit it or crash-land someplace."

"Downtown Washington?"

"Don't tempt me."

"But we only have so many SRBs. You used too many catching up with me."

"What about that thing we're tied up to?"

Sin's eyes widened. "Even if there's nobody in there, how do you know we can live in it, breathe the air, or anything else?"

"It's got to have a propulsion system."

"Could be broken down, worn out, out of fuel. Why does it even have to have one? It could be a life raft. Even some kind of beacon."

"It's not emitting on any band we can pick up."

"Batteries run down; just like civilizations."

"Thank you, Herr Spengler. How long since

you sent word to Jeff?''

Sin turned on a light. "About six hours." As she said it the recorder chirred its signal. By the time they had gotten to the CRT the message had been winnowed from its protective garbage. Army looked at Sin. She looked at Army. Then they put their clothes on and went back to work.

M'Meath spent the afternoon cleaning out the car. When he had come home from seeing Gus the children were already there. He fussed over them a while and then went out to the garage. He didn't know whether Tina had missed him. Then he remembered Albert had explained to her that it was him or the children. He had not felt so useless since he had discovered that it made no real difference in family lifestyle whether he had a job or not.

He was not stupid. Just thorough. But to be eternally three topics behind everyone else was enough to make a man forego partygoing for more sober pursuits. And he hadn't even done well at making money, which is often deemed the dullest task of all. He had tried to save the business for the family—and botched it. He had tried to infiltrate ECPAD for old Gus—and botched that. He wondered if that Ivy League bastard in the hospital knew he had been secretly working—screwing up—for Gus.

M'Meath didn't know exactly how but he knew that phallus was using him—extracting information in some sly manner. And he was not even privy to any of Gus's secrets. Why had they bothered to steal the scrambler and call attention to their ability to penetrate company security?

Right in the hospital parking lot too, while he was
visiting Philps Averill.

It suddenly occurred to M'Meath that in all the
time he had been dealing with that plausible bastard he had not once really looked into him. He
went into the library and punched up whatever
was available.

Half a dozen families were practically incestuous. Even then he almost missed it until he remembered that there had been a Philps in that raid
on a younger and more trusting Gus. He ran
checks on those dead or senile thieves and—
correlation! Still, it was hard to believe. Philps
Averill: WASP, Ivy League, Establishment . . .
everything going for him. Would he dedicate so
much time and effort to revenge? M'Meath had
thought only the Irish were like that. And it
wasn't . . . then he understood.

Of course! If it had been himself, Philps Averill
might have shrugged, smiled, and taken his
lumps. But they were an incestuous lot of in-
breeders. Averill was not avenging himself. He
was striking a blow for status quo, God, country,
WASPdom. Not to mention Dad and Granddad.
Even an Orangeman might get a little worked up
over that.

So what to do? He went back out and moped
about the garage looking for something to do.
There was only one thing left for him to do. He
checked his watch. There was time to do it this
afternoon. He took special care showering and
shaving. He picked one of his better suits: blue
and dark enough not to stand out but enough to
call attention to a man of substance who would
brook no more nonsense. He checked the pistol

Albert had given him. It was clean, oiled, and loaded. He looked into the family room where Tina was still mother-smothering restless children. "See you later," he said, and drove past the extra security men, off to the hospital.

Averill was just finishing his evening meal. His leg was still suspended from pulleys but today it hung a trifle lower. "Throbbed like hell for the first few minutes," he greeted, "but if I keep it up in the air any longer I'll decalcify like an astronaut."

"I kept a company scrambler when they kicked me out. Thought it might be handy."

"Always nice to know what the opposition's up to. I believe they call it military intelligence—if that's not an internal contradiction."

"Somebody stole it while I was here."

"Tough. Get anything else?"

"Locked the car up afterward so I'd be sure to notice that was the only thing they took."

"Nothing very intelligent about that."

"No. I'm not. But sooner or later I work things out."

"Oh?"

"Somebody was afraid I might not even miss it."

"Afraid you're losing me somewhere."

"Distraction. To keep me from noticing that they had another better pipeline into the company."

"Oh?"

"Me."

"Just who is it you think's using you?"

"At first I thought it was Nadar and ECPAD. Now I know it's somebody else using Nader."

"Now why would anyone do that?"

M'Meath remembered the sour taste of anger the day he had strolled across the lawn with Averill. This time he was not going to blow his cool. "It's beyond me. Only thing I can think of is something small and mean and Irish. How do you stay mad for twenty-five years?"

"Practice and proper breeding, old cock." Averill halted and studied him for a moment. "I see you've been digging up old dirt. Do you believe it?"

"The courts did. Himself and your Old Gentleman both did time for robbing Gus Dampier."

"It's not the sort of thing we boast about but every family has its ups and downs. I meant, do you really believe I'd piss away eighty-nine percent of my life plotting revenge on an old man who did me no harm—who was quite possibly closer to the right than my forebears?"

"A man's poor and unprincipled, he'll kill for money. A man's never had to work wouldn't. What does that kind of man do to fill his empty days?" M'Meath's hand began moving imperceptibly closer to his shoulder holster.

"Don't."

"Don't what?"

"Don't jump to any simplistic conclusions about motivation."

M'Meath noted that Philps Averill's hands were both under the sheet. "Wonder whatever happened to that guard used to sit by your door."

"He's there," Averill said with unwavering eyes. Then abruptly they were both looking toward the door as it burst inward.

Not again, M'Meath thought. It was another

dark-haired, dark-skinned assassin. This one did not shout. Instead, he aimed the burp gun and left monied, advantaged, Ivy League Philps Averill dead in several places. The body jerked and the sheet slipped to reveal a pistol. It clattered to the floor.

Failed again. M'Meath was so disgusted with his incompetence that he couldn't really get excited over the knowledge that he was next. Couldn't even get up enough steam to say an Act of Contrition. A moment passed. "Well?" he demanded.

The assassin was handing him the burp gun butt first. M'Meath was so startled he nearly shot him. "Do you speak English?"

"Little bit. Please."

"Be goddamned!" M'Meath muttered. He put the gun across Philps Averill's riddled chest and opened the door. Incredibly, nobody was there. Then he remembered how well soundproofed were these walls and doors. Had Philps Averill tired of games and disabled the squawk box? Then as he led the sleep-walking assassin toward the elevator he saw the nurse returning to her station from a pieshaped room across from Averill's. She smiled. M'Meath smiled back. Twenty-two minutes later he led the darkhaired man stumbling into Gus's building. Gus, Albert, and Mansour were waiting.

Mansour barked a question in raucous Arabic. The killer shook his head and the only word M'Meath caught sounded like *farsee*. "He's Iranian," Mansour said. "We can as easily speak English."

Albert had already set the wheels of 'justice' in motion with a call to a high voltage specialist in criminal law. He wished M'Meath could have had sense enough not to leave his prints on that burp gun. But the young Irishman was not so used to being shot at as Gus and Albert. "Who do you work for?" he asked the killer.

The story was not easy to extract but finally with Mansour's limited *Farsí*, the killer's stumbling Arabic, and patching the gaps with English, they learned what happens to those who go along, hoping someday to see a modern country and perhaps even a little democracy. No Iranian had ever been that enthusiastic about hunching with his hands over his gonadia lest the shah irradicate them with his luminous presence. But few were eager for a return to the Middle Ages.

Those in US schools when the ayatollah reestablished the kingdom of God were stuck, their families hostage. By Islamic law a *murtadd* has three days to return to the paths of righteousness—or face execution. Visas expired, deportation was the price for their loyalty to Western ideals. Only one man in the government had seen fit to help them. And Philps Averill had kept them in a vise for years, even furnished the drugs to get them psyched up for each big assignment.

"So what finally made you kill him?" Gus asked.

"Mail come from Iran. My family—"

"What're we going to do with this poor bastard?" M'Meath asked.

Gus had asked himself the same question only this morning. "Teach him a few words of Spanish and the government will send him to safety at no cost to anyone except our future relations with Latin America."

"You cannot," Mansour protested. "The Mexicans will just send him back. But you are not serious."

"Of course not."

"Need him here to clear Mr. M'Meath anyhow," Albert added.

Gus sighed. "Why should the Communists monopolize all the show trials? Nothing like a good murder case for publicity. By the time we're through people may be disgusted enough to make the government lay off us. We haven't been able to afford justice for ourselves but we can buy him some."

"'Member Oswald?" Albert asked.

"Your criminal law friend can fix that with some sworn depositions on video tape. Spread the word that we're keeping a little dirt in reserve just in case anything happens to our boy before trial."

"And I suspected my brother."

"Don't worry," Albert said. "King Omar will be sending some of his just as soon's he gets tired of waiting for that desalination plant."

The criminal specialist was shown in. After introductions Gus, Albert, and Mansour went to another room so the hotshot lawyer could work it out with M'Meath and the drawn, drained Iranian.

Gus felt grumpy and deflated. "Why couldn't it have come along a year sooner and saved us all the trouble?" he growled. "Now that we've killed all our own snakes those babes in the woods have finally stumbled onto something that upsets the whole scoreboard all over."

"You've always looked toward the future," Albert said. "Getting old?"

"Speak for yourself!"

"I am. Mansour and I have both wanted to start a few projects that just might come to fruition someday. Now, thanks to those two babes in the woods"—*and don't forget whose money and skulduggery it was put them up in those shuttles*—now they've found the magic that makes it possible during my lifetime. Maybe *you're* unhappy," Albert concluded. "But *I'm* going to live long enough to see a few people quit eatin' dog food!"

"I suppose you're right," Gus said. "But it takes a little getting used to. I wonder if we can master a whole new technology without ruining everything we now have."

"I don't know about ruining everything," Albert said. "But now that you're going to have more money than you ever dreamed of, what about all those lovely people who've been trying to ruin you?"

Gus began to smile. "Keep it up. You may make my day yet."

Albert turned to Mansour. "Has Jeff gone back up again?"

"Yes. He waits for more news from our "babes in the woods". We have also agreed upon a new and undecipherable code."

"There's no such thing."

"Possibly not. But pages and word numbers from an obscure novel are meaningless without knowing from which book we select the words. This sort of code is useless for a spy in the field since his book will invariably be captured. But Jarfi has no neighbors to snoop his possessions."

A phone buzzed. It was the engineer in telemetering again. "I wasn't sure anybody'd be there this time of night but—he just sent down another batch." Moments later the floppy arrived via the pneumatic system.

They crowded around the printout. Army and Sin had gotten the counterweight loose and into the cargo bay of her orbiter. Three hundred twenty-eight days from now Jeff would have to check out the OMS and RCS systems by remote and decide whether to orbit it around Earth or bring the ancient and overloaded shuttle to a crash landing.

"We'll have to select a spot," Gus said. "Once it's on the ground no land transport could move a thousand-ton chunk. Thank God it's easy to melt or saw."

"Why do we not land it in Alaska where the iron will be coming?"

Gus pointed at the globe in the corner of the office. "Hard enough to get the United States to observe its own laws. I have even less confidence in the Russians."

Mansour studied the globe. "I had not realized how close—But how can we protect ourselves?"

"Small deliveries and no advance notice. We'll probably get hijacked at least once but I suspect it won't take the US long to learn they'd better come out on our side unless they want the dollar to continue its conversion into Kleenex."

"But how do we hold out that long? We're scraping bottom now." Albert thought a moment. "Iron won't be here for another six months and everybody's—"

"Oh Albert, for heaven's sake, think!"

"I must be getting old." Albert began punching the phone. Mansour was already on another line selling gold futures several points shorter than any operator in a printing press money market would dream of. "We gonna be investigated," Albert murmured.

"By then we'll be able to wreck them all."

"I pray we do not. I want Arabs in space but we cannot all go. Our investments are in money. Can we eat or drink it?"

"Montezuma's real revenge," Gus said, "was not the Aztec Twostep. It was Aztec gold: foreign goods suddenly cheap while Spanish industry withered and the peasantry starved. But I have to live on this planet, too—at least until we get a look at the other end of that thing."

"What do you suppose they'll find in there?" Albert asked.

"Cholera and syphilis," Mansour guessed. "I wish they would leave it in peace. Do we not have troubles enough with our own inventiveness? That ship is—" He searched for a simile familiar to Western ears. "Pandora's box will be as nothing. That ship may be to Western technology as yours to us—or ours to you a thousand years ago."

"Be more like the first whaler in Hawaii," Albert said.

"The only ones who complain about Western technology are Westerners," Gus snapped. "Every Third Worlder carries a ballpoint and a transistor while he struggles to climb from moped to limousine. To hell with those who won't trade their old flat rock for a washing machine. That's not our problem right now. The old guard can still hurt us. We won't be safe until we have factories and farms off planet."

"You dream," Mansour said.

"Is that forbidden? The technology is already here. All it takes is money. There's nothing from Earth that we won't be able to produce cheaper and better, and without having to lift it out of a four-thousand-mile gravity well. What's not in the asteroids we'll get from the Jovian satellites. And of course they're irradiated. Robots are immune. Before long, trade with Earth will become an expensive form of charity."

"Same old ghetto," Albert muttered.

"Not necessarily. Emigration never solved Europe's or Asia's problems. But with laser elevators and wheel colonies we can offer transport that, in real purchasing power, is cheaper than a cruise in chains from Africa to America—or England to Australia. And a somewhat better life on the other end." Gus got up and drew coffee. "Once the heavy industry and pollution are out in orbit where they belong, Earth can be whatever people want: ghetto or garden.

"Lately even Third World population curves are flattening. Sociologists all pontificate on cultural inertias. What they never see is that Third Worlders are governed by self interest even as you and I. Once there's no advantage in large families, they still bow to Pope, mullah, or bonze—then go home and quietly take the Pill. In another generation Earth could be where we go on vacation—or retire to if our feet can still take all that gravity. But nobody would try to make a living there."

Albert scratched his head. "That Army, he really is something!"

Gus looked at him.

"Been going over these numbers. I'm no engineer but it seems to me that if he wasted a lot of

his fuel catching up with that girl then how come
they got enough to send one shuttle back to us
with that gold? You think they're planning on
staying up there with the big prize?''

Suddenly Albert had their full attention.

Army and Sin were still trying to get into the big
prize. They had stayed strictly away from the
million possibles from accident to anthro-
pophagy that could emerge from the big end.
It had taken days to get the gold counterweight
loose, into the doorless maw of Sin's orbiter,
strapped down, and SRBs back in place. Then Sin
had spent another half day programming the orbit
close enough for Jeff to take over. Finally the gold
and Sin's ship were on their way. Now they had
Army's orbiter and enough rockets for a low
power, years-long loop home. They had done
their best for Gus and his partners. It was time to
do something for themselves.

Roped together, they made their laborious way
across the convex bottom. The cone was of some
metal that had once been highly polished but was
now sandblasted. Having inspected the gradual
deterioration of paint and polish on his own ship,
Army knew something about erosion rates. He
wondered if this one had been orbiting for
thousands or millions of years.

The makers had put eyes and handholds at
more or less human distances. There were iris
diaphragms over a set of large holes and another
set of smaller ones. Motors inside? He had found
hatches. Or were they inspection plates? No
screws or rivets.

Sin's voice came tinny through suit radio.

"We're on the wrong surface. People don't put doors in floors."

She was probably right. They had just about covered the bottom anyhow. Army pulled around the edge and began working his way up the conical side. "I'm hooked on," he said. "Turn loose and come around to join me."

"Radio was nearly dead around the corner," she said as she drifted past hunting for the next place to hook on. "Aha!"

It looked like a cargo hatch. At least Army hoped the inhabitants were not that big. They ranged around it hunting for a latch and found none. A hundred feet closer to the apex they finally came to a reasonably man-sized hatch. This one had a latch which Army struggled to twist. It was so totally unyielding that he was afraid to use the wrench he carried lest he twist the wrong way and the entire universe tilt. He tried pushing and pulling with every possible combination of twist. After a full minute of frustration he slammed it with the head of his spanner. The next time he tried the latch turned easily.

They were in an airlock. "How's your air?" he asked.

"I came out the same time you did."

"Better change bottles here so we don't pick up a whiff of whatever poison they breathe inside." With the outboard hatch still open they switched bottles and were good for another hour. Army was switching on his suit light when Sin closed the hatch. A blue-white light came on in the airlock. "This ship's still alive!"

"Why shouldn't it be?"

"They didn't shoot at us."

Sin was having trouble securing a new bottle one-handedly. Army buckled it for her. "Perhaps," she said, "hostility is not a universal reaction to visitors. In any event, we've still to open the inside hatch."

"Just so they don't serve chicken a la king," Army muttered. He opened the hatch. Lights came on in the next compartment, which was not a compartment: it was a hallway.

"Call me Ariadne," Sin said as she began unrolling a ball of string.

Why was he so nervous? They could only kill him. Hadn't he been enduring slow death on Earth as long as he could remember? Still he knew the girl was as uptight as he was. A door opened. Sin gasped. When he could think coherently again Army realized that supermarket doors open on Earth without frightening anyone. He pushed away and the door closed. He approached and it opened.

Inside, the small cabin seemed to be living quarters or at least a sleeping room. There were curtains with no windows behind them. Finally he saw they were nets for storing things. Three of the larger ones could be strung crossways for hammocks.

"Tourist class?" Sin asked.

"Sure don't believe in privacy."

Sin had been inspecting the sliding door. "I think it locks from the inside." She was right. They could not get out.

Army checked his watch. Fifty-five minutes of air if he didn't panic and start gulping it. They ran gloved hands around the edge of the door hunting some hidden latch. Nothing. He pried and the door was unyielding. He rapped it with the wrench. Nothing. He backed to the opposite bulkhead and pushed purposefully toward it. The door did not open. "Come on you miserable SOB, open up!" Army growled. The door opened. They pushed hastily back out into the corridor.

"That's frightening," Sin said in a thin flat voice.

"Want to go back?"

She shook her head, then grunted a no when she remembered she was in a space suit.

"It's not reading my mind," Army said. "I just did something else at the same time. But we could die trying to figure out what." He was sure no machine would ever read minds.

"Where do you suppose the controls are?"

Doors opened invitingly as they pushed down the corridor but the cabins were all identical, all empty, and they were not eager to be trapped again. The corridor ended with another sliding door. This one gave onto a spiral, half staircase– half ladder like some nightmare vision of a lighthouse. There were no guards nor hand rails. In full g a fall could be spectacularly fatal. They floated in. "Up or down?" he asked.

"Might as well be thorough," she said. They went the shortest way, which was three levels down to what was probably the slightly convex floor of the cone.

It took Army a while to realize what had created such utter chaos, then he realized this must have been the garden, air-exchange section, several other things. Great tiers of hydroponic vegetation run riot, so long untended that the decaying mass of unharvested crops had long since turned to humus. But in the zero g since he had removed the counterweight loose packed soil, water, mud, plants had all gone adrift. "Wonder how many more things we ruined?"

"They'll live a while. They're green. Do you suppose there's oxygen around us?" Sin put a cap on one of the bottles she had brought across the vacuum from one ship to another. "Let's go see if the controls are up in the nose."

Fifty minutes of air left.

They pushed up through the open center of the spiraling ladder toward where they had entered and the door in between opened. Dim light flickered for a moment and then they could see the interior of the huge pillared expanse of the second level. There were grooves in the pillars for sliding board partitions. Gritty black dust rose in blinding clouds as they disturbed it.

Army glanced at Sin. "Not much fuel left." He pointed at one small section where boards still stood in place between the pillars.

"How do you know it isn't cargo?"

"Could be. But let's see if we can find the engines."

"I'd like to find the people."

"You will."

Three levels up the door had a stylized lightning bolt. Army moved toward it and the door failed to open. "Restricted area?" Sin asked.

"You read absolute zilch for radioactivity, didn't you?"

"Just normal background for this far from the sun."

"Then that jagged lightning means what I think it does." He began prying and poking, then remembered what had worked last time. "Come on you SOB, open up!"

This time it didn't work. He hadn't really expected it to. "Time out," he said. They pushed back down to the level where they had entered. Back home, while Army netted a supply of air bottles, Sin ran spectograms on the gases she had trapped in bottles, fed cultures into other bottles, and did what she could to forestall infection and/or suffocation.

"It's air," she said when Army came through the lock and began exhaustedly peeling off his clammy suit.

"Earth air?"

"Richer. This is 25% oxygen, 72% nitrogen, and the rest is bits and snippets of carbon dioxide, argon, neon, the usual traces. I haven't found anything dangerous."

"Pressure?"

"Equivalent to about 14,000 feet. With Earth's 20% oxygen we'd have trouble breathing. Even with 25% it'll be no picnic but I think we could manage as long as we don't play too much fast tennis."

"How about the cultures?"

"Give them a few hours to fester."

"I've got a feeling you won't find anything dangerous."

"Why?

Army couldn't explain it. His mind was on that huge unwalled level with black gritty dust. "But we've got to be careful. And if that greenery down there is a working air machine, while we're waiting for those cultures to hatch we'd better get some spin back on that ship."

"Without a counterweight?"

"We have this orbiter. And we need some spin on us too unless you want your bones to turn to mush again."

Sin sighed and began dogging down her helmet.

"You stay inside and do the piloting," he said. "With one arm you can't do much to help me horse that cable around."

"Going to use our cable or theirs?"

"Theirs was taking a full g and it's easier to handle than the hybrid abomination I strung together." He locked out and went to work.

What you doin' here boy?

Screw off! He was too busy for hallucinations. Would he ever rest again? Space was supposed to be months and years of unrelieved boredom. It took four hours and four bottles of air before he had the eye in the end of the alien cable pinned through the harness that held their orbiter horizontal. He snapped both ends of his lifeline well away from any RCS nozzles and told Sin to start firing.

The ships drifted apart and ten minutes later the cable was taut. There was less stretch in this one than in the nylon and graphite he had spliced. The orbiter did not yoyo so nauseatingly. He locked inside and peeled off his suit while she began firing the main RCS jets to push the orbiter sideways.

It took half an hour for their orbiter and the larger ship to settle into a stabilized spin but finally things were falling much straighter down than they had with the older, shorter cable and g was up to nearly .3. Army had planned on doing something else once he got out of his suit but he was so tired that he fell asleep first.

Gus was feeling pretty good this morning. He had even been able to turn down his hearing aid until he was in less hazard of those feedback squeals that threatened to coagulate his eyeballs. And for once his partners seemed in good humor too. "Either the media haven't guessed what's up or else somebody's leaning on them," Albert said. "I haven't seen a single call for an investigation."

"They feel no need to push an already toppling structure," Mansour said.

Gus raised bushy eyebrows.

"We have shorted gold futures," the Arab said. "Without the intervention of some major power there is no way we can deliver that much gold at the agreed-upon price. Ergo we must bankrupt or default."

"In two-hundred-ninety-nine days," Gus added.

Albert laughed. "Bet they've got us already cut up among themselves."

"What do you hear from our babes in the woods?" Gus asked.

"Army's very careful with what he beams Earthward," Albert said. "And once I decipher what he's saying it's hard to decide whether he's crazy or if it's just all the rest of us."

Gus and Mansour were studying him. "Either of you know anything about imprinting?" Albert asked.

"I presume you're not talking about our government's unfortunate ways with quick money—" Gus began.

"Psychological imprinting?" Mansour asked. "Hatching duck eggs beneath chickens to add to the world's neuroses?"

"Something like that," Albert agreed. "Now Army doesn't come right out and say that ship's alive but . . ."

As usual, Gus was four kilometers down the road ahead of anyone else. "Damn!" he exulted. "A direct mind-to-machine link for production without all the bunglings and screwups and failed inspections and—why, it could even keep the engines from falling off the DC-10s!"

"Or deliver the mail on time," Mansour added. "But does Army understand the process?"

"No more than the average driver knows what's happening inside his transmission."

"Impasse," Mansour muttered.

"How so?"

"We cannot send up experts to dismember that ship. Even if they did not damage it beyond repair, how much loyalty can we buy?"

"If that ship ever gets within grabbing distance of Earth there'll so many dislocations nobody'll even notice when we're gobbled up or legislated out of existence."

"Oh, I don't know," Albert said. "I'm sure you'll rate an asterisk on a John Sutter monument somewhere. Anyhow, it isn't hoepless."

Gus and Mansour waited.

"Well, it looks to me like we've gotten more loyalty than we deserve. They're sending us the gold. And we don't really want the ship down here where a bunch of hamfisted experts can frighten it to death. Seems like you're forgetting Sin's and Army's IQs."

"But won't they want to come home someday?"

Albert shrugged. "I knows you never been young," he told Gus. "But haven't you ever been in love? Anyhow, they don't seem in any big hurry to come down."

"Perhaps," Mansour guessed," by the time they are ready for a holiday the ship will understand enough to exclude all others and let only them back in."

"You still using that book code with Jeff?" Albert asked.

Mansour shook his head. "Gus was right. I asked and Jarfi said every volume in his library had been pawed over by some NASA freight handler."

"No great loss. He can still bring the raw data in his pocket whenever he comes down."

"But since he has put his ship spinning against a bundle of SRBs he does not come down so often. We must create other medical problems."

"Why not just tell the truth—say he comes down for conferences on company matters?" Albert asked.

"It's better if they think we have no secrets," Gus said. "We should all be bravely struggling to conceal our unhappiness. Shouldn't we be out trying to scrounge short term loans or somesuch to keep them sure we're ready to collapse?"

"My brother has already agreed to give a noisy refusal to my request for more money."

Albert raised his eyebrows.

"The sheikh is old fashioned but he understands discretion. Especially when I explained that we do not need the money."

"How about that desalination plant?"

Mansour smiled. "On its way. It is fortunate that our recent discovery out there makes nuclear fuels unnecessary."

"They know." Gus said it flatly.

"How can they?"

"They know but they don't dare make waves as long as we have that Iranian assassin in our hip pocket. But somebody pushed through those export permits because they knew we couldn't deliver a nuclear desalination plant. Now we are delivering it." Gus grinned. "Somewhere in a smoke-filled room evil old men are going nuts trying to figure just what got us off the hook." He turned to Albert. "If those children can't understand how it runs, what are their chances of getting home in one piece?"

"Fair. Last I heard, the girl ran every test she could think of on the air and water. Couldn't find any microbes or viruses."

"Perhaps they could send samples back to Earth for more careful analysis—" Mansour broke off when Gus and Albert rounded on him. "Of course not," he agreed. "We have enough plagues on Earth now."

"Anyhow," Albert continued, "she and that Army figure they're going to run low on food and air—maybe even kill one another if they have to spend three years cooped up in that shuttle."

"Perhaps Mansour could take their place for a while?"

"Boosters, man, boosters!"

"Army said he'd gone out there to accomplish something and he was going to see it through. He figures somebody's got to be first and take the risk.

If they're dead by the time it gets close to Earth then everybody'll be better off just to let it go on by."

"Unusual," Gus said.

"That they are not afraid to die?"

Gus shook his head. "We only fear death in new and unusual forms. Apparently those children aren't even afraid of that. Perhaps—"

"Perhaps what?"

"Perhaps we do not fear death at all. But if I were young I might cavil at the thought that I had never lived."

"They lived," Albert said.

"I suppose that explains it."

"You know," Albert said thoughtfully, "there's one way to make sure nobody gueses what we're doing." He ran a hand over grizzled hair. "Little risky but I think it would work."

Gus and Mansour knew that if they were dealing with individuals there would be no danger. They had sold futures. Nothing legal could be done until delivery day came and they failed to come up with the gold or its going price. But when free-wheeling business tangles with the total amorality of government . . .

"We could prepare a press release," Albert said. "Tell them we just discovered a solid gold asteroid."

Gus and Mansour stared. "Why not?" Gus asked.

"I think not," Mansour said. "What if someone with another ship were to attempt an informal acquisition?"

"Piracy? Who'd believe that kind of cock and bull?"

"There is always at least one person who will believe anything. And if someone did—and blundered onto two unarmed young people in a defenseless alien ship . . ."

"He's right," Albert said.

The phone buzzed. Miss Jepworth's voice came over the speaker. "Mr. M'Meath," she said. "Are you in?"

Gus picked it up. "What can I do for you?"

M'Meath was hesitant. Gus reminded himself that his son-in-law was still facing possible charges. "Is this line secure?"

"Of course not. But we have no secrets. Go ahead."

"I found some of Averill's papers. The Old Boys are getting set to do a number on you."

So what else is new? "How'd you happen to find them at this late date?"

"Entirely too easily. I think they were planted."

Every once in a while M'Meath did show unmistakable signs of intelligence. "What are we supposed to believe they're up to?"

"They're going to investigate foreign ownership of an aerospace industry vital to national defense. If there exists a clear and present danger then the government may be forced to take over."

Mansour's eyes widened. "They can do this?"

"Governments can do anything. Some tinpot dictator do it to us, he call it expropriation."

"Well, thanks for warning us, Francis. We'll keep our eyes open and try to be prepared." Gus broke the connection.

"Now what you s'pose them eggsuckers really up to?"

Gus shrugged. "Nice to know we're vital to

national defense. When we were going under nobody gave a damn."

The phone buzzed again. This time it was company intelligence. The nondescript, balding little
man on the other end of the line was sweating.
"The news'll be public in half an hour," he said. "I
don't know how they managed to keep it secret
this long."

Unlike his son-in-law, Gus would not play one
upsmanship with company intelligence. "What
news?"

"The president has invoked wartime emergency powers. They're taking over the entire defense and aerospace industries."

"So?"

"Every other company has been warned to pay
no attention and not to worry."

"And we're the only ones didn't get the word?"

"That's about it," the balding man said. "Is
there anything I can do?"

"Afraid not."

Gus, Mansour, and Albert faced one another.
"Apparently they don't care how much dirt that
Iranian can uncover," Gus said.

"By now they will have altered enough birth
certificates to prove Philps Averill was a Black
Panther." Albert was bitter.

So was Mansour. "Haroun and Yassir were the
only totally honest men I ever knew. What can we
do?"

"Nothing. Government pulls something like
that it means they don't care what people think
any more."

"I've tried to be a builder," Gus said. "I thought
I could leave the world better than I found it."

"Then it is hopeless?"

"I'm older than Howard Jarvis. How many more fights have I got in me?"

"What must we do?"

Gus shrugged. "Every man for himself."

"I am the only—You are both US citizens, are you not?"

Gus and Albert nodded.

"Give me a dollar. Each of you."

"It won't work," Gus said. "And even if it would, we trust one another but what would happen to you if I or Albert were to die before we could put your shares back in your name?"

There was a long moment of silence. "My brother does not merit my death on his conscience," Mansour said as he prepared to depart.

"That's enough doom and destruction! We can do something as long's you don't mind seeing a few people get hurt."

"My people?"

Albert shook his head. "Nor mine. And in spite of skin color I've never thought them Gus's kind of people."

"They're determined to force a showdown," Gus said. "You may as well go ahead."

"I don't understand it," Army said.

"Liquidation? They strip the company of everything usable, then let the auditors sort it out. The government inherits a bunch of angry employees all pressing claims, an old building, and some aging machinery. Put them all together, they spell mother."

"But where do we stand?"

"On top of the machinery that made that old plant obsolete. And, as shareholders in the totally new mining company that's going to exploit a gold claim due for discovery in about a hundred more days."

By now they had gotten full g back onto the alien ship, were breathing its air-and drinking its water. Army had labored mightily getting part of the hydroponics back in shape. He had been mystified at its size. Perhaps the aliens had different metabolisms and needed a hundred times more oxygen than would be required for three humans in each of the eighty cabins.

Under near normal g Sin's bones were stiffening until she could occasionally and vocally wonder if splints might not be more appropriate on Army's wilting member. He had a suspicion by now of how the drive worked. But understanding it and making the ship run were in different orders of magnitude. Sin had been unbelieving. "A coal-burning spaceship?"

"Fifty years ago there were lots of coal burners on Earth," he explained. "The bunkers all looked just like that big open section with all the loose coal dust and the removable bin boards."

Sin understood magnetohydrodynamics, in which a jet of powdered coal and air flames past supercooled magnets to make electricity. She had no trouble seeing the hybrid nature of this ship's engines where the coal jet provided primary thrust, plus direct current for secondary ion rockets—with possibly enough left over to electrolyze small amounts of oxygen from water "But where do you get enough oxygen to flame off all that coal?"

Army didn't know. There were still unexplored

parts of the ship where they had been unable to force their way. For the first few days they had expected momentarily to discover an occupant—dead or alive, devil or dust. There were none: nor personal possessions, nor bones, nor hint that anyone had ever lived aboard. If there were any books or records in the control cabin they had not mastered the necessary spells to call them up.

There were no chairs—only backless stools too high for Sin and almost too high for gangling Army. With g restored Sin's exploration had been curtailed, thanks to a still gimpy arm and that nightmare spiral ladder which was the only way from one level to the next. Unwillingly, she had accepted that she could more efficiently serve their enterprise by staying aboard the shuttle to monitor instruments and make sure nothing went wrong while Army prowled the ship and tried to trace what might be fiber optics on some unknown wave length but was most assuredly neither electric nor electronic as a hotshot computerman saw such terms.

The iron alloy of the alien ship was nearly half manganese and could not properly be called steel. It absorbed electromagnetic radiation until radios were nearly useless. Finally Army had strung wire along the cable from one ship to another and put a repeater inside the main stairway. Even then he could not hear Sin's voice around a corner.

The control room was so totally alien that he knew any attempt to take something apart would undoubtedly ruin it. He moped about the bunkers, poking at what were obviously hatches—maybe even chutes to where the main engine was locked into inaccessibility.

From time to time there were incomprehensible

noises—just enough to remind him that parts of this ship were still alive and functioning. Even if he could open one of those hatches to the MHD engine, would he dare enter? The makers must have had their own excellent reasons for putting locks on all the doors. If Army could just get it back near Earth the company—or whatever heir phoenixed from the company's ashes—could put a crew of experts to work.

There was a louder than usual shriek-groan. He spun but there was no movement in the dimlit bunker deck. He strode back toward the central staircase to see if anything visible had happened elsewhere. Even now that he walked about the ship with his helmet off, breathing alien air, Army had never quite screwed up his courage to go back into one of those cabins and try to figure out what it took to make the door open.

"What you doin' here, boy?"

"Screw off!" he shouted. Out in the staircase he heard Sin's voice. The loop returned to the beginning. "Something big coming up on us. You'd better get back inside."

As long as they didn't run into it. . . . He had already hooked two far bigger prizes than ever they had expected. Who cared about another chunk of rock or metal? But Sin was right. Small stuff tended to gather near any big rock. He didn't need a load of hypersonic buckshot as he shinnied up and down the cable between ships.

He moved down the corridor toward the airlock, trying to ignore cabin doors that hissed invitingly open as he approached. He was startled only when, near the airlock one door did not open. Broken? Or was somebody-thing inside?

"What you doin' here, boy?"

He locked out and went back to Sin and the orbiter. "What is it?" he asked as he locked through. "Another spaceship?"

"I think we've gotten our quota for one trip. This's about a mile across. The usual junk."

"Rock?"

"Still checking. At first glance I'd say carbonaceous chondrite."

"Come in handy someday," Army said. "But I don't know what I'd do with one just now." He stood beside her studying the CRT display, then walked toward the bow and tried to find it in the refractor. "Give me a bearing."

Six degrees off their spin axis would not give him too stiff a neck. He cranked the information into the equatorial mounts. After a moment he found it and locked on. Just another piece of black rock with white veins. It drifted out of view. He checked the tracking mechanism and reset it. The rock slid slowly out of view again. "What in hell's going on?"

"I don't know. Can you hear it?"

She meant the grunts and cackles of their solar panel tracking. Now that he noticed it seemed to be moving faster. He took his eye from the scope and studied the rotating star field. Someday maybe he could program something to make those stars stand still. Or at least take out the apparent motion, for the stars were standing still; it was the orbiter that was spinning. And now it was spinning faster!

He staggered back to the CRT. Why was he staggering? The accelerometer was still at .8g. But he felt a slight dizziness.

Sin held up a pencil and dropped it. It fell in a visible curve. "Coriolis," she said.

A grain of sand clanged somewhere.

"Only one thing could be happening," Army said.

"Conservation of angular velocity." She meant the same force that makes skaters spin faster by pulling in their arms.

Army was dogging down his helmet. "Put yours on," he said, and ducked into the airlock. A moment later he was back. "Yup," he said. "That ship's reeling in its counterweight. Looks like we're getting ready to move."

"And we're the counterweight. How long did it take you to hook us up?"

"Several multiples of how long it's taking to pull us in. No way I can cut loose in time."

"I don't think I'll put my helmet on. It might as well be quick."

"If this orbiter's going to get wrapped around a winch why can't we be inside the other ship before it happens?"

"I hadn't thought of that." Sin began suiting up.

By the time he had helped her across the ships were only half as far apart as normal. He had been afraid something else might have changed but the airlock let them in without quibble. "You first." He followed her up the spiral ladder-staircase where he could grab in case she slipped. But Sin's arm was almost back to normal now and she made the climb without difficulty.

From the control cabin they could watch their shuttle draw closer. Army squinted through the slightly smoky 'glass' and knew the shuttle was going to block most visibility when it came close.

It weighed about the same as the gold counter-weight but was not so compact. He wondered if whatever was reeling the cable in would stop in time, or if it would try to draw the orbiter down through the eye.

"Going to be a mess even if they don't crunch it," Sin said.

He didn't need explanations. The orbiter swung decksdown. If it was not crushed it would still be taking acceleration from the wrong direction once this ship started moving. But why was the ship preparing to move? The alien ship was down to its last gasp of fuel. Evasive maneuvers for an asteroid that would pass thousands of kilometers away?

But . . . this ship was thousands, perhaps millions of years old. It had not survived by playing chicken with near misses. The ships drew closer, spin accelerating as angular velocity squeezed into an ever smaller circumference until Army could almost feel his bones warp from the differential between his head and feet. "Better lie down," he warned.

Then suddenly there were alien noises. The ship was firing to kill spin. As the stars' apparent motion slowed they began to float. Cable reeled in faster now that centrifugal force no longer worked against the winch. Arms unfolded. Claws grasped their orbiter and held it twenty feet away.

"Looks like this isn't the first time they've used something odd for a counterweight," Sin said.

There was another deeper roar and they drifted down to the deck. "Wish I had the refractor," Army grunted.

"What for?" The large section of blank bulkhead above the incomprehensible controls was flickering. "I think we're going to have a view soon," she said.

The alien ship matched asteroidal velocity with more adroitness than ever Sin or Army had achieved with overage shuttles. They had a perfect view from the screen Army had always taken for a bulkhead.

"So now we find out what a chondrite is good for," she murmured.

"I already know," Army said. "I just can't figure what they use for an oxydizer."

"You know?"

"Man's carbonaceous chondrite is an alien's coal mine—would you look at that!"

The cargo hatch was opening. Something midway between lobster and scorpion emerged, jetting steam between its claws as it backed from the big hatchway towing a strand of web.

"Is it alive?" she asked.

"If it is we won't be for long." But even as he said it Army knew that whatever it was, that monster could never squeeze into this pilot house.

Troubled with vermin? Call your friendly neighborhood fumigator. He watched that creature jetting steam and wondered why the screen had waited till now to come on. A warning? But he was plagued with a *déja vu* feeling that he had seen that lobster-scorpion before. Where could he have seen it apart from a nightmare?

The clanks and groans of the sleeping ship had given way to shrieks as dormant machinery returned to life. Army wondered if it was always this loud or if this was the result of a million years between oil changes.

"Ariadne," Sin said suddenly.

"Huh?"

"The first day I brought a ball of twine in case we got lost. The original Ariadne gave Theseus a ball of twine to find his way out of the Labyrinth."

"You think that's the Minotaur?"

"I just remembered what was odd when we came in this time."

"I'm not given to overstatement," Army said, "but don't you see several odd things?"

"The cabin doors didn't open."

"So?"

"During moments like this the ship doesn't want passengers cluttering things up."

"Maybe they're prisoners."

"Given the run of the ship at other times?" She paused. "Remember those ball bearings?"

"To hell with the ball bearings. That lobster isn't an arachnid."

"Spiders aren't the only animals that spin webs."

"That's not an animal and that's not a web. But if you'll watch closely there is an evolution."

"From what?"

"An automated coal miner has two claws and a chute-conveyor belt. In zero g any machine would have more claws and a closed tube conveyor. Ah, there it goes."

The lobster-scorpion jetted steam from its other end as claws attacked the carbonaceous asteroid. The filament of "web" swelled as crushed coal began streaming back into the ship. "But I still don't see where they store enough oxygen or how they reduce it."

"Perhaps it is not given to Man to Know All

Things." Sin was given to uttering portentuous twaddle in absentminded moments.

"Not unless he works at it. Wish I knew what that oxydizer was."

"You will. I left the chromatographer on back in the orbiter. Just looking I'd say it's nitrogen tetroxide."

Army supposed it was. "That exhaust looks like the hydrazine-tetroxide much from our RCS verniers."

An hour later the lobster was drawn back into the hold by its hose. The milesized carbonaceous chondrite was now a honeycombed rock and appreciably less black. The cargo hatch closed and the main, presumably magnetohydrodynamic, engines came back on. "Surprises are not over yet," Sin said. "Care to guess where it's taking us?"

"Home, I suppose."

"Whose home?"

Army shrugged. "We wanted adventure."

He really couldn't understand his lack of excitement. This was a first. Unless you were a flying saucer nut how often did humans get shanghaied aboard alien space ships? But since Albert had caught him with his hand in the computer, Army's life had taken so many unbelievable turns that he was numbed. He just could not get excited. "Do you really believe this is happening?" he asked.

Sin gave him an odd look. "I know what you mean. We ought to be oohhing and ahhing and gee-whizzing all over the place. Maybe our generation just saw too much TV."

"Almost as if some part of my mind were telling me to cool it and not to worry."

"If I were building a trap—" She shrugged. "It's too elaborate for that."

"What do you think it is?"

"Rent-a-car? U-drive? They've gone to some pains to keep passengers from fiddling with things they don't understand."

"Those ball bearings—"

"Probably a fleet and most of them broke up."

"I was thinking of something else."

The drive had been blasting away for over an hour, putting a half g on the combined weight of their ships. Army wished he were back in the orbiter where he could calculate how many times faster they were moving than ever he had moved in the shuttle. But he had never measured out the exact null point on the cable. With the ships drawn together and not spinning there was no easy way to work out weights. The alien ship was heavier than his. But how much? What kind of acceleration was it capable of without all the extra weight? What difference did it make? He had no idea where the ship was taking them. Did the ship know? Would he ever be able to tell the company what had happened? If that engine didn't shut off he wouldn't even be able to lock outside to reach the orbiter. There was air and water here. How about food? Even if the engine did shut down he wouldn't dare go out until the alien ship signaled its intention not to fire again. Would it let out the cable and start a spin?

"I wonder what they look like," Sin said.

Army shrugged. They must be taller than humans, or else they sat with legs dangling. Why not something as simple as a chair back? Inflexible spines needing no support? For all he knew they could be pygmy versions of that coalmining lobster. *Let us make robots in our own image.*

"How many hours is this burn going to last?" she wondered. "If they keep it up long enough we could get close to light speed."

Army was not enthused at the prospect of a slower-than-light run to another star. The nearest he could remember was over four light years away. "Besides," he grunted, "I don't know anybody on Alpha Centauri."

He wasn't learning anything here on the bridge. Could he possibly get into the engine room or peek into the coal bunkers now that the burn was progressing? "I'm going below if the ship'll let me," he said.

"The door into here's closed."

Army glided toward it in a half g walk and the door opened. Why, he wondered, couldn't a ship as automatic as this have an elevator instead of that lethal ladder-staircase? He hooked his life line at the top and rappeled down, ignoring the steps. Doors opened invitingly on every level: several that had never opened before. He experimented with jamming a spanner into one. When he retreated the closing door sheared the tempered steel wrench in two.

The big door where he thought the engine room was refused to open. "Come on, you SOB," he growled. The door ignored him. He lowered himself to the bottom, hydroponics section. And finally was sure that he knew where the ship got at least part of its combustion air. Must need a long recovery time between burns.

But the main magnetohydrodynamics engine could not be providing any of the CO_2 that made breathing difficult in this chamber. MHD jets would exhaust reaction mass outside. This had to be exhaust from some internal auxiliary. Fuel cell? He had not seen anything like a solar collector. But if this really was a star ship then solar collectors would be useless for the greater part of its time. Where was he going?

What would happen when he got there?

"What you doin' here, boy?"

"What are *you* doing here?" he snapped.

"Taking care of you."

Of all the goddam times to be hallucinating! Must not be enough oxygen down here. He ignored the voices. Even if it were to turn out to be a long trip, he had congenial company. Was Sin . . . ? He went back out and started climbing, then as he was snugging his lifeline he was struck with another inspiration. He went down the corridor toward the airlock. Cabin doors were opening again now. He looked for the one that had closed on him and the girl. "Sin?"

Either the walls were absorbing it or she just could not hear over the continual roar of the MHD engines. He considered writing a note but he hadn't seen a piece of paper in months. But by now Army knew that the ship *knew*. He left his helmet in the corridor to give Sin some clue, then stepped into the empty, three passenger cabin. The door hissed shut behind him. He remembered the way another door had sheared through a hardened steel wrench. "Open up," he said.

The door opened.

He stepped outside and it closed. He turned back and it opened. This time he faced the far bulkhead away from the door, his face practically buried in the nets. "Open up."

The door opened.

He tried it again, just wishing.

If the door was reading his mind it was not ready to admit it.

He went back up where Sin waited. "We've been here long enough for the ship to learn English and imprint on our voices."

"Voices?" She gave him an odd look.

He remembered his suspicion of a moment ago. "You been hearing them too?"

"Somebody asking what the hell you're doing here?"

"Son of a bitch!"

"Didn't want to lay another problem on you," Sin said. "But I thought I was going flaky." Abruptly the burn stopped and they were weightless.

"He didn't say he knows how to fly it," Albert explained. "He only said he's gotten it trained."

Mansour gave him an odd look. "We Arabs train horses or camels. Much as I admire Western civilization, for me its weakest point is that your lives are arranged for the convenience of your machines. You live where the bus, train, or plane can come. You spend half your substance to feed an automobile that works not half so hard for you as you for it. Your factory hands work nights and lay awake days—all for the convenience of machines. Your machines have trained you."

Albert shrugged. "And yet the whole Third World rushes to catch up with us."

"Machines are training us too," Mansour admitted. "They are more seductive than the Prophet's promise of paradise. But when you cannot master your own machines, how can those young people have broken a strange machine to the bit?"

"There seems to be some kind of obedience built into that ship," Albert said. "Once it got to know them—decided they were there to stay, it opened up and does just about anything they ask."

"It obeys either of them?"

"No. The girl's still a little frail. I guess the ship imprinted more off Army because he spent more time in it. But it's getting used to Sin too."

"And it does anything they demand of it?"

"Altered course three times already. They've caught up with Sin's ship already so we'll have all those tons of lovely yellow metal several months before schedule."

"Coal-burning spaceship," Gus mused. "Have you any new figures on when they're due?"

"They're not," Albert said pointedly. "That ship's not coming within several million miles of anybody he thinks might grab it."

"Our ace in the—"

"Our ace in space," Albert said. "But let's not show it till we have to."

"But the gold—"

"Is going to plunk down on that piece of Montana where our pigeon partner optioned mineral rights."

"Mineral rights?"

Mansour smiled. "People enjoy selling worthless land to a rich Arab who cannot even see that the low-grade lignite seam is too thin for economical mining."

"Aha!"

Albert looked at Gus.

"That coal-mining machine of theirs. It can nip the counterweight into bitesized chunks and we don't even have to send a crew up. They can drop it one inconspicuous ton at a time." He hesitated. "But what about heat and friction? I'd hate to see all that gold vaporized."

"Jeff's been packaging drogue chutes. He sent off a load of them with an SRB under remote."

"Every radar on Earth's going to track it," Gus said.

"Not during a meteor shower. Everybody been dumping on us. Now we gonna dump. Not big enough to do any damage but when a chunk of coal comes in at two million miles an hour it really burns."

"But we must not give all the gold away," Mansour said.

"Course not. That's as crazy as communism. Give every poor Arab and poor black a piece of gold and it'll just end where all the rest of the gold is within sixty days."

"Selective philanthropy," Gus said. "Every aspiring politician wants to do the right thing but before he can do anything he has to be elected. By then he's a totally owned subsidiary of the same people who've always run the world. All we're doing is buying TV time and votes for a new lot. Be interesting to see what a new generation could do if they got in without being owned."

"But will we not own them?

"Of course we will," Gus said. "But there have been many freeings of slaves. The washing machine was more effective than Mr. Lincoln. And in any event, the only totally owned—other directed, I believe, is the buzzword—the only class left in this country with no control over their own souls are the politicians. I propose to buy some of the better and free them."

"You'd trust them?" Albert asked.

Gus grinned. "Ever notice what happens when a tired old hack gets into a bombproof slot where he knows he'll never have to kiss another fund raiser's fundament again?"

"Makes a difference," Albert conceded. "Man don't have to worry about getting reelected, he can afford to turn honest. But how you gonna do it?"

"Buy the elections for the right men. The Old Guard hates me now so I won't have much choice over what history says about me. But I never thought I'd go down as the man who dumped on Earth."

"They won't call you that," Albert said. "All that money starts flowing around to the wrong people, they're going to remember old Gus Dampier was the man who corrupted Earth."

Army and Sin had been busy. Even with the ship understanding and obeying there were things beyond the capabilities of its machines— like rigging drogue chutes on those ton-sized snippets of gold. But with each day the telepath link became more used to Sin and they could share the job of controlling. Finally, to Army's surprise, there came a time when he had slept a full eight hours and awakened to the knowledge that there was nothing that just *had* to be done.

He wondered why it had taken him a full day after that first burn to understand that they were not being taken to another star—or anywhere else, except back home much faster than they had departed Earth. Someday when things settled down on the planet, a team of real brains could be brought up to try to understand how a coal-fired spaceship was getting a hundred times as much energy from its fuel as was possible with simple magnetohydrodynamics. Had to be a nuclear process . . . but without radiation? To hell with it. He was wrung out. Drained.

Who had built it? When? He decanted from his sleeping net and strode down the corridor in full g, savoring clean fresh air.

And a wall opened. Not a door.

Sin was coming from the other direction with a tray. The coffee was from their own supplies since the ship's hydroponics did not seem capable of producing coffee beans that tasted as good as the other and infinite vegetables. She gasped. "Did you do that?"

"I don't know," Army said. "I was just wondering who built the ship."

They stepped through the opening into an unsuspected compartment. "Looks like you found the confidential file," she said.

Army stared at 3-D pictures—or were they holos? They wore clothing of a sort. So these were the builders of the ship. How many millions of years ago had they lived?

"They look almost human," Sin said.

"Almost," Army agreed. He turned away.

"I didn't mean it that way."

"I know you didn't."

The builders of the ship were almost human. They were tall and thin. They looked just like Army.

"Poor Leakey," Sin sighed. "At least he died before this came along to wipe out a lifetime's work."

"Poor Darwin!" Army snapped. "Poor Marais. Poor Howard. Poor Lorenz. Poor Dart. Poor me!"

"You?"

"Can you believe in a God whose eye is on the sparrow, who counts the spawn, who makes it always come out right and ensures that there's never a loser in the spermatozoan sweepstakes? This puts us right down there with flying saucers, pyramid power, von Däniken and all the other mental masturbators."

"Some of my best friends believe in God."

"Do they believe in people?"

"Do you?"

"Did God create computers? I'd feel myself diminished if we all turned out to be some botched experiment or it was all handed us on a silver salver along with the Host. I happen to believe the only real difference between me and my million-year-old grandpa is technology. His IQ was probably higher than mine because the Stone Age didn't have any Head Start programs for also-rans to dilute the gene pool. You were either pretty smart or pretty dead."

"So who are these people that built the ship?"

"I don't think they're human. And I don't think they're our ancestors. I'd rather be wrong with Leakey's skulls than right with von Däniken's fantasies."

"Parallel evolution?" Sin asked.

"We're eating their food and breathing their air. Where they came from couldn't have been too different from Earth. But close enough to crossbreed? If you'll believe that, you won't believe it took the geneticists over thirty years to achieve the first hybrid between a rabbit and a hare."

"But why are you so bitter?"

"Aren't you?"

But of course Sin didn't understand.

"Europeans created a hitherto unrecorded crusade to explain the ruins at Zimbabwe. Some experts even dredged up Solomon and Sheba. They were willing to accept any drivel except the truth all around them—that black men were still building stone forts like Zimbabwe all around that part of Africa."

"But nobody still believes that nonsense."

"Whenever some dingbat insists the pyramids or Zimbabwe or anything else was built by strangers with magic machines he's denying all the sweat that went into everything on Earth built by humans. Sure we're territorial, aggressive, petty. But civilization was not built by ants, beavers, or aliens. And it wasn't even started by white men. We did it all the hard way. And if I had my way about it every von Dänniken who thinks it couldn't be done ought to do thirty days in a road camp just so he can learn what humans are capable of when properly inspired.

"I'm not bitter about softhanded intellectuals who insist it's impossible for blacks to cut stone or lay brick. Flying saucer nuts are sure no human could build a pyramid. It's the same fuzzy thinking that has Shakespeare by Bacon and Whitman by Salami."

"So what do you want to do with this evidence?" Sin asked. "Bury it?"

Army was running out of anger. "No," he sighed. "I just want to understand it."

"They don't look exactly like you," she said tentatively. "A little taller and thinner—what the old anthropologists used to call an Ohio Valley jaw."

Army had heard of it: too many teeth crowded into a too narrow jaw to give the colonial and barely post-colonial American a look quite different from his European ancestors—until 18th century immigration drowned that emerging type's genes into a new homogeneity. "There were skulls like that in Africa ten million years ago," he said. "Small jaw, large brain—like some man-of-the-future caricature. They were apparently another of our loving God's failed experiments."

"Or shipwrecked survivors who couldn't or wouldn't get it on with the natives."

Army shrugged. "Do you suppose this *is* a lifeboat?"

"The mother ship would have to be the size of a planet."

"They all say there wasn't ever any planet here."

"But they change their minds every time a probe lands somewhere new."

"What's the difference between a ship and a planet?"

"I don't know," Sin said. "But even if you turn it inside out like a Dyson sphere or a ringworld—any way you look at it you've got to take your own star along."

"Or go where your star's taking you."

"That makes Earth a spaceship."

"As several writers have remarked."

"So where's this lifeboat's ship?"

"Scattered to hell and gone between Mars and Jupiter. They used to say the asteroids were a broken-up planet. Looks like the natives had time to make at least some preparations."

"I've got to learn how this machinery runs."

"It would be nice to get home."

"Sooner or later," Army said, "we're going to find some bigger pieces of wreckage. Some of them may still be in working condition—without all the ball bearings missing."

"There is that," Sin said. "But no matter how slowly and carefully we reveal the "gifts of the gods" there're going to be some ungodly dislocations in Earth's technology and economy."

"Tough. Protect our local bronze industry: help stamp out iron. The Philistines had it; the Hebrews didn't. Iron could have saved Samson's eyes."

"And gunpowder could have saved Africa from the slavers. But what's going to save us right now?"

"Learning to read these records," Army said.

"Here it is," Albert greeted.

"Here's what?" Gus growled.

"Your invitation to go back and explain to congress just why we ain' got no more company for them eggsuckers to grab."

"I'd almost forgotten."

"You will go?" Mansour asked.

"Wouldn't miss it for the world," Gus said. "I think we should all go."

"I jus' drives de car," Albert said. "But they issued a subpoena for Mr. Mansour too. Even spelled his name right."

"When's it dated?"

"Two weeks before G day."

"G day?" Mansour asked.

"The day when the futures contracts come due on all that lovey yellow stuff your boy's been droppin' down onto Montana."

"You think someone knows what we do?"

Albert shrugged. "They see us with our neck stuck way out on the gold futures and they see us optioning mineral rights on the most worthless piece of land north of Texas. And no matter how we try, it's hard to look as worried as we ought to."

"Then why do they not wait for the due date to fall?"

"Because somebody knows," Gus said. "They may not know exactly what's up but this's a government fishing expedition. And meanwhile, I'd see about posting a little extra security around our worthless gold mine."

"They would steal it?"

"Thieves steal. Governments expropriate."

Mansour sighed. "Whatever happened to ancient concepts like honor?"

"History celebrates them," Gus explained. "Because of their extreme rarity. Would there be any point in parables about Samaritans if the citizens of that region were renowned for their hospitality?"

"I suppose you are right," Mansour mourned. "But if this is all the trust we can have, perhaps we should make our drops in some other country."

"Like which one—" Albert began, then abruptly stopped. Gus and Albert studied the Arab for a moment. "It is mostly your money after all," Gus said.

"You agree?" Mansour asked. "I will not go against your wishes."

"As the principal stockholder I think you should outvote us," Albert said.

"And as the principal non-citizen."

Mansour grinned and began punching numbers into a keyboard.

And in due course the joint committee convened in all its sovereign majesty and splendor to inquire just how it turned out that when they decided finally to steal Gus's company there had been nothing left to steal.

"My company?" Gus replied to the senator's question. "My company has been stolen three times. The third time found me too old and tired to fight. I was grateful when the new majority stockholder invited me to stay on in an advisory capacity—with no salary, no title, and no responsibility."

There was shuffling of papers and whispered consultation among the committee. Finally the Grand Inquisitor demanded, "You knowingly and willingly allowed control of a company vital to national defense to pass into foreign hands?" He drew himself up to a proper camera angle and thundered, "This skates the edge of treason!"

Gus smiled and turned on his benevolent walrus look. "Eh?" he asked, and fiddled with his hearing aid. "Did you say reason?"

"I said treason!" The senator was having difficulty holding his pose.

Gus waited long enough for the senator's neck muscles to start quivering. He waited a little longer. When the cameras had finished recording the silvermaned solon's collapse they turned on Gus.

"I deny all counts, angles, and facets of any such question," Gus snapped, "coming from an august body which has taxed me unmercifully throughout my lifetime, has shut me out of every lucrative defense contract, which has stampeded over my civil and corporate rights, which has never found me important enough to rescue from raiders or bankruptcy. I hardly see how I can be accused of treason when, finally, through governmental neglect, one lot of raiders managed to acquire control against my will and my votes."

The senator was on his feet but Gus had the floor and no intention of relinquishing it. "Where were you when I asked for help to beat off these carpetbaggers? Where were you when I delivered on time and for the agreed-upon price? Where were you when everybody but Dampier Industries was 85% into cost overruns? Did I hear one voice from this floor advocating fair treatment?

"I never sought favors—only fairness. You never gave it to me so now you can deal with the new owner of the company—whose brother supplies this nation with a large part of its oil. Do I see any ears pricking up at the magic word?"

Gus bowed to Mansour and sat down.

In full native dress with gold-trimmed *agal* holding his *kuffieh* in place Mansour was impressive. He stood and smiled. He smiled for several minutes while the inquisitors shuffled papers and held muttered conferences. "If there are no questions," Mansour finally said, "then perhaps someone could move to adjourn?"

The consternation was louder but still none saw just how to attack this new menace. "You deal in gold futures?" a congressman finally asked.

Mansour smiled. "We Arabs see much useless paper."

"You plunge heavily and have no visible hopes for recovery."

"Then I shall have to surrender to the ineluctible laws of the marketplace. Is that not true?"

A longhaired congressman in granny glasses muttered something about letting that arrogant bastard go broke any way he wanted to. The man next to him hastily muffled the mike.

A page entered the committee room and handed a slip of teletype paper to the Grand Inquisitor. The old man's face lit up with illconcealed triumph.

Albert, in black chauffeur's uniform, leaned forward and whispered to Gus. "Look like the news's out."

"Mr. uh—Mansour, I'm afraid we must interrupt this meeting for a moment. There's been a disaster of some kind."

"Strictly a matter of interpretation," Mansour said. "No lives were lost, I trust?"

"You uh—knew this was going to happen?"

"My company deals in aerospace," Mansour explained. "But not in weapons."

"You have the effrontery to stand before the United States Senate and—"

"I do indeed. As you know, my country is short of water. For a time Sheikh Omar has brought it in as ballast when the oil tankers return empty. But obviously this is no long-term solution. Unfortunately, both the Straits of Hormuz and Bab el Mandeb are shallow enough to render impractical any scheme for towing Antarctic icebergs to the Arab states."

"I must ask what all this has to do with killing

American soldiers and wiping out a radar station."

"It has everything to do with it." Mansour's manner was as bland as Gus's. "Read your report closely and you'll see all Americans, as well as all our own citizens were evacuated from the *wadi* before the missile struck."

"But you wiped out a radar station!"

"I believe spy station is the correct terminology. In any event, your soldiers are safe and well fed in the capital. If you want another spy station we'll buy you one."

"Atomic weapons in the Middle East," a senator groaned. "Thank God I'm an old man."

"Atomic? Someone detects radioactivity?"

By now xeroxed copies were circulating among the inquisitors. "Has to be," a congressman said. "What else could do that much damage?"

"Something did along the Tunguska river on June 30th, 1908," Gus said. "That's in Siberia."

"Are you trying to tell us this is a meteorite?"

"A rather carefully aimed one," Mansour said. "But then we Arabs have always shown a proper respect for water. We were building dams and irrigating when your ancestors were still trying to learn how to drain a swamp."

"I fail to see the point of all this obfuscation—"

"When all else fails, try listening," Gus suggested. He bowed to Mansour.

"As I was saying, we need water. Though your government was kind enough to authorize delivery of an *atomic* desalination plant, not even petrodollars can keep this kind of equipment safe and clean forever. We now have a nonpolluting solution to our water problem."

He paused to taste a glass of water and make a

face. "Either clean up yours or you may find yourself buying water as well as oil from my country."

"You control water?" The senators were incredulous.

"My country," Mansour said, "owns the technology that allows us to divert an ice asteroid and fine tune its entry so that the landing plows a pressure ridge down the *wadi* ahead of itself, thus creating dam and reservoir—and filling it in the act of landing."

"Unbelievable!"

"Only if you lack the skill to fire a braking rocket first so the drogue chute does not burn up. You Americans invented computers but most English words that begin with *al-* are of Arabic origin."

"I fail to see the point of—"

"The word to which I refer is algebra."

Guys stood. "In the days of our innocence it was suggested that we demonstrate our new weapon on some uninhabited island instead of Hiroshima. There were even those silly enough to believe that, sentimentality aside, our survival might someday hinge on our treatment of those beneath us."

The silence in the committee room was turning glacial.

"Now surely," Gus continued, "there's none among you so innocent as to believe this committee has any jurisdiction over the prince of a friendly country—a man who appears here merely from politeness and of his own free will. Is there among you any one who doubts we can drop an iceberg or a million tons of stone or iron on target? If doubts remain, pick a site for the next demonstration. We can dump it *anywhere.*"

There was stony silence as Gus, Albert, and Mansour left the hearing room. They stood on the steps of the Senate office building waiting for a government employee to bring the Mark V around. Albert would have been just as happy to have come in a cab or an airport limo. This way he would have to sweep the car for government 'improvements' before they could talk.

"Looks like they'll leave us alone for a while now," Gus said.

"We're being listened to forty ways from Sunday," Albert growled with a glance at all the empty windows that stared from both sides of the street.

"But we have no secrets," Mansour said.

Gus's laugh was ten years younger. "Totally unChristian—no doubt unMoslem too, but isn't it lovely to know we can dump on any of the holier-than-thou hypocrites who've been dumping on us?"

"Feels even nicer to know there's more people interested in keeping us alive and happy than the other way around," Albert said.

"And suddenly we're policemen to the world." Augustus Dampier laughed. "Wonder if they'll call it the pax augusta."

"Fraid that'n's been used before," Albert said.

Mansour sighed. "All I ever wished was to live a quiet and private life."

"Takes a little getting used to," Gus said. "Way back in '45 when the dirt first started coming out of Los Alamos, Dr. Bainbridge turned to Oppenheimer and summed up in a single sentence the fate of those who change the world."

"I remember," Albert sighed. "Looks like we've finally achieved true equality."

Mansour looked at them.

"Now we are all sons of bitches," Gus quoted.

A government chauffeur pulled up with the altered Mark V.

Fred Saberhagen

☐ 05404	Berserker	$1.75
☐ 05407	Berserker Man	1.95
☐ 05408	Berserker's Planet	2.25
☐ 08215	Brother Assassin	1.95
☐ 16600	The Dracula Tape	1.95
☐ 49548	Love Conquers All	1.95
☐ 84315	The Ultimate Enemy	1.95
☐ 52077	The Mask Of The Sun	1.95
☐ 62160	An Old Friend Of The Family	1.95
☐ 86064	The Veils of Azlaroc	1.95

Available wherever paperbacks are sold or use this coupon.

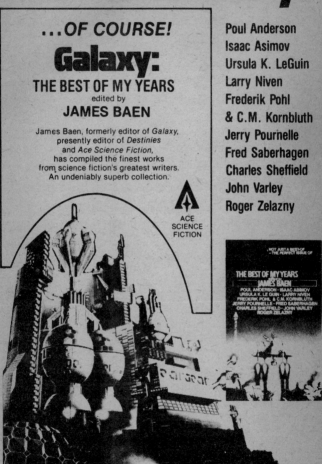